The Rain That

Clears The Chaff

AC O'Neill

The Rain That Clears The Chaff

ISBN 978-0-9573629-1-8

Acknowledgements

My thanks to Jessica Trusler, for her help and for pointing me in the right direction, and to Shelley and David and Maria and Colin for their hospitality on my trips to southern Africa.

Any errors are, of course, my own.

London, July 2012

To Ali

It's come to this. This is where it works. Or it doesn't...

The line of thunder clouds were now swollen on the northern horizon. As he had walked they had darkened, and they now looked like a vast angry bruise across the sky.

This pregnant backdrop, deep amethyst in colour, made everything else seem more intensely bright. It was as if all he could see had suddenly been flooded with colour.

It was a much better vantage point than he'd thought possible, but it wasn't built for comfort. The rock behind him was sharp and uneven. The earth beneath him was deeply corrugated by gargantuan serpentine roots which anchored the trees to the basalt bedrock. A paperbark tree reached over him like an oversized parasol. But while it shaded him it also trapped the heat. He was sweating as if he had just reached his perch by climbing up the cliff face in front of him.

The pilfered t-shirt was in a damp bundle next to him, abandoned in a vain attempt to cool himself down. Beads of sweat were now running freely down his back, sinking into the waistband of his shorts. The hair on his arms glistened. His legs shone with moisture. Again he shifted himself against the rock, knees drawn up to his chest, searching for the least painful position.

He fancied he could smell the sweetness of the spray behind him. But the scent was elusive, and there wasn't a breath of air to relieve his discomfort.

Drawing his hand slowly across his scalp and face, he wiped away the perspiration through three days' worth of stubble. He traced the scar on his head softly with his fingertips. It finally appeared to be healing. But the weals on his shins were still livid. They throbbed incessantly and he couldn't fully flex his legs to ease the discomfort.

Glancing to one side, he checked for the fourth or fifth time that the chalky swimming-pool-blue helmet was still buried under a pile of dead leaves in a crevice between two tuberous roots. It had been a silent colourful alibi as he walked onto the peninsula, but the pretext was no longer needed.

Or even valid. It was one thing to be seen with it on the path down from the main road. Here, off the path and with his presence no longer explicable, the incongruous colour was best hidden.

He knew that only someone actively searching for him would be able to pick him out amongst the rocks and vegetation. Even that would be a difficult task. All the same, he felt helplessly on show on the towering spines of rock rising like some overblown gothic cathedral from the black water boiling on three sides below him.

He looked over his right shoulder up the gorge. There, settled between the opposing cliffs like a jeweller's confection in filigree silver, the girders of the bridge reflected the filtered sunlight against the smoky spray rising in vast delicate clouds, like steam from a subterranean cauldron. It looked beautiful – nothing like its workaday appearance when he had walked across it.

He picked up the binoculars, shifted round, and, bracing his elbows against his knees, searched through the lenses until he found the span.

He adjusted the focus and then followed a lone figure pushing a low flat barrow, heaped with groceries, slung between a pair of bicycle wheels. He watched until the barrow and then the figure disappeared from view.

A hazy torpor descended over the empty crossing. No trains, no cars, no pedestrians, no cross-border traders.

Bored, he turned back in the opposite direction. Pressing his eyes hard against the rubber, he inspected the opposite side of the gorge. Though less sheer than the buttress on which he was perched, the facing bank still rose sharply from the dark waters below.

He could make out here and there amongst the patches of dun vegetation a path switching back and forth. He followed the traverses from side to side as they climbed the slope until he found the flagpole centred in the lenses, standing brilliant white through the haze. A flag dangled bleached and limp from its tip.

Around the pole on a stone-built viewing terrace sat a circle of fat red Alibaba pots. Dull green vegetation, unidentifiable over the distance, sprouted from the top of each.

Behind the flagpole and the pots he could see a substantial lawn. It was brown in patches and in need of watering. It ran up to the warm white walls and red tiled roof of the hotel, which sat like a *grande dame* casting a proprietorial eye over a late-imperial garden party. More imposing than the bridge, and just as incongruous in the surrounding primeval countryside.

Waiters clad in brilliant white, vividly coloured sashes brightening their uniforms, floated serenely up and down the steps of the veranda ferrying trays of drinks to guests, most of whom appeared to be seated unseen in the shade of the vast ancient trees which hid the most part of the central block of the hotel from his view.

A faint shimmer of smoke rose vertically from behind

those trees as the lunchtime *braai* drums were stoked up. To the right he could see part of the car park to the side of the main building. Multi-coloured, highly-polished steel was just discernible through the shrubbery.

He remembered as a boy setting traps to catch birds on the fringes of the mission compound, where the trampled dirt ended and the bush began. What seemed then to be endless watching, hidden and still - although probably a fraction of the time he now imagined - until a sparrow, finally succumbing to temptation, hopped up to the pellets of mealie meal. Then pulling the string to dislodge the twig propping up the fruit box, catching the bird before it fled.

He focussed on the two short steel supports bracing either side of the foot of the flagpole.

Come on, bastards. You've all been invited and the party's about to begin. Where are you..?

He let the binoculars swing back on their strap, and fought the urge to sleep.

One

Three months earlier

The stitch in Themba Sibanda's side was really starting to hurt. The pain spiked up into his ribs from just above his waist, between his loose-fitting shorts and his too-tight shirt, both worn to the weave. Glancing up, he fixed his eyes on an isolated clump of undernourished trees a dozen or so yards ahead and made for them, his bare feet thumping in rhythm on the hard-baked path.

Reaching the trees, he stood in the tiny patch of shade underneath their spindly branches, feeling the relief as the soles of his feet cooled. He bent over and waited for the pain in his side to subside. Gradually he caught his breath. He picked up his feet in turn to extract the paper thorns he had picked up along the track.

Slung low from both shoulders, the straps adjusted for a larger torso, he carried a small blue nylon back-pack. He slipped off the straps and rubbed his neck to relieve the ache. Then, wiping the sweat from his brow with his forearm, he looked out over the short-cropped islands of scrawny grass punctuating the bare earth of the wide gently-sloping valley he was crossing. The only sound was the incessant low-level din of cicadas. The heat had driven almost everyone inside.

Some way below where he stood he could clearly see the crossroads where the tarred highway from town to the border crossed a sandy road leading into the communal lands on either side. Like a child's building blocks, several small buildings rubbed close up against two opposing corners of the intersection.

Furthest away from him, the district police camp stood white-washed and squared away within its high-fenced compound. In the centre a miniature khaki-coloured figure leant on a shotgun, standing sentry over a Lilliputian gang of hard-labour prisoners in dusty white shorts and tunics. They were hoeing listlessly at flowerbeds marked out by borders of whitewashed stones. Running between the flowerbeds, a crazy-paving path led to a flight of steps, burnished weekly to a mirror-like ox-blood red by the same gang of convicts. The steps rose sharply to a walkway running the width of the main building, which was covered by a short angled roof.

The building housed the charge office and the cells. There were large trees standing to one side of it. In their shade three grey police Land Rovers were parked side by side in a neat rank. A sentry-box stood next to a boom at the gate, inside which, Themba knew, a constable would be fighting off heat-induced slumber, with occasional success.

But the sentry box and the boom, both neatly finished in broad blue, white and gold stripes, were redundant. The Member-in-Charge, Inspector Deliverance Mpofu, was as suspicious of the surrounding countryside as he was doubtful of his sentry's vigilance. The gate was held shut by a giant padlock and a substantial chain.

Facing the police camp diagonally on the other side of the intersection stood an altogether grubbier building topped by a roof of faded red corrugated iron. Across it, in bleached white letters several feet high, the words 'General Store - Garage Prop: M Ndlovu' were emblazoned.

A band of black paint two or three feet high circled the

filthy white walls at ground level. It was spattered heavily with an enveloping brown stain where raindrops from innumerable thunderstorms had bounced up against it, making it seem as if the building had burst through from the surrounding dirt. Such a thunderstorm would have been welcome. But there hadn't been one so far this season, and the waiting was testing tempers in the district to the point of eruption.

Fronting the building, a cement veranda was raised like a rampart above the dirt. Themba could almost feel the dark coolness trapped under its generous canopy. A knot of local youths, the usual Saturday afternoon crowd, leaned against the outside of the veranda walls. But Mr Ndlovu, purveyor of over-priced sundries to the local populace, would be profiting little from them. Their interest lay with a group of teenage girls perched together on the exposed roots of the grand fig tree sitting imposingly to one side of the building.

Just in front of them, on the side of the recently-graded sand road nearest to him, Themba could see the large blue-painted rock that was the signpost for the mission. He surveyed this road as it rose from the police camp and the store up the valley towards him and then veered away from the higher ground where he stood. He looked back along the track he had run along as far as the point where it too dropped away again into the dead ground beyond the rise.

He could no longer see the spurt of green splitting the dusty countryside which marked the banks of the meagre stream where the communal washing took place, just below where his family drew their water. The water trickled - no more than that - down into the communal lands from the farm away to his right, where the boundary was marked by a low three-strand fence. The real divide was not the fence itself, but the vegetation on either side of it: scrubby, sparse and overgrazed on this side, thick and abundant on the other.

St Cuthbert's mission, with its church, clinic and school, was also out of sight beyond the rise. He had passed it earlier on his run. It being a Saturday, the school that he attended with his sister was closed, but Father Barnabas, a figure clothed entirely in black, sleeves rolled down in defiance of the heat, was tending his kitchen garden and had thrown him a quizzical glance as he ran past.

Themba knew there would be polite enquiries on Sunday morning when the district trooped in for Mass as to why he had been running past in the heat of the day. Themba looked forward to the attention with some pleasure, and briefly formulated his answers in his mind. The more he dwelt on it, however, the more certain he became that the news would already be spread around the district well before then. Not much remained a secret around here for long.

Anyway, there would still be a story to tell.

Squaring his bony adolescent frame, he slipped his arms back into the straps of the pack, and ran off with renewed purpose along the track. He jogged steadily for a further quarter of an hour before he caught the first sight of his destination.

A smudge of woodsmoke rose from within a head-high boundary fence closely woven from acacia branches. The fence stood dark and distinct against the dull khaki of the thick tangle of grass, bushes and trees which ran behind it up to the light grey backdrop of a low range of exposed granite hills that flanked one side of the valley.

As he drew nearer, several thatched conical roofs, sagged and sorry-looking, came into view above the fence. He could also now see the upper branches of a tall shade tree standing near them. Two lean hunting dogs, slumped in the shadows near the entrance, registered his approach from under eyelids drooped in near-terminal boredom. It was a scene of sweltering domestic tranquillity.

Themba slowed to a brisk walk. His father, sitting erect on a straight-backed wooden chair in the shade outside the nearest hut, did not look kindly on unseemly haste. But as he walked through the gap in the fence, Themba found it impossible to still his heaving chest or contain his near-to-bursting excitement.

Two

D aniel Hove, consultant orthopaedic surgeon at St Botolph's, was extremely annoyed. It was a condition from which he had suffered increasingly frequently in recent months. As he sat on the train he was ranting to himself, replaying the earlier events over and over in his mind.

He had spent the last part of the evening before he left work for the day defending himself before a star chamber of two hospital managers.

'Mr Hove? A word?' one of them, Clarke, had enquired, peering round the door to Daniel's cupboard of an office as he tidied the files on his desk. The tone was not quite courteous. It was an instruction rather than a request. And Daniel had bridled at the mispronunciation of his name. He had glanced up at Clarke.

You know damn well it's Hov-ay. I'm not a bloody seaside town.

Clarke's expression was neutral. Daniel hadn't been sure whether Clarke was deliberately trying to rile him or not. But he was riled nevertheless.

He had made an obvious show of finishing what he was doing.

He now realised that had been a mistake.

Daniel had walked silently beside Clarke to the hospital's 'Executive Suite' where Grainger, Clarke's superior, was waiting. Beyond the entrance doors, with those two words on a heavily varnished plaque above them, the decor became abruptly more luxurious. The lighting gave off a warmer glow, the furniture was of a superior quality. And the deep-pile carpet, Daniel had thought, not for the first time as his shoes sank into it, was probably harbouring more resistant strains of bacteria than was acceptable this close to a hospital.

Grainger and Clarke, rarely spotted out of each other's company, had then sat themselves down facing Daniel across the table, in a meeting room which must have been at least five times the size of Daniel's office but which only contained a table and six well-padded, but nonetheless uncomfortable chairs.

His capital crime, set out in double-spacing on the sheet of paper which Clarke had slid menacingly over the desk to him, was titled 'Slippage in 360-Degree Stakeholder Information Pathway Management'.

As evidence, late and incomplete submissions of compliance forms.

Daniel had stared at it in disbelief. It was beyond parody, he'd thought, until they proved him wrong with the cherry on their indictment cake; several occasions on which he had failed to ensure that post-operative questionnaires were reclaimed from patients on whose limbs he had operated. The questionnaires asked those patients, amongst other matters of equally vital bureaucratic necessity, to rate their 'operative experience' on a scale of one to five.

Daniel had almost burst out laughing. Another mistake.

Daniel had never liked Grainger. Shadowy and viper-like was a description he had heard someone else use, and he couldn't better it. His opinion of Clarke was less charitable. And he'd probably let it show.

You moron. Incapable of anything except menial tasks, and even then only under supervision. I bet you don't change your

11

underwear unless Grainger's cleared it first. You're a moron managed by a dangerous political snake.

Daniel was a serial offender. He'd decided after a disastrous previous arraignment on charges similar to these that there wouldn't be a next time. He'd made a suitable show of contrition, and vowed to get his paperwork in order.

He had, for a while. And then he'd let it slip. Nothing had been said, so he'd put it out of his mind. Until they pounced again.

And this occasion was slightly different. It came to him suddenly, fifteen minutes out of London. There was a vacancy in the department for which, so the rumours went, he and a colleague, Stewart Ainslie, were being considered.

Bastards. Ainslie put them up to it. Bastard.

So. Another entry in his personal file. Another reason not to consider him for advancement.

Daniel had been fuming ever since, cursing the three of them, and then himself, so vociferously that midway through the journey he'd noticed a pair of his fellow passengers exchanging knowing arched-eyebrow glances. He realised he must have been venting his frustrations visibly, probably out loud. He wondered how many of the other passengers crowding in on him from every side were in on the joke.

And that was the second reason for his irritation. Two stops away from its terminus the carriage was still packed to bursting with commuters, some still standing after more than an hour's travel. He'd managed - against the odds - to secure a seat for himself not long after the start of his own journey. That should have been a cause for celebration. But it was between two other passengers on a bench only really generous enough for a courting couple engaged in intimate conversation.

Even the sight at eye level of a seductively curved rump in a pencil skirt and sheer black tights, from which he felt it would be churlish to avert his gaze, failed to dilute his mood.

The train resumed its journey with a lurch, and then, with as much lateral movement as forward motion, the carriages rocked and swayed their way up the final incline. He prised himself from between his two fellow sardines, who immediately relaxed to fill the space he had vacated. He picked a delicate path through the assault course of limbs and luggage that separated him from the doors. Once there he stood, arm raised to the grab rail, braced for an early exit.

Between the patches of condensation on the window in the door in front of him he could see the pier pushing cold and lonely out to sea. The beachfront was deserted, the amusement booths along the strand tightly shuttered against the lack of custom and the weather. A bitter easterly blew unhindered up the estuary and across the mud flats, chilling all in its path.

The windows of the train were momentarily dashed with raindrops blown horizontally across the embankment. And then the view disappeared and the spatters turned into forlorn drips down the glass. The tracks swept inland into a shallow canyon cut between pebble-dashed terraces of narrow Victorian cottages huddled tightly together with their backs to the weather, their slates slick with rain.

The train passed Shoalview Terrace, the street where he lived. He looked down it, as he did every evening on his journey home. The sea was again briefly visible at the bottom of the road.

Anything to eat in the fridge? He couldn't remember. *Probably not.*

Since his divorce three months previously this had become a regular occurrence. He still kept assuming such chores would invisibly be done for him.

Dammit. That means the bloody supermarket. In this weather. Just what I need...

The train slowed on the ascent to the station. When it stopped he was first out of the carriage door, and he joined a flood of alighting passengers washing down the platform.

There was a small knot of trench-coated, briefcase-wielding individuals in the crowd, all tightly buckled up, looking like so many members of a Hollywood sleuth re-enactment society. Daniel was swept just behind them through the exit barriers and down the station stairs into the street. In unconscious imitation, he pulled the wide collar of his coat up around his ears, and with his gloved hands stuck firmly into his pockets, he made his way across the road and down the pavement.

Short of stature, he was nevertheless a figure of some presence. His shaven head, a polished horse-chestnut brown, gleamed in the weak light from the street lamps. He carried a canvas attaché case slung on a long strap from his shoulder, which he pushed behind him onto his hip as if he was constantly about to enter a narrow doorway.

He wore, at an angle not quite perpendicular to his nose, a pair of rimless glasses, over the top of which he was in the habit of glaring when focussing on anything closer than the reach of his outstretched arms, or, as now, when spots of rain obscured the lenses.

The casual observer would have been taken by his lips which appeared to be set permanently just short of a smile. His eyebrows were sceptically arched. He wore the guileless air of someone unused to gladly suffering fools. But his outward, almost cynical, demeanour was belied by his eyes. They were those of an idealist, wary of disappointment lurking around the next corner.

Walking rapidly, he was about to turn into the final stretch of his journey home when he felt his phone vibrating against his thigh. Cursing quietly, he ducked under the awning of a corner shop and fished it from his coat. Finding he could not operate the keys with his gloved finger, he swore again, pulled off one glove, stabbed at the phone again and raised it to his ear.

'Hello,' he answered grimly, his lips chilled.

The connection was filled with static, but he recognised his mother's voice. 'Daniel?' he heard distantly through the interference.

'Yes?' he answered, impatience replaced with concern.

'Daniel?' she said again. 'Oh, Daniel. It's Patricia. She's dead.'

Three

He saw her first as he walked down the steps from the lunchtime shuttle from Johannesburg and began the short walk to the terminal building. Her familiar silhouette was leaning forward over the balustrade of the first floor balcony. Daniel could see she was tense from fifty yards away. No effusive waving to attract his attention, as she had greeted him on previous arrivals. No wide beam of welcome. Instead her smile seemed forced and deliberate and her posture self-protective.

Heat was radiating from the apron, so he walked across it as briskly as he could into the stuffy heat of the terminal building and the less than welcoming queue for the immigration officer.

The queue edged forward intermittently, each person second in the queue halting at the white line painted on the floor. Transgressors were firmly directed back behind it by a *mdala* whose sole responsibility this appeared to be.

Daniel finally reached the line. He looked blankly at the official standing behind a lectern which stood barring the way forward. The studied languor, the insolent flipping of passport pages; he looked like a bored croupier in a downmarket casino.

Daniel stepped forward. Perhaps a little too far forward, for the old man was about to put his arm across to stop him when the official warned him off with a curt wave of his hand.

Daniel offered up his passport and immigration form. The official eyed him up and down in between snatched glances at the documents.

Daniel began to worry. But the official's hardening expression must have been in disappointment that he hadn't found anything out of order. He reluctantly picked up his visa stamp and hammered it down with practiced accuracy and exaggerated force.

There was a delay at baggage collection as they waited while a vintage electric cart hauling three ramshackle trolleys clattered heavily across the tarmac from the plane. The bags were dumped without ceremony onto a track of ancient brass rollers leading nowhere. Daniel retrieved his suitcase, and made his way through to the foyer, after queuing again, this time for a customs officer in a threadbare shirt, a safety pin standing in for a button which had gone astray. He brought another stamp thumping down.

The foyer was adorned, as it had been for as long as Daniel could remember, with huge tourism authority posters that looked as if they pre-dated the luggage cart. One wall was still dominated by a gigantic mounted kudu head which stared unblinkingly past a large portrait of His Excellency on an adjacent wall. Below them both, his mother. Grizzle-headed, diminutive, and despite her uncharacteristic unease, irresistibly in charge. His questions about his sister were firmly headed off.

'Not here,' she said quietly. Then louder, changing the subject. 'How was the flight?'

They walked out into the sunshine to the car park, which was laid out optimistically over a large expanse of ground. Daniel doubted it had ever been even a quarter full at one sitting.

Ignoring his offer, his mother took the driver's seat, and

drove slowly out of the airport until they turned onto the main road into town. They accelerated past high yellow grass advancing towards the verge on one side. The other side, closer to the airport, had been closely scythed. A bush fire here would leap the road and devour the airport buildings within minutes if the grass was any higher. Heaven knows the conditions were right. The vegetation was tinder-dry and the heat lay heavy across the countryside. Daniel had almost forgotten quite how physical the summer could get.

'I had no idea she was even here,' his mother began once she had settled into the journey. Her voice cracked over the first few syllables and she coughed to regain control. 'I thought she was in Cape Town. I'd heard nothing from her for a couple of weeks. I certainly knew nothing about her coming up here. Absolutely nothing. She would have called. You know. She never did things impulsively like that.'

Daniel took that as a personal, if mild, rebuke, and then thought badly of himself for doing so.

His mother was still talking. 'She would never have made the trip without telling me first. I just don't understand it.' She slowed to allow a small trip of goats to decide whether to cross the road. They blinked at her with opaque eyes, and then came to the collective conclusion that the cropped grass on the other side wasn't worth the bother. They resumed wrenching the verge-side vegetation from its roots. She accelerated again.

'And then last Monday - that night just before I called you - there was a knock on the door. It was your friend Henry. Henry Mliswa. You know, the one you used to work with at the hospital. He just said 'I'm sorry Mrs Hove.

Something terrible has happened'. He came in for a few minutes, and he told me that Patricia had been found dead. He said he would pick me up in the morning and take me to the hospital. Next day – two days ago - when we got there he took me through to the mortuary, and there she was… Oh, Daniel, she was dead, and I never had the chance…'

Tears were brimming in her eyes. She pulled the car over to the side of the road and stared straight ahead, her hands still gripping the wheel. Then she took her head in her hands and began to sob.

Daniel reached over and put a hand on her shoulder. He couldn't remember ever seeing his mother in tears. Not even when his father had died. Her age must be catching up with her, he thought. Almost thirty five years in a nurse's uniform, married to a teacher at a rural mission. Then widowhood. Finally, retirement to the city. Daniel stared at her. There was no real sign of any physical decline. But he got the distinct sense that her legendary ability to deal with everything that was thrown at her was beginning to fail.

They drove in silence for the remainder of the journey. They parked under a heavily bleached shade-awning next to her flat, and made their way inside. After an age spent making sure he was settled in the spare bedroom, emptying his suitcase, and plying him with tea, he eventually persuaded her to sit and tell him everything, from beginning to end. Her hands grasped tightly around a mug, her eyes now dry, but puffed and red, she began.

It didn't take long. She didn't have much to tell.

'Henry said something about her being brought from another hospital. The district hospital in Gwanda? Is that where he works now? I'm not sure now. I wasn't taking much in by then.'

Daniel shrugged. He hadn't heard from or of Henry in years.

She sniffed, and sipped from the mug.

'Henry said he recognised her when her body was brought in. He arranged for her to be brought into town. He thought it would be easier for me that way. Then he came round here.'

'He recognised her...?'

'That's what he said. She had no ID. No passport. Nothing. So he said. They found nothing with her body except a shirt she was wearing. He remembered her face. If he hadn't seen her, maybe we wouldn't even have found out. I just can't understand it. When we went to the hospital there was another doctor there, but Henry did all the talking. The other one hardly said a word the whole time. Wormy little man. Glasses. Moustache.'

'Sounds like Henry. The talking, I mean,' said Daniel. 'Where did they find her?'

'Henry said somewhere on the side of the road. I'm not sure exactly. On the side of the Beitbridge road. Oh Daniel…'

She broke down again and wept silently. Daniel offered a tissue and she pressed it against her eyes.

'Didn't they tell you how she died? Did they give you a death certificate?' he asked.

'Yes. I'll get it out for you. It said something about a traffic accident. Hit by an unknown vehicle…'

'Nothing else? No bag? I mean, she must have been carrying a bag if she came from Jo'burg. Surely? How could she travel without a bag, or something? Why would there be a shirt and nothing else?'

'That's what I thought. But there was nothing else, Henry said. Just the shirt she was wearing, he said. I don't know, Daniel. Maybe everything she had with her was stolen. But why only a shirt? What about the rest of her clothes. It's all so strange. What could have happened to her?'

'Did he say anything else?'

'Not really. But he was full of questions. Asking after you. And Patricia. What you'd both been doing, where you were now. I said you'd probably be coming out, and he wanted you to give him a call. I've got his number somewhere. He was very keen to talk to you. Said you would both have a lot to catch up with.'

* * *

Daniel thought back fifteen years – more? - to when he was a freshly qualified doctor working at the general hospital in Bulawayo. Henry and he had both started on the same day, and, though often on different shifts, they had formed a sort of a bond.

Invited to the same parties, eating in the same canteen, they had at one stage considered sharing a bachelor's mess together with two other doctors. But that idea had fizzled out amongst the shifting sands of romantic entanglements and developing ambitions.

Once he left, the relationship had subsided. There had been one occasion years later when Henry had looked him up while on a visit to London. They had gone out one night, got roaring drunk, and after that Daniel had not heard from Henry again.

A few shared experiences. More than an acquaintance, but hardly a lifelong friend.

His mother's voice brought him back to the present. 'It's happening again, Daniel. Your father... it's happening all over again.'

'No, it isn't,' he said bluntly. 'That was a long time ago. Things are different now.'

'You've forgotten what it's like, Daniel,' she snapped. 'You haven't lived here for years. Half this country spies on the other half. Especially here. You don't know who people are. You don't know what they're mixed up in, what they might do.'

'All that is finished,' he said, but it sounded as if he was trying to convince himself as much as her.

She was having none of it. 'Oh, sure. Things look OK. You can't talk to anyone without them telling you how back-to-normal things are. But I don't care what they say. You still can't speak your mind. Some big chef might hear, and then you're for the high jump.'

Daniel smiled briefly at the word.

First time in years I've heard that outside a restaurant review...

The word, borrowed from Portuguese, was the common term of contempt for members of the political class. Contempt, but guarded contempt. Said under the breath, from the corner of one's mouth.

Other gloomier thoughts took over, racing around his mind.

Why do I resent her so for bringing it up? He was my father. But he was also her husband. She has as much right as anyone to talk about what happened to him. Yet I can't even tolerate the subject being mentioned. All I want to do is blank the whole thing from my mind, and all the know-alls and conspiracists can go to hell. What the hell is the matter with me?

But the brief episode of self-examination didn't change his response.

'I'm sure you're worrying about nothing,' he insisted. 'I'm sure there's a proper explanation for all this. Look. I'll go to the hospital tomorrow. I'll give Henry a call. We'll find out exactly what happened to her. Try not to worry. Get some sleep tonight and we'll start again tomorrow.'

He spoke as reassuringly as he could, lapsing into a bedside manner that, if truth be told, had never been his strongest skill.

Four

D aniel returned to the conundrum of his reaction to his father's disappearance during a sleepless night, induced as much by his own uneasy feelings of guilt as by the hot still air stifling him in his mother's spare bedroom. He turned it over again and again in his mind, as often as he rolled and turned on the sweaty sheet beneath him.

Gilbert Hove had disappeared one March afternoon in 1984, twelve years before. He was on his way back to the mission after a visit to town. He had phoned to say he was leaving, a miracle in itself being able to get through on the party line.

The bus had arrived, but he wasn't on it, nor on the bus after that. Nor on any buses the next day. There was no-one to confirm he had boarded any of them, no evidence at all as to what had happened to him if he had. He had simply vanished into thin air and no-one knew why.

Except that everyone did.

The countryside he would have travelled through was occupied territory, district by district taking turn and turn about to submit to the depredations of what amounted to an invading army.

The Fifth Brigade, a self-contained force outside the usual army structures, had fanned out across Matabeleland, laying down a rolling regime of intimidation, arson and murder. They were separately trained by North Korean instructors, differently armed and equipped, and were under the control, it was said, of the highest political office, bypassing the military chain of command. Even their radios, it seemed, were incompatible with the rest of the military.

Their purpose, it was publically claimed, was to deal with bands of armed dissidents - former guerrillas who had returned to the bush. But the lack of a weapon was no proof of innocence, and speaking Ndebele was prima facie evidence of guilt.

In the wake of the Fifth Brigade came the Central Intelligence Organisation - the CIOs – and the Special Branch, and all the other gimcrack groups who claimed an expertise in intelligence. They went to work on those the Fifth Brigade gathered together in the holding camps scattered throughout the province.

There were other targets. Anyone with influence in a community - priests, teachers, nurses - whatever their tribal roots. But at heart it was a pogrom against a minority tribe. The mission was to crush political, not military, dissent.

It was the North Korean connection which added the final excruciating mental twist to the horror - even though they could probably teach their pupils little about the finer points of terror. Unknown, foreign, alien – their involvement honed the dread to a fine edge.

Gilbert must have been picked up, hauled off the bus. It was a daily occurrence. It had happened to so many others. But enquiries with the district authorities were met with flat denials, and warnings that any further probing would be considered prejudicial to state security. To suggest that officers of the state might be responsible...

After all, if you didn't know where a close relative was, then either he had been abducted by dissidents, or he was one himself. In the paranoid logic of state security, it stood to reason. Everyone knew what that meant.

They had kept quiet after that, forced themselves as a family to bury the distress. Perhaps it was fear of a resurgence of that pain that made Daniel refuse to discuss the subject. Perhaps...

* * *

He was still brooding the next morning as he drove through town in his mother's car. He had tried calling Mliswa before he left, but got only as far as leaving a message on his voicemail, so he had set off for the hospital on his own.

It was as he remembered it. It stood cream and solid and quiet, unadorned buildings planted foursquare in a featureless landscape of open veld, the doors and window frames picked out in gloss municipal green. He found a parking place in the dappled mid-day shade thrown by an ancient thorn tree, and, armed with Patricia's death certificate, walked up to the front doors.

The mortuary would be in the same place. Through the entrance and down the passage to the right.

Mortuaries don't move. Like their contents.

Daniel stopped and drew his hand down his face from his forehead to his chin, wiping away the blasphemous thought. Recovering his composure, he entered the building.

He followed his instincts, and sure enough, he soon found an arrow directing him down an intersecting corridor, closed off at the end by double swing-doors. A sign hand-painted onto them in an unsteady script confirmed it as his destination.

Daniel tentatively pushed open one of the doors. A

white-coated attendant seated behind a small table just inside the entrance looked up at him with a sullen expression.

'I'm Daniel Hove,' he said as pleasantly as he could. 'My sister Patricia's body is in the mortuary. I'd like to see her, please.'

'ID,' the attendant demanded flatly, his tone pitched perfectly on the divide between indifference and incivility.

Daniel produced his passport from his jacket pocket. The attendant glanced at it disdainfully. 'You need a doctor to come with you,' he said eventually.

When Daniel had worked in this hospital there had been two categories of despot. The Matron and her deputies were one. Those at the bottom of the pecking order, the ones who ground out the menial duties that kept the institution functioning, were the other.

If Daniel's memory served, this man had been guardian of the mortuary when Daniel was a junior doctor here. Daniel tried to remember his name. Benjamin? Benedict? Something like that. He couldn't recall it precisely, so he played safe.

'I'm a doctor,' he said coolly. 'I used to work here.'

The attendant examined Daniel suspiciously, but betrayed no sense that he remembered him. 'You need one of *our* doctors to come with you,' he said, his words dripping with condescension, as if Daniel suffered from learning difficulties. The unspoken message was: 'Go and find one yourself.'

Daniel stood his ground, returning the attendant's gaze as directly as he could, trying not to blink. As Daniel had learned the hard way, would-be despots are best dealt with early, and by preference directly.

After an uncomfortable interlude, the attendant slowly eased himself out from behind the desk.

'Wait here,' he said, as he slowly pushed through the doors and disappeared up the corridor. It was more than ten minutes before he returned in the wake of a bespectacled, moustachioed man who barged officiously through to where Daniel was waiting.

Daniel took the initiative, mustering as much charm as he could from his dwindling reserves. He removed his glasses and smiled. 'I'm Daniel Hove,' he said, extending his hand in greeting. It was ignored. He went on. 'I was a junior doctor here years ago.'

The man's face tightened at the word *doctor*.

'Ncube,' the man said coldly. 'Duty Doctor.'

The name triggered a response in Daniel's memory.

'Patricia Hove was my sister. Her body's in the mortuary. I'd like to see her, please,' Daniel repeated.

Ncube beckoned with a quick flip of his hand. The attendant leaned over to the table, retrieved a large ledger with a scuffed cover, opened it, and handed it ingratiatingly to him, supporting one wrist with the palm of his other hand. Ncube snatched at it and surveyed the open page.

'The body has already been identified by the family. It is now up to you to make funeral arrangements. As soon as possible. We can't hold it indefinitely.'

Daniel nodded. 'Yes. My mother came here a few days ago, with Dr Mliswa. But I wasn't with her. I have travelled a long way and I would like to see her.'

Ncube was quiet for a moment, and then pushed rudely between Daniel and the attendant. Maybe it was the name

Mliswa which made the difference. Daniel couldn't quite tell. But he and the attendant followed Ncube up a short corridor until they came to a large cold-room door. The attendant scurried forward to open it.

Beyond was a low-ceilinged room that had once been painted white. Three fluorescent tubes hung down from the ceiling, only one of which showed any sign of life, and that was spluttering a dull intermittent yellow at each end.

The door swung shut behind them with a resonant expulsion of air.

At least the refrigeration's still functioning.

A row of dented steel doors stood shoulder to shoulder from one wall to the other. Behind each, Daniel remembered, there would be space for three bodies to be stacked one above another. The attendant scanned the cardboard labels tied to the doors until he found what he was looking for. He pulled on a handle, and then put some effort into sliding out a tray that ground forward on corroded steel rollers.

The body was enveloped by a flimsy off-white plastic body-bag. Ncube took hold of the zipper and pulled it, parting the bag sufficiently to reveal Patricia's face. Daniel looked and then briefly closed his eyes, visualising his sister when he had last seen her.

Long braided hair, wide smile, shocking white teeth. And now you're dead. Patricia. Eight years my junior. Dead. Lying on a mortuary tray in front of me.

He opened his eyes again. Her long braided hair was there, splayed and folded beneath her head, but there was no smile. Her eyes were closed, her mouth shut, and she appeared more at peace than he had expected. It was his sister, but at the same time it was only an approximation of her, like a figure in a waxwork museum.

Daniel blinked, and his professional detachment took over.

Ncube started to close the bag. 'No,' Daniel said firmly. 'I want to see the rest.'

Ncube ignored him, tugging the zipper further towards the top. Daniel put out his hand to stop him, and there was a moment when it seemed they would come to blows.

Eventually Ncube withdrew his hand, and Daniel pinched the zipper between forefinger and thumb. He pulled it fully down to the bottom of the bag, feeling the clamminess of the plastic as it slid against his knuckles. He parted the opening, gently paring the plastic sheeting away from her form.

She was naked, but with no injuries immediately apparent.

Traffic accident? What on earth are they talking about?

Then he saw the discolouration on the edge of one thigh.

'Help me turn her over,' he said.

The attendant glanced at Ncube. There was another pause, and then Ncube nodded slightly and took a step back.

Reluctantly, the attendant moved around to the other side of the tray, and helped prevent the body from falling off as Daniel rolled it over. He looked in horror at what was revealed as her body rolled face down.

* * *

Daniel fished in his jacket pocket, pulled out the death certificate and unfolded it. 'Are you the Dr Ncube who signed this?'

Ncube plucked the paper from Daniel's fingers as if it were infected. He extended his arms and focussed on it. He grunted noncommittally.

'You examined her before you signed it?'

'Of course,' Ncube replied, defensively.

'Then how could you say the cause of death was a traffic accident?' said Daniel baldly, staring at him, waiting for a reply.

Ncube swung sharply on his heel and began to walk out. Daniel grabbed his arm, and forced him back round.

'Fetch security,' Ncube barked, but Daniel glared at the attendant and it was enough to stop him leaving the room.

'Look here,' he said, pointing towards the wounds on Patricia's body.

There was another delay. Ncube stared straight at Daniel, refusing to look down at her body.

'Don't look away. Look at these injuries. Do they look like they were the result of a traffic accident?'

'The investigating officer…'

Daniel could barely contain himself. 'The investigating officer!' he scoffed. 'And if the investigating officer told you the moon was made of green cheese, you'd write that on the death certificate too, would you?'

Ncube stared back with undisguised fury. Daniel glanced past Ncube's shoulder to see the attendant struggling unsuccessfully to wipe a smirk from his lips.

Interesting relationship you two have. Grovelling one minute, taking immense pleasure in watching your boss being humiliated the next.

Daniel returned his gaze to Ncube. 'I'll tell you what caused those injuries. I've seen these kind of wounds before.'

He made a quick estimate of Ncube's age. 'I bet you have as well. Listen carefully. I want you to remember exactly what I say.'

Daniel pointed to two large, almost circular, bruises, one on each of Patricia's buttocks. Dark and mottled, almost black, they stood out aggressively from the lighter brown of the rest of her body They covered almost entirely each mound of flesh.

Daniel indicated a series of thick, almost parallel, marks within the circumference of the bruises.

'Do you seriously think these were caused by a traffic accident?' he said, glaring at Ncube, who remained mute. 'I wouldn't. I'd say they were caused by severe and repeated beating. Maybe something wooden, maybe an iron bar. Difficult to tell. But something like that, straight and regular.'

Ncube started to protest, but Daniel held up his hand. Ncube closed his mouth.

'The underlying tissue has probably been damaged so badly that there'll be necrosis under those bruises. I can't say categorically – an autopsy would be needed, and there obviously hasn't been one - but I'd be willing to bet on it. If she'd lived she'd have had to have all that dead tissue debrided. Then substantial plastic surgery to repair the damage.'

Ncube said nothing.

'And these.' Daniel traced out several of a large number of cuts across Patricia's shoulders, some as if made by a single blade, others perforating her skin, all darkly clotted with blood. They crossed each other at oblique angles, shredding her flesh.

'That's a simple one. No-one could say those wounds were the result of a traffic accident. Looks like she was whipped with a bicycle chain.'

Again he looked at Ncube, who stared back at him defiantly.

'The point is,' Daniel continued, 'there is enough evidence there, for any fool to see, to show that the cause of death was not a traffic accident, as you wrote on her death certificate. She was very severely assaulted, and it looks as if she died soon afterwards. I don't know with precision what the cause of death was. Maybe an embolism caused a heart attack or a stroke. Maybe she died from shock. I don't know.'

'But neither do you, and that's the point. Your duty, your *legal* duty if there is *any* doubt about the cause of death, is to write your doubts on the death certificate and recommend a post mortem. That used to be the law when I worked here. I bet it hasn't changed. I hope you remembered all that. Because now you're going to write out another one. Let's go to your office and do it right now.'

'No,' said Ncube, finally regaining the power of speech. 'I will not be intimidated. What is on the death certificate is consistent with the injuries. The injuries are consistent with what the investigating officer wrote in the police report. I will not write out another one. If you have a problem, then take it up with the investigating officer.'

He turned to the attendant. 'Get him out of here!' he shouted. 'Now!' He marched out.

Daniel, shaking his head in disbelief, watched him disappear. He turned to the mortuary attendant, who was by now beaming uncontrollably. He obviously had no intention of ejecting Daniel from anywhere.

'What about her clothing? Personal effects?'

The attendant reached up to the top of the mortuary cabinet and pulled down a large opaque plastic bag, the top of which was tied loosely in a knot. Daniel could see fabric through it, but when he took it from the attendant, it weighed hardly anything. It was clammy and cold, like the body-bag.

He loosened the knot and extracted the contents. A faded blue denim shirt. Nothing else.

'That all? No trousers? Skirt, underwear? Shoes? Bag?'

The attendant shook his head. 'That was all the police brought in with her.'

'And who exactly is this investigating officer that your boss spoke about?' Daniel asked.

'Inspector Mpofu' he replied. 'Jahunda Police Camp. South of Gwanda.'

He turned and walked from the room, and Daniel could have sworn he detected a swagger in his step that hadn't been there before.

* * *

Gwanda is a leafy, house-proud little town that looks as if it might once have been an outer suburb of the city that had somehow slid down the road and come to rest against a range of low hills that blocked its passage further south.

Precisely how little it is, is a matter of constant local debate. Not as small as that, says the chairman of the local council, pointing to the official census figure and claiming a conspiracy to deprive the town of development funds. Smaller than that, claims a persistently unsuccessful candidate for a council seat, indicating the voters' roll, padded as it is with the underage, the fictitious and the already dead, who loyally turn out for the ruling party at every poll.

Whatever the exact figure, and although a little scruffy in places, the colourful parade of shops along one side of the pleasant main street was doing a brisk trade as Daniel drove past. Parked up on the other side of the road under an extended rank of trees were several gargantuan long-distance trucks pulled over for a break in their journey, huge black tarpaulins stretched like elephant hide over their towering loads.

Several drivers lounged against the heavy-duty shoulder-high cow-catchers, chatting with small groups of people sat on the edge of the road in the shade of the trees.

But the main street was short and Daniel was through the town in minutes, emerging on the other side into countryside bristling with spark-dry bush.

South of Gwanda, the attendant said. That could mean anything, but then again, it shouldn't be too difficult to find.

There hadn't been much traffic since he had left the hospital and, after unsuccessfully trying Mliswa's number again, had begun the journey south. He hadn't passed many roadside buildings before he had got to Gwanda, and he knew there would be even fewer before he hit the next small town. Twice he had seen the headgear of an isolated mineshaft standing proud above the surrounding bush, but apart from those there were very few signs of habitation. A police camp should stick out like the proverbial.

It wasn't long before Daniel saw a red-roofed store appear ahead on the right hand side of the road. Opposite the store on the other side of the dirt road leading off to the right was a large rock, painted entirely in blue, with a long wobbly painted arrow and the words 'St Cuthberts Mission' above it, both picked out in white.

Daniel smiled briefly. An apostrophe had at one time or another been placed both before and after the final *s*. Both attempts at grammatical precision had now been abandoned, painted out in a fresher blue.

Facing the store on the left hand side of the tar was a compound fenced in by tall chain-mesh topped by a narrow coil of razor-wire. A sign warning of the approaching intersection became legible as he neared it, and Daniel began to slow. He saw that the entrance to the compound lay just around the corner of the junction on the dirt road.

He turned and drove up to the fence. A sign on the gate spelled it out: Zimbabwe Republic Police. Jahunda.

There was movement in the sentry box, and the guard shambled out. He walked to the gates, unlocked the huge padlock and unlooped the forbidding-looking chain. He pushed one gate open and then stood in front of Daniel's car.

Slowly and fastidiously he copied the car's number-plate onto his clipboard. He closely examined his handwriting and finished it off with stabbed full stop, which he then ground into the paper with the point of his pencil. He walked slowly to the side of the car. His questions were perfunctory, but he wrote Daniel's answers down on his clipboard with the same fussiness.

He turned and pulled open the other gate. He walked through the entrance, pushed up the boom, and allowed Daniel to drive through and park. Daniel was soon in the charge office asking the duty sergeant for Inspector Mpofu.

Mpofu eventually entered through a door behind the counter, at the back of the charge office. As Mpofu strode into the room, the sergeant and another of his subordinates retreated to lean against the back wall, observing with smirks on their faces, arms folded disdainfully across their chests. They had obviously seen Mpofu perform before.

He stood with a bored expression on his face, hyperthyroid eyes staring out contemptuously from under hooded eyelids. He wore a light grey short-sleeved shirt that had been ironed to geometric perfection, the faultless creases giving the sleeves a sharp edge. The front of his shirt presented an almost perfect plane that gleamed with accumulated starch. A cloth slide embroidered with his badges of rank sat neatly centred on each of his epaulettes.

A dazzling set of polished brass force initials stood picket at the end of each shoulder. A short line of medal ribbons were pinned above the precision-pleated centre of his left breast pocket. They were exactly horizontal. They could have stood in for a spirit level.

The very model of a police officer, except for the fact that he was digging the grime out from under his finger nails with the end of a matchstick, and dropping the result onto the countertop.

From his demeanour, it was plain that he had been warned of Daniel's visit. He dismissed Daniel's questions with unconcealed irritation.

'I myself went to the incident.' He tapped his chest with a substantial forefinger, while his other forefinger and thumb held the matchstick poised for action. Daniel worried for the perfection of the finish of the shirt, but the starch had been skilfully applied and didn't crack.

'We get a lot of those things round here.' Mpofu sniffed, as if mystified as to how people managed to get themselves into such situations. 'People walking at night on the side of the road, not taking proper caution of the traffic. Drunk, maybe. There is a lot of drunks. Walking crooked on the road, and then a truck comes and they get it.'

He clicked his thumb and middle finger loudly across his chest to emphasise the finality of such an event. He resumed his labours on his fingernails.

'She wasn't hit by a truck,' objected Daniel. 'She was severely assaulted. Beaten repeatedly on the buttocks, and whipped across the shoulders with what looks like a bicycle chain. You saw her body. You know she wasn't hit by a truck.'

'The cause of death is on the death certificate. Ask the hospital. There was a traffic accident,' Mpofu said, his voice now carrying more than an edge of menace. 'Just down the road there,' he said, gesturing vaguely towards the door without looking up.

Daniel shook his head in frustration. 'Not true,' he said. 'You know that's not true!'

'You were not there. It was a traffic accident,' said Mpofu, staring straight at Daniel. 'You are very mistaken.'

Daniel changed tack. 'She was wearing just a blue shirt when you found her?'

'That's what we found. We don't know why she was half-naked. Maybe she was in a shebeen.'

Daniel let Mpofu's obvious insult wash past. 'And the truck? Whose truck was it?' he continued.

'We don't know. Plenty, plenty trucks drive up and down this road all night. We don't know which truck hit her.'

'And there was nothing else? No Bag? ID?'

'Nothing. Only that shirt. It was very very lucky for you the doctor knew her face. Otherwise no-one would know her.'

'And what are you going to do now?' asked Daniel. 'Are you going to look for this truck?'

'The docket has not been closed. We don't know why she was there. We don't know which truck hit her. If we find out anything you will be told.'

With that he flicked the matchstick down behind the counter. There must have been a bin there, because Daniel heard it land with a dull metallic ring. Finally, Mpofu brushed the fingernail shavings from the countertop in Daniel's direction, turned on his heels, and left Daniel staring at the flawlessly pressed back of his shirt as it left the room.

* * *

There it might have ended, in anger, frustration, but ultimately in resignation.

Daniel began his journey home. He stopped briefly in the town to fill up with petrol, anxious to get under way before the light disappeared completely. Even though Mpofu was an unabashed liar, he was right about one thing. Driving at night on a country road, with unlit obstacles around every bend, could be fatal.

Broken down cars, wandering cattle, abandoned scotch carts, staggering drunks. You name it, everyone knows someone who's met his maker by colliding with it on a dark country road. And on a Friday night...

While waiting for the garage attendant to finish filling his tank he noticed two white twin-cab pickups parked one in front of the other on the side of the road. They were sat where the gargantuan trucks had been parked earlier when he had driven past in the opposite direction. They were shiny and new, and they carried no number plates.

Twin twin-cabs! Must be on their way from the showroom to their new owners...

He then forgot about them completely.

Until one of them overtook him as Daniel drove past the town limits and accelerated onto the open road. He watched it speed past, and felt it too, his car swaying slightly as if it had been sideswiped. He cursed as the vehicle swung back in front of him and immediately began to slow down.

Daniel angrily flicked on the indicators, then checked his mirror, intending to overtake and put the twin-cab in front of him firmly behind him. But as he was about to swing out, the second twin-cab pulled up next to him, the occupant of the front passenger seat gesturing for him to pull over. Daniel looked to left and right, rapidly considered his options. He had none. The rolling roadblock was forcing him to stop.

As he came to a halt his door was jerked opened and he was pulled out with shuddering force. Before he could gather his senses, someone else was sat in the driver's seat, and Daniel was wedged into the back seat behind him between two large men, with his glasses missing and a blindfold partly covering his eyes. They started up again, and the three vehicles left in convoy, the twin-cabs bracketing his mother's car in front and behind.

A short distance further on they turned off the main

highway onto a dirt road. Daniel felt a rattle of sharp bumps through the seat and thought that they must just have driven over a cattle grid. But as they went further he saw through the side of his blindfold that it was a railway line that ran parallel to the road.

They stopped violently. He was hauled out, uncomprehending and unsteady. He had his legs kicked out from under him and was pinned to the ground. Someone unseen grabbed his left ankle and jerked his leg off the ground.

'Take him halfway,' a voice said behind him.

Shortly afterwards a crowbar slammed down onto his shin midway between his ankle and his knee.

* * *

He came to unable to see out of one eye and at a total loss as to what time it was, or even what day. He had a terrible ache in his back, his groin was swollen, his head was thumping. There were bruises and cuts along the length of his arms. But knifing through every other anguish-filled sensation was an excruciating pain centred on his left leg. Bolts of agony were radiating out from it, and when he tried to move the pain was so intense that he felt he was about to pass out again.

He tried to think logically.

Complete fracture of the fibula, he concluded, as if studying an invisible x-ray. *Could be worse. Could have been the tibia as well.*

He tried to look down to see whether the skin had been broken. But as he did so another spasm passed through him.

And there was nothing he could do to help himself, because his wrists were strapped tight to the steering wheel and to each other by yellow plastic cable ties.

As he looked fuzzily out of the window with his good eye, he saw in the gloom that the car was straddling the railway line. In one direction the rails ran towards each other and the horizon. In the other, they ran straight for a short distance before bending gently away behind a hillock and out of sight. The keys were in the ignition, but he couldn't reach them because the steering wheel was locked and the ties around his wrists were too tight.

The permutations began to run through his fazed brain.

How often do the trains run? Which direction will the first one come from? Will it be able to stop?

More than one inconvenient politician or General had met his end when 'the vehicle in which he was travelling was in a collision with a moving train', as the announcements in the official newspapers sombrely put it. Disbelievers, which included almost everyone, knew there must have been some other cause of death, and not accidental. The worn out joke was that it would be impossible for a car to be hit by a moving train, since the trains never ran.

In a moment of absurdity, Daniel prayed that the jokers were correct.

* * *

The two twin-cabs were already dispersed across the countryside, visiting every headman in every village in the district. Warnings were given, exhortations made. Anyone seen asking questions, any strangers noticed, must be reported to Jahunda Police immediately. Hats were removed, heads were uncovered, all nodding in assent.

'Of course, of course. We know our duty, sir,' they said obediently. A few meant it.

Five

D aniel thought he was hallucinating. As the sun rose, and he was still calculating the odds on his fate in the gathering light, a large black 4x4 drove up. Two men climbed out and walked towards him. One did look familiar, but without his glasses Daniel couldn't be sure. Their faces were blurred, as if they were mirages.

But he wasn't dreaming. As the figures drew nearer Daniel recognised the features, older and a lot fuller, of Henry Mliswa.

The door next to him was opened. One of the men looked in and then returned to the 4x4. He returned with a stubby knife which he used to cut Daniel's manacles.

The two men began to help him from the car, but the movement re-energised the pain emanating from his leg and he screamed in agony. Mliswa bent over him to look down at the leg, and rose again shaking his head in concern. When he looked back up at Daniel his expression was serious.

'We'll make up a litter for you,' he said. 'Then we'll get you to hospital. Your leg needs a bit of patching up. Pretty quickly.'

He was back a few seconds later with a large sheet of canvas, which they laid out next to the car. The two men manoeuvred him out and onto it as he shuddered and arched with pain. It wasn't long before he was lying flat on the back seat of the 4x4, willing, with all the concentration he could muster, that the spasms which were spearing through his body would stop. He waited what seemed an eternity while Mliswa's companion drove his mother's car clear of the railway tracks. Then the two vehicles drove in tandem back to the main road.

'You OK back there?' Mliswa said, glancing over his shoulder from the driving seat once they had turned onto the tar and Daniel was able to relax his grip on the sides of the seat a little. 'Lucky we found you.'

Daniel stared back through his unswollen eye, dumbfounded.

'I got your messages on my cell yesterday evening, I tried phoning back but I got no answer. It's obvious why, now. So I phoned your mother,' said Mliswa, anticipating Daniel's questions. 'She was very worried. She told me you hadn't come home. She said you'd gone to the hospital, and that you might have driven down to Gwanda after that.'

'I live down here now. I've got business interests round here,' he continued. 'I try to keep on top of what's going on. They're saying in town that a driver was abducted from his car on the road out of town yesterday evening. I put two and two together, and we've been having a look round this morning. Lucky you weren't very far from the main road.'

Daniel was speechless. But even if he had managed to formulate the words in his brain, he doubted whether his swollen lips would have been able to utter them.

'I'm taking you to hospital. It'll be like old times, except this time you're going as a patient. They'll sort that leg out. And the rest of you,' said Mliswa.

Daniel groaned. This time it wasn't from pain. The thought of being anywhere near the tender mercies of Dr Ncube in even the most marginal way filled him with dread. He tried to speak, and this time he managed to get something intelligible past his lips.

'Not there,' he said. 'Somewhere private. There must be somewhere private.'

'As you wish,' Mliswa said.

He pulled out his phone and tapped in a number with his thumb while he drove.

'Mrs Hove,' he said cheerily after an interval. 'I've got your son with me. He needs a bit of attention to his leg. No, no – he's fine. Nothing that can't be fixed. Once I've taken him to hospital we'll drop off your car. Here, have a word with him.'

He thrust the phone back over the seat to Daniel, who painfully held it to his ear. He mumbled into it, and then returned it almost apologetically to Mliswa, who finished the conversation for him.

Shortly after they left the railway line, a train emerged from behind the hillock. Driven relentlessly forward by the momentum generated by the locomotive and several hundred tons of fully laden freight wagons, the juggernaut bore straight through the void where Daniel's mother's car no longer sat stranded. The driver wouldn't have been able to stop, no matter what he tried.

* * *

Daniel lay in a hospital bed, his leg in plaster and his other injuries an abstract patchwork of startling white dressings and the dull red patina left by swabs of antiseptic. He examined himself. There were rows of stitches in several places which twinged and caught every time he moved. The pain in his leg had been stilled, but he still felt groggy and nauseous.

Must be the hangover from the anaesthetic.

He looked around, suddenly anxious about which hospital he was in. But his room wasn't decorated like any that he remembered. A movement in the corridor beyond the door attracted his attention, and he saw a nun in a wimple walk past the doorway.

They don't wear those in government hospitals...

He relaxed.

He gradually became aware that someone was observing him. He turned awkwardly, trying to twist his torso without moving his leg. Mliswa was sitting silently in an armchair next to the bed. Daniel was finally able to draw his thoughts together.

'Do you remember we used to get those people brought into casualty who'd been beaten so badly? Backsides and shoulders whipped until there was hardly anything left?'

He was slurring his words, but Mliswa appeared to have understood what he said, and nodded.

'Someone did the same to Patricia,' Daniel said. He paused. 'I'm surprised you didn't see the marks on her body.'

'Really? I didn't see anything like that. There was nothing obvious,' Mliswa replied smoothly. He, too, paused, then continued. 'I do the occasional duty shift at the Gwanda hospital. The police brought Patricia's body in while I was there. When I saw her face I recognised her straight away. I knew your mother was still living in Bulawayo, so I arranged with the police for your sister to be taken to the hospital there. I thought it would be easier for everybody that way.'

'But I didn't examine her. She was in a police body-bag.

Perhaps I should have done. I left that to the doctor in Bulawayo, since he'd be taking responsibility for her body. And when I went with your mother they said it would have upset her, so I didn't insist. I read the death certificate and just took what it said at face value...'

'That death certificate is a load of bullshit,' said Daniel. 'Traffic accident, that doctor put on it. Fucking liar. I know what I saw. Those injuries were from a very severe beating. Not a collision with a truck. And now this. I ask questions, and this is what happens.'

'It certainly looks like more than coincidence…'

'Please!' Daniel protested, and immediately regretted it as a spasm of pain passed through his body. 'Of course it's not bloody coincidence! You don't beat someone like Patricia was beaten just for the hell of it. She was being punished – tortured - for some reason. You know how they used to do it. What could she have done for them to do that to her?'

'And if the attack on me was just coincidence, what were they after? Why didn't they steal the car? They took my phone. Emptied my wallet – not that there was much in it – but they left my passport. And why strap me up and put me on the railway line? Why go to all that trouble for a bit of foreign currency? From the look of the cars they were driving, they don't need the money. The only other things missing are my glasses.'

'Not even those,' said Mliswa, grinning.

He reached up from his chair and handed Daniel his spectacles, or what was left of them. They were broken in two at the bridge. One lens was missing – just the arm remaining - the other lens was heavily scratched, the arm very bent. 'Unfortunately, that lens is in the wrong place for your good eye,' he joked.

The joke fell flat.

How on earth did you get them?

'They were on the back seat of your car,' Mliswa said, as if Daniel had asked the question out loud.

Daniel didn't know whether to believe him or not.

Stop it. Stop it. This is sheer paranoia.

'You tell me, Henry. What do I do?' he demanded, returning to his point. 'The hospital and the police deny the obvious truth. And when I try to find out what really happened to her, this happens. That bloody policeman was lying through his teeth. I knew he was and he knew I knew. But he must have cared that I knew, because look what happened to me. This was a warning to me to shut up, to stop asking questions. Just like it used to be.'

He remembered with some embarrassment his earlier conversation with his mother.

'They do what they want, nobody can stop them, and they don't give a shit. Total impunity. But why am I being warned? What's this all about? You tell me, Henry. What do I do now?'

'Concentrate on getting back on your feet again. That's the most important thing,' said Mliswa. 'But you're right. This whole thing stinks. I'll ask around. I'll keep my ears open. Maybe I'll hear something.' There was a pause. 'But what can you tell me? Do you know why she had travelled up here? Your mother said she hadn't told her she was coming. Why do you think she was here?'

'I'm ashamed to say I don't know anything at all,' was Daniel's subdued reply.

She was living in Cape Town. She had finished studying. She wasn't married. That much I think is true. As to the rest... She was working. She was looking for a job. She was unemployed. Maybe. Maybe not. Relationships? Who knows? Any or none of the above might be true.

'But whatever she was doing, nothing deserves what they did to her,' he went on.

They both sat in silence again. It was Daniel who broke it. 'Business interests, Henry? You given up medicine?'

'Not completely. I still have a small practise. Keeping my hand in. But I also have a couple of businesses in Gwanda, a few other projects. There's better money in those than in a medical practice, I promise you. Moving out here was the best thing I ever did.'

'If you find out anything, please let me know,' he continued. He stared directly at Daniel. 'I'll try and find out what I can. But, as I said, it would help if I had some idea of what she was doing, And if there's any other way you think I can help, please just ask. Now. We need to get you back to your mother. How good are you on crutches?'

* * *

There were more mourners at her funeral than he would have thought possible. Elderly relatives and friends of his mother, mostly, mustered by an urban variant of the bush telegraph. Of Patricia's contemporaries, there was only Henry Mliswa and a female school friend of hers who, exceptionally, had not joined the universal exodus of the young to brighter lights. And him.

They stood in a respectful silent group around the freshly dug earth, gently perspiring in the morning warmth.

50

As her coffin was lowered in the crowded cemetery, Daniel felt his grief overtaken by dejection. In the unlikely event that he had ever contemplated where his sister might be buried, he certainly wouldn't have thought of this depressing place.

Grave after grave in rank after ragged rank, most with only a crudely painted metal sign on a steel fence post to mark them. And they were new graves too, the vast bulk of them, mounds of soil yet to fully settle in front of each marker. Daniel did the arithmetic as they processed through them. Thirty years old, forty two, thirty five, younger: men and women alike who hadn't died of old age, buried in the bare red earth carved out of the Matabeleland bush, which was advancing back over the inadequate fence on several fronts.

Accompanying the dejection was embarrassment that he, leaning heavily on crutches and with the bruises and lesions from his beating still angry and visible, was attracting as much attention as his sister's coffin. Nothing was said in so many words, but it was obvious that everyone knew the circumstances surrounding his injuries. He now carried about him, like an invisible leper's bell, a warning that he should be kept at a distance by anyone who wasn't a close family acquaintance, and some of those who were.

The only mementos of Patricia that he had - if he could call them that - were several photographs that he had taken once her body had been released from the custody of the hospital mortuary. Daniel had again insisted on her body being rolled over so he could make a record of her wounds, much to the undertaker's open dismay. No doubt that story had also already done the rounds.

And so Daniel returned, downcast and sore, to a wintry England. He was mobile and off his crutches again more quickly than he had thought likely, and on his return to St Botolph's he requested a short sabbatical. It was granted a little too rapidly for comfort by the management inquisitors.

But he no longer gave a damn.

Six

D aniel slept fitfully until they began the descent from the escarpment, but after the sight of the first baobab he was wide awake, and tense and alert. The bus was packed, and he was wedged into a sticky plastic seat by a woman of substantial girth. There the similarity with the commuter service from Fenchurch Street ended. The temperature had risen as the altitude fell, and the bus seemed airless despite the open windows. The red late afternoon sun was beating strongly down through them. They seemed to magnify its force.

The interior was a travelling street scene. Snacks purchased from vendors at the last stop were being unwrapped and devoured straight from their greasy wrappings. An inharmonious cacophony of conversation in half a dozen languages was being shouted joyously from one end of the bus to the other. Most startling of all was the overwhelming smell of humanity, a not-so-delicate blend of cheap soap, perspiration, sorghum beer and Vaseline.

Outwardly, his wounds appeared to have healed well in the intervening weeks. But he still limped, favouring his left leg, and there were still the occasional unbearable spikes of pain. A long vivid scar was visible on his scalp, and scabs still covered the weals and scars on both of his shins. His eyes were both now functioning again, and he had replaced his rimless glasses with a pair with thick black plastic frames. Not the least bit stylish, and with the desired benefit of completely changing his appearance.

His clothes were cheap and ill-fitting, purchased in a

bargain clothing shop in a distressed Johannesburg city centre street the morning before. He had walked some considerable distance from his hotel room in one of the city's swankier inner suburbs before he found, on a well-watered golf course, a place private enough to roughen them up on the soil and grass. He needn't have bothered. Six hours on this sweaty bus would have been enough to reduce the most robust of clothing to limp and filthy rags.

He no longer projected any presence at all. He looked dishevelled and forlorn, one of life's victims. But although there was nothing in his appearance to mark him out from the other passengers, Daniel felt as if he was permanently on the brink of being exposed as an impostor.

He had devoted some considerable effort into steering a line between appearing to be affable and maintaining his anonymity. He had slept and pretended to sleep. When spoken to, he shook and nodded his head and grinned rather than spoke. Better to appear to be a gurning idiot, he reasoned, than reveal an accent and attitude that didn't fit with his appearance.

The miles accumulated with agonising slowness as they pushed on through the flat countryside below the escarpment. Eventually he saw a plume of industrial smoke on the horizon, and not long afterwards the low dusty border mining town of Messina came into view.

* * *

Daniel let himself down gingerly from the bus, feeling his left leg twist with a sharp stab of pain as he lowered his weight onto it. He carried a large multi-coloured bag woven from recycled plastic, purchased from the kiosk next door to the Johannesburg clothing shop, in which he carried only a coat. Apart from a few notes and coins in his pockets, what valuables he had with him, including a cheap plastic camera and several spare rolls of film, he had secreted – he hoped – in a money-belt strapped around his waist.

Making his way through the dust to the rear of the bus, he looked out on a panorama that, even given the queue of vehicles sitting bumper to bumper and extending from one end of a very long thoroughfare to the other, could have been transported wholesale from some ancient eastern bazaar.

There were people disgorging from the buses and people climbing onto them. Drivers stood on top catching luggage swung up at them from the kerbside. Bags like Daniel's, bicycles, all manner of trussed-up packages and suitcases, all being passed up, wedged in and tied down with tarpaulins for the journey. Or untied and dropped down the sides of the bus to their waiting owners, who checked each one briefly to make sure it was theirs and then lugged it away to join a growing pile guarded by some other member of their travelling group. And they were travelling in groups, the vast majority of them. Daniel was unusual in travelling alone.

Shops on both sides of the road were selling every conceivable requisite from kitchen equipment to underwear. They were piled up in the shop windows and advertised on garishly coloured hoardings that ran in an uninterrupted strip above the awnings of the shops as far as he could see.

Like some sluggish worm, the traffic – buses, massive trucks, cars and taxis - nosed its way through the limited space left in the middle of the road, stopping and starting as eddies of pedestrians with no apparent fear treated it as if it didn't exist.

In the middle of it all, under trees surviving by some miracle in front of a fast food shop, a group of women sat straight-legged and serene on brightly coloured blankets laid out on the dirt, some dandling small children on their laps, oblivious to the mayhem going on around them.

That's what I need. Somewhere to sit down and think.

He crossed the street and made his way through the crowds to a shop on a corner. He bought himself a large cold bottle of water and two pastry-covered slabs that lay wilting inside a greasy counter-top warming oven.

As he emerged onto the pavement he was confronted by a beggar, a tall man with no obvious infirmities but with an older woman following dolefully one step behind him, hands cupped in supplication. Daniel was about to refuse, but his conscience pricked, and he thrust his hands into his pocket and gave the man the change from his purchases.

There was an immediate reaction. Daniel found himself surrounded by a besieging circle of beggars, most of them children.

His patience fast evaporating, the final straw came when he felt a dull pressure around his waist. He jerked round to see a young girl running away from him. He felt quickly above the waistband of his trousers. The money belt was still there, but only just. One of the cords securing it had been untied.

Daniel marvelled momentarily at the dexterity of the young girl's fingers, then tucked his shirt into his trousers to secure the belt. He forced himself out of the encirclement, zig-zagged his way through the crowds on the pavement, and then abandoned the pavement for the road, where he found it easier to move.

He scolded himself. *No more philanthropy. Look the part, act the part.*

He made his way up the street until the crowds thinned. Some distance further on he came to a piece of open ground, an inferior sort of municipal park. It was bordered with a low barrier of creosoted gum poles, rising a foot or so above the ground. A large steel notice board listed the forbidden activities. Dogs, footballs, fires, bicycles...

There was some shade under a line of eucalyptus trees. He lowered himself unsteadily to the ground, taking care not to strain his leg, and leaned up against the trunk of one of the trees.

As he bit into his food, which was still hot enough to burn the roof of his mouth, he turned his mind to his next problem.

Where am I going to sleep? And where can I find someone to spirit me over the border?

* * *

As he sat pondering his options, Daniel saw a large man walk past the open ground. He stopped at an oil drum swung between two stout wooden posts which was overflowing with rubbish. The man leaned over the drum and dug into it, his bulk making the movement a little comical. Finding nothing, he straightened himself up and waddled on.

On an impulse, Daniel waved him over, holding out the

greasy bag containing the remaining pastry. The man came nearer, slowly, suspiciously. Eventually he put his hand out to take Daniel's offering.

His appearance on closer examination was anything but comical. His clothes were frayed and torn, black and shiny with grime. His hair was fixed in a thick rigid greasy wave, and he sported several weeks' worth of long filthy uneven beard. He was white, Daniel could see from his features, but it was not obvious from the colour of his skin. It was stained with ingrained dirt. And his bulk was deceiving. His face and neck were very gaunt and Daniel realised he must be wearing several layers of clothes.

He made as if to move away, but Daniel gestured for him to sit, and then waited as the man devoured the food, chewing furiously as if it to prevent it escaping. Daniel offered the bottle of water. The tramp took it gratefully.

Daniel let him drain the bottle and wipe his lips on a crusty soiled sleeve. Then he asked: 'I need to cross the border. Who can help me?'

The tramp surveyed him, weighing up the prospects with an experienced yellow eye. He raised two foul fingers, the nails blackened and cracked, and rubbed them together in the universal language.

Daniel fished in a pocket and extracted a note, which he held out towards the tramp. A hand darted out and snatched the money from Daniel's grasp, and the face broke into a huge grin, revealing two serially-interrupted rows of teeth. They looked like milestones, some of them almost as far apart. None of them were white.

The tramp gestured away from the road, indicating a destination on the horizon.

'Nthabiseng Bar. Barman.'

At least, that's what it sounded like. The tramp's lips were sunburnt and swollen and his words were slurred. He probably wasn't used to conversing with other human beings.

In response to Daniel's quizzical look, he gestured again into the far distance. He mumbled something which Daniel didn't catch, and then looked expectantly at him, wondering whether there was more business to be done. Eventually deciding not, he rolled himself unsteadily to his feet and moved on to resume his trawl through the litter bins.

* * *

Following the tramp's vague directions, Daniel struck out away from the main street and the park. He walked through a small estate of neat houses set apart from each other on substantial plots. There were neatly tended lawns mown into startling green stripes which looked so out of place against the drab brown of the surrounding veld. Sprinklers hissed and waved in an endless dance.

Passing one house, he heard the sounds of shrieking children and splashing water from a backyard swimming pool.

He left the houses behind, and after passing underneath a gigantic pendulous loom of high voltage powerlines, he found himself in open veld with a row of low buildings in the far distance. The light had faded rapidly, and Daniel walked as briskly as he could to reach them. The open space was there for a purpose, he decided when he reached the other side of it. It was a social engineer's *cordon sanitaire*, to separate what he had left behind from what he saw before him.

It was a sprawling slum. The buildings were small rude constructions. Some were divided from each other by sorry-looking wire fences, but the barriers were only notional. The houses were unceremoniously jammed together along the narrow streets. As he walked further towards the centre, the plots became smaller, the houses older and more decrepit. What light there was came from a few tall pylons, each supporting a circle of stadium lights shining down, creating as much shadow as illumination as the natural light faded.

Daniel followed the rudimentary roads for a while, walking carefully to avoid twisting his leg again in the ridges and potholes, but it didn't take him long to find what he was looking for. The steady beat and high guitar notes of a live *mbaqanga* band, and a bright glow showing through the windows where everything else was dimly lit, had attracted a full house.

Immediately he entered the door of the shebeen, after a once-over by a doubtful bouncer on the door, Daniel had to wriggle his way into an almost solid crowd smothered by a fug of tobacco smoke. There was nothing outside that identified it, but on the inside of the door the name Nthabiseng Bar was spelled out in glittery red and silver letters. Make me happy, it meant. From the look of the interior, they were doing a fine job.

He found the bar, in reality a low table from behind which a seated barman was producing cold dripping-wet bottles of beer from an ice-filled zinc bath on the floor beside him. Daniel bought one, nearly dropping it as the paper label and the glass bottle parted company in his grasp. The contents went down quickly. This was summer in the Limpopo valley where the earth is already warm underfoot before a new day's sun has fully risen, and he was thirstier than he imagined.

He bought another and prepared to engage the barman in conversation. He waited until another customer had been dealt with, and then took his chance.

'I need to cross the border. Do you know who can help me?' he asked uncertainly, not sure if he was talking loudly enough to be heard above the music.

He wasn't. The barman inclined his head, indicating he hadn't heard.

'I need to cross to Zimbabwe. Do you know anyone who can help me?' he repeated a little louder.

'The border post is that way,' said the barman, pointing.

Daniel smiled apologetically. 'No,' he said, persisting, as quietly as the din allowed. 'I need to cross... without formalities.'

'You think I can help?' the barman enquired. 'You some kind of cop or something?'

His head, like Daniel's, was shaved. Unlike Daniel, he was tall and extremely well built. Daniel supposed his duties also included ejecting troublesome patrons. But he was wearing a jovial expression, and Daniel detected a teasing tone in his voice.

'No. I'm not a cop. Someone I met said I should ask you.'

The barman looked him up and down, amused. Then he beamed, raising his eyebrows in amusement.

'Famous? Me?' He laughed infectiously and Daniel grinned stupidly with him.

Famous among the tramps.

'Travelling light?' the barman continued.

Daniel looked back, puzzled.

'Travelling light, my friend. No papers.'

Daniel nodded, embarrassed at having his ignorance further exposed. *Sharpen up. If you want to survive this little escapade.*

'Wait,' said the barman. He pointed to a corner of the room. Daniel looked round to see if anyone else had heard. 'You're thirsty, I can see.' The barman grinned broadly and handed Daniel another bottle. 'And one for me.' There was a pause. Daniel fished in his pocket again and paid up.

Daniel moved away and began sipping slowly from his third beer of a very short evening. He kept glancing over at the barman, but saw no evidence that he was doing anything to help him. The alcohol began to have its effect. He began to relax, despite himself.

He smelt her before he really saw her. A bow wave of cheap cloying scent rolled back the reek of tobacco smoke and enveloped him. She arrived shortly afterwards. She wore an impressive glistening synthetic wig. Her face was covered by a heavy application of makeup, but her clothing revealed considerably more than it covered. What appeared to Daniel to be several acres of flesh trembled as she came to a halt.

She was too close - much closer than he felt was comfortable - so he stepped back. But she followed, as if tied to him. He saw her mouth move, but he struggled to hear her voice above the clamour. She moved even closer. The wig was now threatening to bury his face, and he heard her suggesting that he might like to buy her a drink.

He raised both his hands, declining in sign language,

shaking his head in emphasis.

She must be desperate for business, considering how I look, never mind how I must smell. Or maybe I'm undetectable through her perfume.

She took no notice, signalling imperiously to the barman, who came over with a fluorescent red distillation in a tall glass with a straw, and yet another beer for Daniel. Daniel conceded defeat and paid up again.

She took his hand firmly and pulled him towards the door. Daniel made a feeble attempt at resistance, but she was having none of it. Her grip was tight, her will determined. There were leers and crude shouts from the crowd as she pulled him along in her wake. They burst out through the door together and she pushed him provocatively up against the wall.

'I am hearing you like to travel,' she said. Her voice was husky and provocative, camp to the point of parody. She took a long draw through the straw. The realisation of what was going on slowly penetrated Daniel's sedated brain.

'The end of town, that side,' she continued in a more businesslike tone. 'There is a business place. Mechanics, so on. Retreaders. You can't miss it. Go round to the back, away from the road. You will see people waiting, I think. Twelve o'clock midnight. After then. Someone will pick you there, I am sure. Omalayisha.'

'What?'

'O-ma-la-yi-sha.' She spelled it out phonetically, as if he was an idiot. 'People movers. The People Removal Company. Private Limited.' Her considerable mouth fell open and she roared at her own joke.

'How much?' asked Daniel, feeling like an idiot.

She shrugged, 'For the trip? You must ask when you are there. For my introduction - fifty rand.'

She held out her hand, palm upwards, and fixed her eyes on his.

Daniel did the maths. *Steep. Even assuming a generous exchange rate.*

He looked sideways. The barman had come outside. Daniel saw him staring at him, grinning in amusement.

No choice.

He removed a fold of notes from his pocket, and dealt off several of them into her grasp. She folded them up again and tucked them beneath her low-cut neckline without breaking her stare.

Then she looked him up and down theatrically, and smoothed down the collar of his shirt with her plump fingers. A garish ring was wedged onto each one, like a disjointed set of knuckle-dusters. The huskiness returned. 'And as for me,' she drawled. 'Dalling. If you think you can afford it, come and talk to me inside.'

She roared again, pushed herself away from him with a playful shove, then turned and flounced back into the bar, leaving eddies of bad scent behind her. The noise from within rose to a crescendo and then died away as the door swung closed again.

Daniel stood, becalmed, retracing the events of the previous half hour.

How did I not see at least some of that coming? They must be laughing their heads off in there. She'll be drinking out on that story for weeks.

* * *

Daniel was surprised at how simple it had been. Serendipitously, and with minimal effort from himself, both his problems had been solved at once. He had planned on it taking until the weekend to arrange a clandestine crossing of the border, and now he also wouldn't have the more immediate worry about where he was going to sleep. All at the cost of a bit of money and a certain degree of embarrassment. As he walked towards the northern edge of town, he was, if not happy, then a little more confident.

The main road was still quite busy. Some traffic was moving north to join the queue for the morning opening of the border crossing. There were even a few vehicles travelling south, although both border posts had been closed for hours already.

He found the retreaders' yard without difficulty, and walked slowly around the edge of the business estate under dull orange industrial lighting until he found himself at the back of it, facing into a dark expanse of bush.

As his eyes adjusted he could see a few figures sitting low to the ground some distance away. He made his way steadily towards them, all the way hoping that he wasn't stumbling – again - into something he couldn't handle.

They were prospective travellers like himself, he guessed. Travelling light, in the barman's phrase.

There were still several hours to go before midnight, so he settled himself down on the ground, near them, but far enough away for privacy and a decent chance of escape should it be necessary. No-one spoke. Through anxiety before the trip or fear of arrest, it wasn't clear. Or maybe just sheer exhaustion. Even though it was still warm, Daniel put on his coat, folded the bag and stuffed it into one of his coat pockets. He settled back on his elbows to stare at the stars above him.

It was an hour after midnight when Daniel noticed a sudden movement further into the bush. He could see two figures standing upright, their heads and shoulder just visible against the sky above the vegetation. There was noise, too – urgent, threatening – coming from that direction, answered suddenly by a higher, shriller cry of alarm from someone unseen.

Then other forms appeared, running towards the first two, shouting as they closed.

The figures merged into a grunting, heaving maul, which abruptly came to a standstill with one final scream from within it.

Silence descended again. A group of three men emerged, walking casually towards them as if nothing had happened.

They spoke quietly to each small knot of people as they came to them. They moved swiftly from group to group and were soon crouching in front of Daniel.

'Zimbabwe toe?' came the question in Afrikaans, the lingua franca of the southern African frontier badlands.

Though still bewildered by what he had just witnessed, Daniel did manage to dredge up a memory of travelling home by train in his youth over another adjacent border, when the ticket inspector had rapped loudly with his master key on the door of his compartment, bellowing exactly the same words.

He managed a reply in English, and, just as the ticket inspector had years before, the man immediately changed language to suit.

'Eight hundred,' he said curtly. The voice was

emotionless. 'Pay now. Once we go that's it. No going back. You do exactly what we say. We are going now. If you want to go, come there.'

The man gestured in the direction of the thick bush that lay not far away, and then walked away to the last group.

The men were of indeterminate appearance. Baggy clothing, knitted balaclavas rolled up on their heads. Daniel wasn't confident he would have been able to pick them out at an identity parade five minutes hence.

He lay on his side facing away from the rest, and as surreptitiously as he could extracted a roll of notes from his money-belt, not quite believing what he had just seen. He unfolded what he thought was the correct sum, although in the dim moonlight he couldn't be entirely sure, and then stuffed anything else of value he was carrying in its place.

He pushed himself to his feet, and walked in the direction the men had indicated, not far from where the struggle had taken place minutes before.

The money changed hands rapidly. Within minutes Daniel and ten others were jammed together thigh to thigh in the back of a pickup truck travelling along a dirt track that stood out almost white against the darkness of the vegetation on either side.

With two other passengers.

At the open end of the pickup, one of the gang was crouched on his haunches, one hand to the body of the truck to keep himself from falling out. With his other hand he gripped the clothing of a dead body which lay across the opened tail-gate which was bouncing heavily on its chains. There was a large dark stain on the corpse's shirt.

* * *

The track was rutted, and the truck's overloaded springs transmitted every bump directly through to Daniel's spine. He remembered a previous jarring trip in the back seat of his mother's car and felt a reflexive convulsion in his throat.

He turned to face the man sitting next to him. He flicked his eyes towards the body on the tailgate and raised his eyebrows to add a question mark.

His neighbour replied softly, speaking downwards, hardly moving his lips.. 'Thieves,' he said. 'They tried to rob that one.' He raised his eyes, indicating a man sitting opposite them. 'Also, they want to have this business. Gangs, fighting.'

In between the lurches, Daniel took a closer look at his companions. Four women, the rest men. No children. Painfully thin legs and arms. Hair coated in dust. Cheap t-shirts and tops, shoddy skirts and trousers were standard. If Daniel had deliberately tried to dress himself like a poor man, he now had a new lower standard to reach.

Their shoes were pathetic, mostly mean plastic flip-flops or threadbare cloth takkies that didn't look as if they would survive the journey. Although one man was wearing thousand-milers - sandals made of recycled car tyre – which would definitely see him out, and probably his heirs as well. Daniel felt guilty as he looked down at his own shoes, scuffed and filthy, but only two days out of the box.

Is this how Patricia had crossed the border? 'Travelling light' with people like this? Surely not.

He did the calculations. Nearly nine thousand for a few hours work, assuming everyone had paid as much as he had. Although looking at his fellow travellers, perhaps that was assuming too much. These people were much worse off than he was. Daniel wondered how they could afford the cost of the crossing. They couldn't, he decided. It was he who was paying well over the odds. Nevertheless...

There would be costs. It hadn't really been any more difficult than buying a ticket for the bus that had brought him from Johannesburg. Illegal, obviously. Yet it wasn't exactly hidden. It hadn't been difficult to find people who knew people. Which surely meant that some official or other also knew about it. And if it was that open, it meant there was profit in it for them too. So, some official somewhere would have had to be bribed, probably in order for a blind eye to be turned to their gathering point. Daniel didn't know what the resulting profit would be, but even divided by four it sounded like lucrative work. No wonder others wanted to take it away from them.

The track bent away in a gentle curve. As they rounded it, the truck slowed down and then stopped. A door opened and one of the occupants of the cab got out. He came round to the rear, and with the help of the other man they manhandled the corpse to the side of the track, and then further in until they could no longer be seen. They re-emerged a minute or so later, took their places again, and the truck moved on.

Just commodities. Bodies to be moved. Dead or alive.

* * *

As they bumped along, the wide course of the river itself came into view. It stretched away to the side of them, the expanse of sand shining as white as the track they were driving on. In the distance over the border was a low range of hills. And then they swung away and were suddenly dismounting in the lee of a large stand of shrubby trees. The pickup drove off, leaving three men with them. They gestured for everyone to lie down. And then they waited.

It could have been half an hour, it could have been two. Daniel didn't know. His watch was hidden in his belt. The wait was mostly in silence. But not long after they had climbed down from the pickup there was a sudden scuffling noise followed by a brief truncated feral scream.

Not again.

It could have come from yards, or miles, away – impossible to tell. It could have been human or animal. Daniel couldn't figure it out - he had nothing against which he could compare the sudden freakish nature of the sound. Not even the night's previous incident was of any use.

One of the guides urgently motioned them to keep their heads down. The sound didn't recur.

And then Daniel heard, this time definitely from nearby, the deep growl of a large diesel engine approaching, driving past very close, and then continuing on its way, gears noisily double-declutched as it went. Soon afterwards and suddenly, they were on the move again, this time on foot.

Daniel surveyed the group again as they walked, counting them all off absent-mindedly.

Wrong number.

He counted again.

One of the women was missing.

He turned and told the guide behind him, and received a violent shove between his shoulder blades for his trouble. A woman in front of him turned towards him and he stared at her. She wouldn't hold his gaze, and turned her face away, fearfully, as if in shame. But her behaviour was eloquent enough and he knew instantly what had happened to the missing woman.

Poor soul. Fallen prey to one of these men, paid for the trip with more than the exorbitant fare.

As they emerged from the brush a tarred strip was there right in front of them, ragged edges disintegrating into the sand. The engine noise must have been the sound of a passing border patrol.

Just beyond the strip, three fences. Two either side of a wide expanse of cleared ground and topped with barbed wire, the middle one a pyramid constructed of three continuous horizontal rolls of razor wire, two on the ground and another balanced on top. No vegetation, just stones and gravel, exposed and daunting. And beyond the triple barrier the bush grew unmolested again down to the riverbank.

One of the men darted across the tar. Squatting low, he shuffled a short distance along the first fence until he found a trapdoor section expertly cut into the strong square mesh. He bent the section upwards and dived through the gap.

He was soon at the middle fence, where he pushed himself prone through a shallow excavation under the coils of wire. Within seconds he was at the third fence, bending up another freed section of mesh. The practical demonstration ended with him ducking through the second trapdoor.

Immediately he did this, one of the men waiting with Daniel and the others ran forward to the first fence and held up the section of cut fencing. The remaining guide then started urging the group on. 'All the way. Like he did. Through. Under. Then through to the bushes on the other side. Wait there.'

One by one they made the crossing. Nothing to it. Apart from catching the back of his coat on the wire, and a few scrapes on his hands, Daniel managed the crossing without damage. No-one slowed down, no-one wanted to be caught in the open ground.

Daniel looked back once he had reached the other side and was waiting a few feet into the scrub. As the last of the group went through the opening in the first fence, the third of the guides followed. Crouched and shuffling backwards, he switched at the soil behind him with a branch pulled from a tree near where they had hidden, covering up the scuffs they had made in the dirt as they crossed.

He bent down through the first fence and paused to bend the section of mesh back down again behind him. And in a similar fashion through to the third fence.

As if by military drill, it had taken less than ten minutes to get everybody across, although in Daniel's mind the passage had been interminable. He couldn't even remember drawing a breath until it was over.

Then they were off again, moving in single file, winding the short distance through the thick and tangled vegetation down towards the river. They gathered in a tight group, huddled down just where the river bank descended to the sandy bed of the river itself.

Again, one of the guides demonstrated the way by walking out onto the sand, moving briskly without running, over to a thin line of living vegetation tangled up with dead branches that stuck up like a reef from the non-existent river around it.

Daniel could see no water at all between where he knelt and the other side. All flowing underground at this time of year, if flowing at all, although come the rains this whole expanse would turn into an impassable torrent.

A guide on the near bank despatched three of the travellers, all the remaining women, across the sand to join another guide at the way-point. In turn, this man moved off from the island taking the three women with him. The four of them were soon out of sight.

Another group, this time of four including Daniel, moved out from their shelter to the island. By the time they got there, the first guide was back from wherever he had gone, and was leading them on. In stages they passed through two more sanctuaries in the middle of the sand before they reached the far bank. A short wait for the final group to catch up with them, and then they were off again in single file.

There were no fences on this side of the frontier, but their progress was slowed to a crawl by a band, several hundred yards wide, of thick, tangled, thorn-infested vegetation that lined the northern river bank. The guides were now much more apprehensive. Avoiding the more obvious game tracks cutting down to the sand, they moved doubled up, and any noise from the group was swiftly reprimanded with a shove and a threatening glare. They walked a considerable distance in total silence until the countryside began to open up.

There the guides called them together. One pointed to the east, where a faint line of light on the horizon marked the soon-to-be-rising sun. 'The main road is over there,' he said quietly, pointing. He gestured with his thumb. 'That way.

Beitbridge.' His thumb switched direction. 'That way. Harare, Bulawayo.'

And which one of you bastards raped that woman?

But they were gone. Like wisps of smoke, with nothing to indicate they had ever been there. The relief of no longer being in their company lifted Daniel. He and the rest moved off singly and in pairs.

Seven

Some distance past the crossroads Daniel disembarked clumsily from the bus with two others. After passing the last small hamlet on the road north, he had peered surreptitiously ahead trying to judge just where to get off. The bus had not stopped since, and he had resigned himself to having to travel all the way to Gwanda and then walk back again. But just as he saw the buildings at the crossroads and the blue-painted rock appear on the side of the road, the bus began to slow.

He nervously dropped the two feet or more between the bus and the ground, flinching in anticipation of a bolt of pain from his leg as he descended. But the bus had stopped near the edge of a storm ditch, and the loose gravel of the slope cushioned Daniel's descent. He slid down into it, and looked up a little stupidly when he hit the bottom. But he hadn't damaged his leg, which was a distinct bonus and worth the indignity. He didn't know how far he still had to walk.

He scrabbled his way out of the ditch, dusted himself down as best he could, and looked around.

The police compound was a little way back along the road from him. He stared at it, a little mesmerised.

How long since I was there?

As he stood working out the dates there was movement inside the camp. Two white twin-cab pickups appeared from behind the main building and drove up to the gate. The guard had already hastily left his sentry box and was fumbling with the padlock and chain. He shoved the gates open, pushed up the boom, and stood rigidly to attention, arms straightened down his sides, as the two vehicles drove out onto the dirt road, wheels spinning impatiently, gravel spraying out behind them.

Daniel turned hurriedly and faced in the other direction as they turned on to the tar and drove away behind him. Nerves on end, he turned back only once he was sure the trucks were well on their way away from him.

He walked back towards the crossroads.

He was thirsty, and the dark interior of the store was inviting. But he resisted the temptation, and began walking up the dirt road in the direction of St Cuthberts, with or without the apostrophe.

As he went, Mr Ndlovu, leaning against the door of his store, watched him go.

* * *

He walked for an hour before he came to the mission that lay white and elevated against the sunburnt landscape. A square bell tower fronted a church that was topped by a steeply angled steel roof, as if built in error from plans for a building designed to withstand a heavy fall of snow. The bell tower - within which, due to a last minute fit of penny-pinching by the archdiocese, no bell was suspended - was topped by a simple wooden cross. It was easily the tallest structure for miles around.

It had been a simple choice of destination. He remembered only too clearly from his own childhood that, if anyone knew exactly what was going on in a district, it would be someone who lived at the mission. The slow rituals of mission life would have been unbearably numbing had it not been for the steady flow of gossip passing through from the surrounding countryside.

Mothers swaying in through the gates to the clinic, infants tightly swaddled on their backs, packages balancing on their heads. Children scuffing in to school. The district's smartest clothing dusted off for church on Sundays. All brought with them a few words of gossip for broadcast or exchange. Advance news of the harvest. Scandal from the city brought by a visiting relative. Adolescent felonies, impending marriages, marital fractures and misdemeanours; all the ripples and eddies of communal rural life found a ready ear at the mission. Woe betide the mission director who failed to keep abreast of the never-ending soap opera.

Daniel's problem was how to avoid becoming part of the gossip himself. He decided to go straight to the top.

Wire fences originally intended to keep out the goats staked out the perimeter of the mission grounds. But there were also entrances leading in from all directions which rendered the fences meaningless except as boundary markers. Daniel walked straight between the nearest set of gate-posts, and strolled as nonchalantly as he could towards the living quarters that stood clustered just behind the main mission buildings.

It was lunchtime, and if the arrangements at St Cuthberts were in any way similar to where he had grown up, then the mission's presiding priest should be home for his midday meal.

Daniel went to the back of the largest house. He stood outside, hesitant, collecting his thoughts, and then stepped forward and knocked firmly on an open stable-door. No response. A few moments later he knocked again, a little louder, resisting the urge to peer over the bottom half of the door into what looked like a kitchen. This time he heard sounds from within of someone approaching, so he stood back a step and clasped his hands in front of him, adopting what he hoped was a look of pious humility.

A figure appeared enquiringly at the door, dabbing at his mouth with a grubby dishcloth, still chewing on a mouthful of lunch. The priest wore a black shirt, sleeves buttoned tightly at the wrists, and a white clerical collar fastened tightly around his throat. There were faint traces of what looked like several recent meals down his front.

'Good afternoon, Father,' Daniel said quietly.

'How may I help, my son.' The voice was round and gentle, and Daniel, against his newly acquired better instincts, let his hopes rise.

Right. Straight in. Don't waffle.

'The body of a young woman was found near here several weeks ago,' he said. 'I am trying to find out what happened to her. She was my sister.'

There. Committed now. He braced himself for rejection. Or worse.

'Your sister?'

Daniel nodded, and the priest pushed open the bottom half of the door. The wood screeched loudly against the kitchen step.

He was a large shambling man, awkward in manner. He wore a big pair of owl-like glasses which, like Daniel's, sat somewhat crookedly astride his nose. A large metal crucifix on a heavy chain hung from his neck. Daniel for some reason later remembered that the priest's black trousers were almost worn through at the knees. They were also several sizes too short and his ankles were exposed through moth-eaten holes in his socks.

He stepped out and glanced rapidly to left and right. He placed an arm around Daniel's shoulders and firmly propelled them both inside, pulling both halves of the door shut as they entered. There he stopped. He placed a hand gently on Daniel's head and intoned a benediction. They were silent for a moment.

He gestured towards a small table against the wall at the far end of the room. Daniel sat, and the priest settled himself down opposite, after removing a small plate dusted with crumbs.

Daniel looked around him. Spartan didn't fully describe it. One small table with two mismatched chairs. Two cupboards mounted at head height on the wall. Another small table as a working surface. A crucifix on a nail on one wall. Ceiling boards that sagged ominously. No sink, no stove, no fridge. A door leading further into the house stood ajar.

'I am Father Barnabas,' the priest began. 'You are?'

'Daniel Hove.'

'Who knows you are here? Did you ask at the mission office...?'

'No, I...'

The priest stared at Daniel, as if fixing his appearance permanently in his mind. 'What happened to her must have been just horrific,' he said eventually. 'I did not see her myself, you understand...'

He stopped, his brow furrowed again.

'It was a lot more than a few weeks ago. Three months?'

The priest spoke carefully, pronouncing every syllable

with precision. It was the language of the seminary and before that, Jesuit mission-taught grammar.

Daniel nodded. 'I suppose it was. I've lost track...'

'It often happens like that. Anyway... the police came and took her body away. People say that her wounds were terrible, but I don't know how they know that. I don't think anybody else saw her, except perhaps for the boy's father. She was found by a boy from a family who live near here, across the valley, you see. That is certainly what I understood after speaking with the boy's father.'

'She wasn't found by the police? The hospital told me they found her body on the main road. Not that I really believed that...'

'No. That is not so. Whoever told you that was mistaken. You were right to be suspicious. The boy found her a long way from the road.'

So much for that traffic accident bullshit.

The priest paused again. 'You have spoken with the police about this?'

'Briefly. The Inspector at the police camp...'

'Ah...,' said the priest, as if that explained everything.

'Where was she found?' Daniel said. 'I'd like to go there. Can I talk to this boy?'

Father Barnabas' manner cooled. 'You know the history of this part of the country, I'm sure. When the war ended for everyone else, it didn't end for us. It went on for years, and things are still very... sensitive.'

Tell me about it. Daniel almost said it, but caught himself in time. *You don't know the half of it...*

The priest carried on. 'You will understand the difficulty we find ourselves in. We have learned to...' He searched again for a suitable phrase. 'live alongside, shall we say, the powers that be. We keep ourselves to ourselves. It's not a good idea for people to become too interested in things we cannot change. I have to think of the mission, the people who work here, those who live around here. Things are not as straightforward as you might think.'

'But the police lied about what happened to her,' protested Daniel. 'They said she died after being involved in a traffic accident. So did the doctor who filled out her death certificate at the hospital in Bulawayo.'

The priest was silent again, surveying Daniel from the other side of the table. 'I don't wish to be discourteous, but there is something strange here. You are dressed like a vagrant, but you talk like an educated man.'

'I'm a doctor. A surgeon,' said Daniel.

The priest nodded sagely, as he might have done sitting next to a penitent in the confessional. Daniel, for his part, suddenly felt guilty.

'I was beaten senseless because I asked questions.' Daniel said in mitigation, lowering his head and gesturing to the scar, and then pulling up his trouser leg to reveal the wounds on his shin. 'Not far from here. I dress like this because I don't want it to happen…'

'That was you? On the road out of Gwanda?' the priest interrupted.

'That was me.'

'That is exactly what I mean. There are always repercussions. Always unintended consequences. Especially for the innocent.'

He smiled weakly, and then, having seemingly arrived at a decision, pushed himself up from his chair.

'It is not only up to me. I need to speak to the boy's father.' He paused. 'You will wait here. It is better that you aren't seen wandering all over the place. I will send for them. If they come, I will sit with them while they talk to you. And I beg you, please, think of the people around here before you open up this terrible matter any further.'

He called out, and the door swung open. Immediately. A woman wearing a threadbare apron walked into the kitchen.

Shit. How long has she been eavesdropping?

'It will take some time,' continued Father Barnabas. 'You look as if you could do with some sleep. Lydia will show you to a room where you can rest.'

He did need sleep. The last time he had been told to wait had been in the shebeen the night before. The last time he had had any real sleep was on the bus north from Johannesburg.

Had that been 24 hours before? More. It seemed like days...

He followed the woman into the interior of the house. She showed him into another hardly furnished room, this one containing only a low metal bedstead covered with a thin mattress. He lay down and was dead to the world within minutes.

* * *

It was some hours later when he was woken. The woman jogged his shoulder, and he swung himself upright and rubbed his eyes into a semblance of wakefulness. Four chairs of varied provenance had materialised. Three in a small arc, with one chair facing the rest. Daniel guessed which one was intended for him.

A minute or so later Father Barnabas entered, ushering in before him a tall, stooped old man leaning heavily on a stick. He was followed by a teenage boy. The old man lowered himself down onto the chair, the boy supporting him underneath one arm as he bent. It was obviously a painful process, but the man moved without showing the pain he must have been feeling.

The other two – the boy and the priest – sat either side of the old man, leaving Daniel to sit facing them. Rather than them coming to answer his questions, Daniel felt as if he were the hostile witness, about to be skewered under cross-examination.

The priest introduced them. 'Mr Sibanda. His son, Themba. Themba is the one who found your sister's body.'

Daniel exchanged pleasantries with the old man, asking after his happiness and that of his family, gently shaking his hand, acknowledging his superior status.

'May I ask your son some questions?' he asked.

Mr Sibanda looked down sceptically at Daniel, then nodded solemnly.

Daniel turned to the boy. 'Please, tell me how you found her.'

There was no hesitation, no looking to either his father or the priest for permission or reassurance. Themba Sibanda was confident beyond his years. Daniel was impressed.

'There is... ,' he began haltingly, in a deep adolescent voice. He whispered a word and looked inquiringly at the priest, who translated. 'Kopje,' he said, looking at Daniel.

'I understand what he's saying,' Daniel replied. 'No need to translate...'

He nodded at the boy, who continued. 'There by the

fence. I was hunting birds with my catapult. From the top I saw her. She... the body was next to the fence. This side.'

The priest interjected. 'The fence runs straight through this area. On the one side are us...' He waved his hand vaguely to include the two Sibandas with himself. 'On the other side is a farm. They don't come over here. We don't go over there.'

Daniel saw a fleeting change of expression in Themba's eyes which flatly and eloquently contradicted the priest.

Daniel resumed. 'My sister. How was she when you found her?'

'Just lying on the ground. She had a blue shirt.' He lowered his eyes awkwardly. 'Nothing else,' he continued. 'She looked like she had just been thrown there.'

'What do you mean?'

'There was no holes. No snare. No rocks. No branches. Nothing to make her fall. She was just lying on some grass, close to the fence.'

'She was wearing nothing else?'

The boy shook his head.

'Nothing lying around? Skirt? Shoes? Bag?'

Themba shook his head again. This time it was the priest's expression which changed and changed back. Daniel made a mental note.

'Why do you think she was there?' he continued.

The boy shrugged.

'What goes on at that farm? What do they farm?''

'As I said before...' said the priest, shortly.

Daniel finished his sentence for him. 'They don't come here and you don't go there...'

He turned to Themba. 'Could you take me to the place?'

he asked.

Before he could reply the priest had interrupted again. 'Doctor. I must ask you please not to push this matter. You don't know what all this could mean for this boy here. Or his family. The matter is in the hands of the police. You must take it up with them again. We really cannot do anything to help you further.'

It was Themba's father who brought the discussions to an end. He pushed himself up with his stick and then nodded to Daniel. 'We have too much trouble. Too many people telling us this, this, this.' He jabbed the floor several times with the end of his stick to emphasise the point. 'All the time, telling us what to do.'

Daniel wasn't sure whether he was referring to himself, the police, or the priest. Or all three.

The old man finished. 'I am very sorry for your sister. I hope you find what you are searching.' He completed his statement with a slow double-growl from deep in his throat, as if, having reviewed his words, he was satisfied with what he had said.

He turned and led Themba from the room, swinging one leg from the hip with each step.

Daniel rose respectfully to his feet as they left, but Father Barnabas, thinking he was about to follow them, waved him back down and then followed them out himself.

When he returned a minute or two later he laid out his conditions. 'I will not ask you to leave at this time of day. You are welcome to our hospitality tonight, but I must ask you to leave tomorrow morning. Tomorrow is Saturday, and perhaps you will not be so... so obvious when you walk down to the main road. I'm sorry that we cannot do any more than that.'

* * *

Daniel woke very early the next morning, before the priest had stirred and before the first light could be seen on the horizon. He let himself out by the kitchen door.

But rather than make his way to the main road he walked away from it. The thicker vegetation which began at the farm's boundary fence lay some distance from the mission buildings – a mile, or more, he guessed. At first he walked parallel to the fence, but by the time he had put some distance between himself and the mission, he started making his way closer and closer to it, as casually as he could without making any abrupt changes in direction. His passage was marked, if not by human eyes, by the barking of dogs from the homesteads and clusters of huts he passed along the way.

Once the gap separating him from the fence had narrowed to a few yards, he turned towards it. As matter-of-factly as he could, he ducked between the top two of the three barbed wire strands and moved away into the denser bush until he judged that he could no longer be seen by anyone standing on the open ground he had left behind.

Then he began walking back on the opposite bearing, in the general direction of the mission but on the other side of the fence.

On his outward journey, Daniel had only seen one kopje that stood anywhere near the boundary fence. By the time he turned to come back, the small hill was out of sight. But eventually, as he kept walking, it came back into view, sitting just on the communal land side of the fence, about thirty or forty feet high at its peak. It must have been a useful marker for the surveyor who had pegged out the boundary. Daniel made his way steadily towards it.

Once there, he ducked through the fence again, climbed the short distance to the top and looked out over the farm and the communal lands below. No movement anywhere. It was still a bit early, he supposed. But there was now sufficient light to have dispelled most of the shadows, and Daniel began circling the kopje from the summit, searching as he went, and then dropping down a few feet to search in a wider circle a bit lower down, and so on until he reached level ground.

He didn't really know what he was looking for. Some article of Patricia's clothing, perhaps? But he found nothing. There was not a single thing that he could see that had any connection at all to any human being. Nothing discarded, no footprints except for his own which he encountered at head height on every successive circuit of the rocks.

When he reached the bottom, he retraced his steps, this time moving upwards and in the opposite direction. Still nothing. At the top, he sat down under a tree and pondered.

His preoccupation was interrupted by a short low penetrating hiss. He looked round to see Themba Sibanda grinning at him.

Eight

There was no stopping him. The boy could barely contain his excitement as he recounted everything he had said the day before, and more, at speed. Daniel eventually had to slow him down to make sure he took in everything he had to say.

Sat together in the shade of a tree at the top of the tumble of rocks they could look out over the surrounding land on both sides of the fence. Themba pointed to where he had found Patricia's body, some distance away from the base of the kopje on an open piece of ground in the communal lands. Close to the fence, just as he had said the day before. Away from anything that could of itself explain why she had ended up there. Except perhaps the fence itself.

Daniel remembered that the day before Themba had said that her body might have been thrown there. Seeing it for himself, Daniel now understood what he had meant. Not just thrown, but thrown over the fence. If two men had put sufficient effort into swinging her, Daniel guessed, her body could easily have cleared the fence and fallen where Themba said it had.

Dumped, like a piece of trash.

'So she was on the other side of the fence.' he said.

Themba nodded. 'Yes. But she was here before she went there,' he said.

'Why do you say that?'

Themba stood up. Looking over his shoulder, he beckoned with a small movement of his head for Daniel to follow. They walked a short distance around to the opposite side of the top of the kopje. Themba indicated a long indentation, slightly off-vertical, in a large granite boulder.

But it wasn't just an indentation. It was a fissure which divided the boulder almost in two. Daniel could see that now if he looked more closely. He was embarrassed to recognise the crevice as something he had glanced at then disregarded during his own search not twenty minutes before.

Themba thrust his hand obliquely into it, and then his arm, which disappeared up to his elbow. Daniel looked on bemused as Themba withdrew his arm slowly from the cleft, pulling hard and twisting his wrist occasionally as he guided something out. He grinned up at Daniel in triumph and then, as if in a magic show, pulled a blue nylon back-pack out of the cleft. He offered it to Daniel. It wasn't particularly heavy, nor very tightly packed.

'When did you find this?' he asked.

'Before I saw her body. I came up here hunting for birds. While I was here I checked in the rock. Sometimes I keep things there. It was there. Then I saw her. You can see a lot from here. I saw her lying there by the fence.' He pointed.

'Tell me what goes on over there,' Daniel said, turning his face towards the dense bush that stretched away below them. 'Who owns that farm?'

'I don't know. Some people say it is a woman. I have never seen her. There was a white man, before I was born my father says. He sold to this woman. She lives in Harare maybe.'

'What do they farm?'

'Some cattle. Not many. But they don't let them here.' He gestured to the thick ungrazed vegetation. 'Nothing else.

Some vegetables near the house. Some maize. The boss-boy has some goats, some cattle.'

Boss-boy. Amazing how things change, and the language doesn't. Colonial words in a post-colonial world. Or maybe it's that things haven't really changed after all.

'How far is the house?' he asked.

'Not far. Close, close.'

'Been there?'

Themba nodded again.

'Where does the boss-boy live?'

'That side.' Themba gestured. 'Too far. Not near the big house. He has some houses for his family that side. Too far.'

'So not much goes on there. No farming. And the owner doesn't live there.'

'The owner never comes. But there is a man who is the manager. Sometimes he comes there from Gwanda. Sometimes a plane comes when he is there. Then he goes.' He looked up at Daniel, stretching his thumb and little finger sideways, mimicking a plane gliding in to land, to make sure Daniel understood.

'A plane,' Daniel acknowledged 'Where does it come from?'

Themba pointed. Daniel worked out the direction. South, as near as he could estimate.

'How often does it come?'

'A few weeks, nothing. Then it comes every Sunday. Then sometimes a long time before it comes again.'

'When do you think it will come again?'

'Soon, soon. Maybe tomorrow.'

'Tomorrow?'

Themba nodded vigorously. 'Before the plane comes

there is a bad smell from there. Too bad. Very strong. Then a few days later, maybe seven, the plane comes. The smell is there now.'

'What kind of smell?'

'Like the toilets at the school when they are blocked.'

'Big plane?'

Themba shook his head, and held his fingers an inch or so apart in mock measurement. 'Small. One man only.'

'Where does it land?'

Themba gestured again, his arm elevated to indicate some distance. 'Near the bossboy's house.'

'When did the plane come, last time?'

'Last Sunday. It was here about one week after I found your sister. Many many times since then.'

Daniel looked at the bag. He unclipped the covering flap and opened it. There was a thin woollen jersey folded on top. He removed it and put it next to him. Inserted against the back edge of the pack was a slim leather document case that he pulled out and placed on top of the jersey. He pulled out all the other items and made another pile with them. There were two t-shirts, some underwear, a pair of leggings in lurid striped colours. A few personal toiletries. No shoes, no trousers, no skirt. He opened the external pockets of the bag. Nothing in any of them, except one. It contained a plastic bottle of water, almost empty.

One by one he examined each item of clothing, feeling his way along the seams with his fingertips and turning everything inside out. There were no name tags, nor anything else to link any of the clothes to his sister. But if, as Themba said, it had been found near where her body had been found, it must be odds on that the bag and its contents were hers.

But it was inconceivable that she would travel without shoes. Themba was not wearing any, but he was a teenage boy used to walking in this countryside. She was an urban creature and the soles of her feet wouldn't have lasted ten minutes walking barefoot around here. And what about the clothes she had been wearing just before she was beaten so savagely? She must have been wearing something else apart from the shirt. But there was nothing of that sort in the bag. Which meant they had to be somewhere else, probably close to where she had been beaten. Wherever that was. And her shoes would probably also be close by.

Daniel picked up the document case. The leather was finished in a deep polished burgundy and looked expensive. A handsome desirable case that wouldn't have looked out of place in a shop window in Bond Street. It was neatly folded in upon itself and held shut with a brass lock on the front. There were no identifying marks. No monogram, no label. A few recent scratches on the brass facing of the lock that secured it shut.

'Do you have a knife or something?' asked Daniel. 'Something to open this?'

Themba nodded. He carefully unbuttoned one of the breast pockets of his threadbare shirt and probed inside it. Eventually he withdrew a bent piece of thick fencing wire. He took the case back from Daniel and settled it flat across his knees. Inserting the wire into the lock, he wiggled it around until it caught. He exerted some force, and the lock bounced open. He lifted up the flap and peered inside the case, before inserting a slender hand and withdrawing a passport. He opened it and showed the back page to Daniel.

It showed the holder's personal details. It was Patricia's.

Daniel feigned a sideswiping cuff to Themba's ear. The boy ducked his head in response. His face broke into a gleeful grin.

Daniel reclaimed the case and looked into it. There were two transparent folders, each containing a few pages of paper. There was a small pocket diary, and a few notes and coins in a pouch close to the top of the case. A ballpoint pen was stuck into a fold in the interior leather.

He pulled out the folders and withdrew the papers, first from one, then the other. He skimmed through them rapidly, and while he did so Themba looked enquiringly on, hoping for some explanation. But Daniel could not fathom their meaning, and he replaced them in the case, none the wiser.

'When you found it the first time - everything that was in it then, is in here now? Nothing missing?'

Themba nodded again.

'Why didn't you give this to the police?'

'My father says this is not the business of the police. This is for her family. For you.'

'No-one else knows about it?'

'My father. Me. Now you. Maybe Father Barnabas saw me carrying the blue bag. But he doesn't know about that red thing.' He pointed to the document case.

'What would your father say if he knew you were talking to me?'

'He told me to find you. He thought you might come here.'

'He's not worried about the police?'

'The police, the CIOs, they hurt his legs. So he walks like that. They are too bad.'

'Why did they do that?'

'He said something against the party man at a meeting for an election. He said he was a rubbish. Afterwards some CIOs came. They beat him.'

'I don't think he likes the priest either?'

'Father Barnabas – he's a good man. He has done good things for us, for my father, many times. After he was beaten, the clinic by the mission treated him, even when the police told people not to help. Once someone says something like my father did, I think that person can go and meet God. So Father Barnabas saved my father from death. But my father... my father says Father Barnabas sometimes stays quiet when he should speak.'

No wonder you are so self-assured. Not much chance of a childhood with that going on around you.

'What about the housekeeper? That woman in the priest's house. Lydia'

Themba made an obscene gesture with his fingers. The action was so unexpected that Daniel burst out laughing, quickly checking himself because of the noise.

'She's his girlfriend? The priest...?'

Themba grinned back in shared mirth.

'Will she keep quiet about me?'

Themba shrugged.

'How do I get to the house over there? Have you been there? I need to see if there's anything there.'

'I can go with you,' said Themba.

'I don't think that would be a good idea,' Daniel replied. 'You have to live here. It's too dangerous...'

But Themba was already on his way down the kopje, and Daniel found himself with little option but to follow. He slung the back-pack over one shoulder and, using his hands and arms for balance, carefully descended the hill behind him.

* * *

The homestead was a modest thatched bungalow with a string of tumbledown outbuildings set back from it, all standing in the shade of an almost complete circle of tall skeletal syringa trees. The sand driveway leading off from the house was overgrown, the *middelmannetjie* in the centre sprouting a spine of dry vegetation. It obviously wasn't often used.

Keeping outside the ring of syringas, Themba led Daniel in a circle round the homestead. As they moved, Daniel recognised an unmistakable odour, that of a filthy overflowing latrine. The further they went, the stronger the smell. Themba led them towards a barn-like structure, much bigger than the other buildings. They kept walking until they were between it and the trees and hidden from the farmhouse itself.

The building was walled and roofed in corrugated iron sheets from which dull green paint was peeling in great flaking sheets, revealing a patina of rust in every conceivable shade of red. This was the source of the ammonia smell, Daniel was sure. It was everywhere, as if leaking from the walls.

They followed the back of the building until they came to the gable-end of it.

Themba peered round, and then motioned Daniel to join him. Themba pointed to a door on the end-face. But to get to it, they would have to walk in full view of the homestead. Themba put his forefinger to his lips and then moved back to the blind side and walked back into the surrounding bush. Daniel followed him.

As Themba walked he moved further round until they could again see the house from the cover of the vegetation. Neither of them had seen any movement so far, but the scars on Daniel's scalp and legs were a constant reminder to him of the tactical folly of his instinct to tackle things head on without thinking. He let Themba pick a place, and they both sat down and watched.

Twenty minutes later they were sure they were unobserved. Themba rose and led them back to the rear of the barn and walked quickly round the corner to the door.

It was also of corrugated iron, a full single sheet supported on a wooden frame, and it wasn't locked. Themba pulled it open, and Daniel's nerves jarred as the hinges squealed and the frame creaked loudly. A few inches, no more - just enough space for them to squeeze past the rotting termite-gouged wooden door frame into the building itself. Daniel pulled the door shut behind them.

Which he shouldn't have done, as it left the interior in almost total darkness. But he wasn't about to risk that noise again, so he let his eyes adjust slowly to the gloom.

The only source of light was filtered through a row of grimy windows set high up in the walls, with what appeared to be several decades' worth of accumulated spiders' webs festooned across them. Here and there, gaps between the metal sheeting and empty nail-holes let in tiny shafts of light from the outside. Each one was a spotlit suspension of dust motes.

Daniel moved to the centre of the space and looked around. A row of light grey forty-four gallon drums was lined up against one wall. Daniel checked, tapping the tops. They were sealed and full. Of fuel, it looked like.

Three wooden trestle tables laid end-to-end lined the wall opposite the drums. In one corner a collection of large glass flasks stoppered with fat red rubber corks stood like gigantic up-ended mushrooms. Bleached dull-red rubber tubing, cracked and almost perished through in places, was coiled around the necks of some of them. A collection of gas bottles of various sizes stood together like artillery shells in another corner.

He walked over to a long wooden cabinet against an adjacent wall and pulled out one of the drawers. It was filled with valves and stopcocks, the glass matt and scratched and filthy. And everywhere the pervading smell of ammonia.

Apart from the fact that this place is a massive explosion waiting to detonate, I'm standing in a lab. This has all the makings of a rudimentary chemical lab. But a lab for what?

Daniel gestured to Themba and they left the way they had entered, Themba making sure the door was closed again behind them. Glancing momentarily back at the house to reassure himself that they were still not being watched, Themba crossed quickly to another smaller brick-built outbuilding standing nearby. The door to this one secured with a chain and padlock, and the windows were set too high in the walls for even Daniel to see in.

They walked around the back of it to put some cover again between themselves and the main house, then made for two other smaller sheds, also close up against the ring of syringas. They were open. Daniel checked them both by peering through the doorways, but they were empty of everything except dust and hot stale air.

Themba then turned their attention to the house itself. Pausing briefly, he walked briskly across a band of closely slashed grass the colour of straw and crisp under his tread. Daniel followed close behind. The grass was not an encroachment from the surrounding bush. Someone had planted it to bind the dark soil on this side of the house, but the exercise had mostly failed.

The nearest entrance to the house, a stable door like the priest's, was locked but the sills of the windows near it were set low down and the windows themselves were uncurtained. Daniel could see clearly into the rooms, and, through one of the windows, straight across a large room to another large picture window on the other side of the house.

Must once have been a sitting room.

Although there was nothing he could see on which anyone could have sat. Instead, the room contained half a dozen large chest freezers. On one side was a wall of blue cool-boxes, each with a white lid. stacked one on top of the other, as if ready for a church picnic. On the other side, three much smaller drums, of the same sturdy blue plastic material, topped by circular white screw-top covers, with thick coin-like ridges around the edges, which were a little bigger, Daniel estimated, than the palms of his hands.

Themba gestured to him to come nearer, and then whispered close to his ear.

'The boxes come in the plane,' he said, pointing to the cool-boxes. 'Those,' he gestured to the plastic drums, 'go away in the plane. Every time, eight boxes come, four of those go. Same, same. Every time.'

Themba cautiously walked to the corner of the house, and then, after checking first with a quick glance around it, he waved Daniel to follow him and they walked along the side wall to the front. The attempt at a lawn had fared better on this side and there were a few dusty flowerbeds and a rockery marking its borders. Again, the windows were uncurtained, the rooms were empty, and the front door was firmly locked.

Only on the second side wall of the house did he find a window with thick curtains masking it, although by putting his head close to the glass Daniel was able to make out through the gap between the curtains the shape of a bed low down in the room itself.

Goodness knows what the owner, whoever she is, would do if she visited. It's not so much a house as a storage shed.

Completing the circuit, Daniel turned and looked out over the garden. Beyond the flowerbeds, the bush had been cleared of everything except low cut grass, leaving a vast swathe of open ground leading to the south. He stared across it for several minutes, with Themba standing silently next to him, and then they turned and walked back to the outbuildings on the other side of the house.

Using the outbuildings as cover, Themba led the way to the thicker vegetation bordering the open ground on the far side of the lawn and they began walking steadily through it away from the homestead. They left the furthest edge of the open ground behind them and continued walking through the bush.

In what appeared to be only a matter of minutes later the ground opened up again, this time in a long flat open stretch perpendicular to their direction of travel. Themba gestured to Daniel, and, reducing their silhouettes to the minimum, they squatted and looked over the airstrip. Across from them stood a pole from the top of which a very tattered and once orange windsock hung inertly down. Peering past it, Daniel could dimly make out a gathering of brown-walled huts, some rectangular, some circular, a short distance from the other side of the strip. A few goats were grazing at the far end, but of any other life there was no evidence.

'The plane comes Sundays,' said Themba. 'Sundays, always. Tomorrow, for sure.'

'You're absolutely sure about that?'

'Sure. Sure. You can see tomorrow.' He looked at Daniel with a disappointed expression. 'I have to go to the church. You can come by yourself. Come here and see with your own eyes.'

Daniel put a consoling hand on Themba's shoulder, and took last glances to either end of the strip. Then they turned and began walking back the way they had come.

It was some way short of the kopje where they had met that Themba diverted them leftwards from their direct path and took Daniel over to a line of rocks, stained the same colour as the soil set out in a clearing in the bush, which were topped by a low wall of thick intertwined thorn branches.

As they moved closer, Daniel saw that they were arranged in a sort of ragged circle surrounding a depression in the ground which was covered by a multi-layered grid of long-dead tree trunks. But for its rounded shape, it might have been a grave marked in the rural fashion.

'Dangerous. Too much dangerous,' said Themba. 'A big hole there. *Mgodi*. A mine. They put the stones for the cattle. You must be too careful walking here.'

A mine shaft. Sunk in search of gold, decades, possibly even centuries before.

Then they were off again, but not towards the kopje. They walked for about ten minutes before Daniel asked where they were going.

Themba pointed to the low granite hills in the distance. 'There is a place you can sleep. I will bring food. Tomorrow you can see the plane.'

* * *

It was a recess between two giant granite boulders more than fifty feet above the surrounding countryside, protected and invisible from above, hidden and difficult to access from below. Over a floor large enough for several people to lie prone was a thick and luxuriant layer of dead leaves, several seasons' worth, dating back to the last time a bush fire had burnt fiercely enough to sweep as high as this along this range of hills. Obliquely from the front of this shelter the Sibanda's homestead could be seen in aerial view several hundred yards away, and it was in this direction that Daniel was gazing as the sun sank rapidly from sight.

Next to him was a thick blanket, neatly folded, a plate of sadza with relish of uncertain origin sitting partially-eaten, and a chipped enamel mug which had been full of sweet warm tea when Themba had brought them all up to him just before the bottom edge of the fierce red afternoon sun had hit the horizon.

How the mug of tea had survived the journey, Daniel wasn't sure, but it was an inspired time to bring him his meal, he thought on reflection. The shadows were at their longest and the sunset coloured the granite with all the reddish hues it was possible to imagine. He doubted whether Themba could have been seen as he ascended the hill under the cover of the foliage which clung to the fissures in the rock. Certainly, and not for the first time, Daniel hadn't noticed him until he suddenly materialised in front of him.

A vertical column of wood smoke was still rising from the centre of the homestead. Daniel could see the faint glimmer of the embers of the fire from which it rose. But there was no other activity. The Sibanda family must be inside one or other of the buildings, although Daniel couldn't see any light escaping from any of the windows or doors. That was also true of the rest of the countryside that Daniel could see from his eyrie. Even the mission, at the limit of his field of vision, was dark. The rapidly dwindling light had brought an end to the day's activity.

Themba's directions had been meticulous. After guiding him up through the crevices which led to where he now sat, he had pointed out over the fence in the direction of the airstrip, which he said he could see clearly. From this elevated spot the bush looked sparse, like wisps of hair on an old man's head. But still Daniel couldn't quite make out where the vegetation had been cleared for the landing strip, however hard he tried.

A little impatiently Themba had pointed to another distinctive hill visible on the horizon.

'Keep looking at that in front of you,' he had said. 'It will take you straight and you can see the plane. Tomorrow morning. Before 12 o'clock. It always comes on Sunday morning. Always, always.'

'And basop for the mines,' he had warned again.

That was something Daniel could see. The clearing with the circle of rocks and thorns, and the woven platform of tree trunks, stood out among the trees. Daniel thought he could see a second similar gap in the vegetation further away.

'Leave those here.' Themba had pointed to the plate, mug and blanket. 'Tomorrow I will fetch.'

Before he left, Daniel took a blank piece of paper and the pen from the document case. Resting on it, he wrote a few brief lines. He pulled up his shirt and extracted a few notes from his money belt, triggering a wide-eyed stare from the boy.

'Thank you for everything you have done,' Daniel said. 'I wouldn't have got this far...' he pointed to the bag and the case. 'without your help.'

He wrapped the cash in the sheet of paper, and then folded Themba's hands around it, pressing the boy's hands between his own.

'Give that to your father. With my thanks. In case any of you need it, I have written the address and telephone number of my mother. If there is trouble, you must contact her. She will help.'

The boy looked back at him, clear-eyed in full understanding, and put the slender parcel carefully into his breast pocket.

'Who used this place?' Daniel asked, by way of parting conversation.

Themba glanced quickly around him, as if someone might have been listening. 'Bafana,' he said conspiratorially, face down and eyes up, partially suppressing a proud grin and staring up at Daniel to confirm that he understood. Satisfied that he had, Themba turned and was gone.

'Bafana.' Daniel repeated the word to himself.

The boys. The boys from the bush. Terrorists under one government, dissidents under the next. Themba wasn't even born when 'the boys' slept here. What keeps these legends alive? History reaching out to touch the present. You can't get away from it. You're never allowed to forget.

* * *

Daniel slept comfortably, even given his rudimentary sleeping arrangements. As darkness fell the temperature dropped sharply and he was glad of the thickness of the blanket wrapped around him as he lay back on his mattress of leaves, gazing up at the wedge of black sky visible between the curves of the boulders above his head. He was soon unconscious, and slept uninterrupted until he woke with a start early the next morning, before the sun had risen. He rose, folded the blanket neatly, placed the plate and mug on top of it, and placed them all together at the rear of the shelter.

Within minutes he was climbing crablike down the granite, keeping note of Themba's guiding hill on the horizon as he dropped. It took no more than twenty minutes for him to cross the fence again onto the farm, and another half an hour to walk carefully through the bush until he reached the edge of the airstrip.

He found cover in a thicket of low bushes and sat down to wait, in the company of several dozen mopani flies which took turns to try to crawl into his mouth and eyes and nose.

Just before noon, as Daniel's mind and body were beginning to wilt, two vehicles drove onto the strip from the direction of the farmstead. One was a dented weather-beaten pickup. Half a dozen men sat perched on the edges of its open back. Two stood leaning over the top of the cab. It reminded Daniel of the truck on the other side of the border.

Behind it, far enough behind to avoid being caught in the leading vehicle's dust, drove a gleaming black 4x4. Tinted windows, swollen wheel-arches, chrome trim and over-muscular off-road tyres, it was the automotive version of a preening, steroid-pumped gym-addict. Daniel brought his little camera to his eye and took pictures of both, praying to all the guardian angels that the click of the cheap plastic shutter, which sounded shockingly loud as he peered from the thicket, was not audible across the field.

Not long after the arrival of the two vehicles, Daniel heard the sound of a plane, increasingly louder as it approached. Suddenly it appeared low over the compound of huts and then banked sharply away towards the end of the strip, brilliant white in the sunshine. The low-slung cargo pod, plump little spats over the landing gear and a jaunty upward sweep from fuselage to tail gave it a guppy-like silhouette which brought an involuntary smile to Daniel's lips.

It swung around again, aligned itself with the centre of the strip and came in to land over the heads of the men in the pickup.

Once safely down it turned on itself and bounced slowly back towards them over the grass, blowing up a miniature storm of dust and straw. It drew level and then turned 180 degrees again, facing the way it had landed.

The exchange was well practiced. The men jumped down from the pickup, revealing an upright drum strapped to the grill behind the cab. The plane's engine died and the pilot emerged. He guided the pickup as it reversed towards the plane and underneath one wing, then climbed onto the back of it, wrenched the seal off the fuel drum with a large pair of pliers, and unscrewed the cap.

He made a show of inspecting its contents. Satisfied, he stood back and watched as two of the men ran a pipe from the drum to the top of the wing and began working the handle of a pump.

The pilot walked over to the black 4x4. The driver's window slid down, and the pilot leant in through the gap, resting on his elbows while the work went on behind him. As Themba had predicted the previous day, large blue cool boxes with white lids - eight of them - were swiftly unloaded from the plane and placed in the back of the pickup. Four blue cylindrical canisters capped with white lids were transferred from the pickup to the plane. The refuelling finished, the pipe was withdrawn from the wing, and the pickup drove clear of the aircraft.

Daniel kept busy with his camera, but the performance taking place in front of him was so slick that it seemed to be over almost before it began. Ten minutes maximum, probably less. The conversation at the 4x4's window ended. A large Manila envelope was handed out to the pilot, who then climbed back into his cockpit. The engine coughed, was revved up to full throttle, and within seconds the plane was bouncing awkwardly back down the strip before rising elegantly into the air and banking towards the south.

The pickup and 4x4 drove off towards the farmstead, two men on the back of the pickup steadying the pile of boxes, the rest following on foot.

Daniel waited where he was until he saw the men return from the farmstead, walk cross the airstrip, and disappear into the collection of huts on the far edge of the clearing. He backed out of the thicket on all fours and cautiously retreated until he was well out of sight of the huts. He walked in a huge arc, first west, then south, and then eventually eastwards, keeping to the thickest part of the surrounding bush and leaving a wide berth between his route and the huts and the airfield.

Eventually the curve of his path brought him back to the fence between the farm and the communal lands. He ducked through it and rejoined the skein of footpaths that ranged through the countryside. He meandered his way past homesteads and goat kraals at an unhurried pace despite the urgency churning in his stomach, in a circuitous alternative route to the main road.

Play the part. You're just a visitor returning home.

He reached the road in the early afternoon, and began walking along it until he came to a sign near a heavily scuffed patch of gravel that appeared to promise that a bus to the border might stop there. There was no timetable so he sat down at the side of the road, lost in thought, with the tarmac stretching away in both directions into the shimmering heat.

Two mangy donkeys trotted past on the other side of the tar pulling a Scotch cart at a lively pace. The driver shouted a greeting at him. Daniel responded with a brief wave of his hand and then sank back into his reverie.

He didn't have to wait long after that. The morning bus from the city had finally made it this far down the road. He saw it breach the horizon, appearing to levitate in the mirage just above the tarmac. He extracted more cash from the dwindling contents of his money belt.

The bus grew larger during its ponderous approach, no longer surfing in the haze. But it was otherwise defying the normal rules of perspective. A deviation in alignment between the bodywork and the chassis made it appear to be moving in a sort of crab-like manner along the road, while a weakness in the suspension gave it a heavy list to the nearside. Daniel didn't want to speculate what other defects might be less visible.

He climbed up into it after it stopped with a grinding of brakes and gears, paid his fare, and then moved to the back where there were plenty of spare seats. For a weekend, the bus looked surprisingly empty, but he counted his blessings. For the time being, he could stretch his legs over a double seat and rest. With an alarming overture of noise from the gearbox and clouds of noxious blue exhaust from underneath, the bus left the stop.

As it resumed its journey another vehicle - a white twin-cab pickup - pulled out from a lay-by further back along the road and followed the bus at a less than discreet distance in its lopsided progress towards the border.

Nine

D aniel emerged reluctantly from the shower and towelled himself down. He felt as if he had been in it for hours, the hot water jetting from the nozzle washing away the grime of four days' worth of make-believe poverty. He was delivering a silent vote of thanks to providence for the luxury when a sudden drop in water temperature propelled him out.

Wrapping the towel around his waist, he sat on the side of the bed and emptied the blue back-pack onto the bedspread beside him. Very conscious of how he had missed the hiding place in the rock two days before, he went through the clothes yet again, examining each item inside and out for anything that he might have overlooked. But there was nothing, so he pushed the clothing to one side, and pulled the contents of the document case towards him.

He paged through her passport. Eventually, with silent relief, he found a stamp dated two days before Patricia's official date of death. A Beitbridge immigration stamp. She had travelled legally after all, not in the company of those people-smuggling thugs.

But look what good that did her.

He counted the money. Just over a hundred rand, a few notes and coins in Zimbabwean currency. He took a second, closer look at the contents of the two transparent folders. One yielded nothing, just five or six sheets of paper, blank on both sides. He put them back and opened the second. It was more promising. The top sheet was covered in scribbles and doodles, patterns and sketches, but no words, no numbers, no meaning.

Another sheet had been neatly divided into rows and columns with hand-drawn lines. Dates down one axis, symbols as titles to each column. The resulting matrix was incomplete. Not all rows contained numbers in each column, some rows contained no entries at all.

There was a third page, this one much larger than the rest but folded twice to fit into the folder. He opened it out. It had several crosses pencilled on to it, and long lines bisecting the page, but their positions looked random, and Daniel couldn't fathom what they represented.

He repacked the second folder and picked up the diary. It was tiny, maybe an inch by an inch and a half, two pages to a week. Daniel looked at the minuscule area of paper allocated to each day. He went through it painfully and slowly, because it was difficult to separate one page from another. The covers of the diary extended so far out that it made it almost impossible to reach the edges of the pages, and even his surgeon's fingertips were far too clumsy for the job. Eventually, by bending the covers back on themselves, he was able to leaf through it methodically.

There was nothing of interest in the first part. As he began to approach more recent dates, he took more care. A week before his mother had phoned him with the news of Patricia's death there was a phone number pencilled in, with a name below it.

Thinking of which, if Patricia had a phone with her, it's also missing.

Daniel pulled one of the blank pieces of paper from the first sleeve and copied the name and number on to it. Three days before his mother's call was marked by a tiny hand-drawn asterisk. That was the date she had travelled north. Two days after the date of his mother's call was marked with a similar asterisk. Was that the date she had intended to return, a travel plan that she had been unable to fulfil? And a week after that another appointment. 'EA' it said in tiny letters. '9:00 am, CT.'

That was the last entry he could find. Daniel closed the diary. But the covers sprang open again. The spine of the diary was hollow, made to hold a miniature diary pencil. Daniel examined it. There was no pencil, but the tube formed by the spine and the cover wasn't empty. Squinting through it as if through a telescope, Daniel could only see a pinprick of light. His bending back of the covers must have disturbed the alignment of whatever it was that had been inserted into it, causing it spring open and block the clear daylight that he ought to have been able to see.

He looked around the hotel room for something he could use to extract whatever was hidden there. He found nothing in the bathroom. He investigated the clothes hangers in the wardrobe, but they were of the variety that could only be detached from hooks permanently attached to the rail. There was nothing on the dressing table in the bedroom. His search of one of the bedside tables yielded only a Gideon's Bible.

On impulse, he picked up the blue back-pack and upended it. A small pencil fell out onto the bedspread. As he stared at the pencil, Daniel felt something caught inside the corner of the back-pack where he held it upside down. He turned the bag right side up again and rummaged around in the deepest recesses of the bag, and pulled out what he found wedged there.

It was like an oyster shell, but bigger, the shape and size of an old man's pendulous ear. A line of small holes pierced a gently curved outer recess in the shiny interior. Daniel turned it this way and that, watching the light catch its surface. Then he placed it in order next to the other items laid out on the bedspread.

Cursing himself, he picked up the bag again, and checked every crevice and seam for anything else that might have escaped his notice.

But he found nothing more, so he picked up the pencil. Blunt end first, he pushed it slowly and carefully into the hollow spine of the diary and, sure enough, as he pushed, a small tube of cardboard emerged from the other end, catching at first on the diary's thin leatherette binding and then sliding out more freely.. It was a little over an inch in length. He unrolled it. It was a business card. She must have hidden it there, not wanting to discard it and keen to protect it from casual discovery.

'CaNRU' was written across the top, large bold letters in a faded shade of green, an explanatory 'Cape Narcotics Research Unit' just below it. There was a street address and a telephone number in Cape Town in black type at the bottom, and, in the middle of the card, 'Ellen Arendse: Director'. Daniel turned it over. Blank. He rolled it in the opposite direction, and then flattened it out on the bedside table.

Ellen Arendse. Is that what 'EA' refers to?

Daniel picked up the phone. He dialled the number he had written down. There were several rings at the other end. Daniel was about to break the connection when it was answered.

'Williams' residence?' a woman said breathlessly. 'So

sorry... I was in the garden.'

'Sorry,' Daniel echoed her apology, mystified. 'Who am I talking to, please?'

'This is the number for Dr and Mrs Williams,' the woman replied, a little warily.

'So sorry,' said Daniel again. 'I must have dialled the wrong number.' He returned the phone to its base.

Older than I am. But not elderly. Early sixties, perhaps? Dr? Medical doctor? Had enough of those for the moment, even if I say so myself.

He thought a moment further and then dialled the number on the business card. Engaged. The continuous wavering tone reverberated in Daniel's ear, and he slowly extinguished it by pressing gently on the telephone rest. He sat unmoving for a minute or two and then tried again. This time a woman answered.

On Daniel's query she asked him to wait while she transferred his call to Ellen Arendse. The line went silent, and then a woman answered, in English, but with a high-pitched lilting Afrikaans accent. 'Hello. Can I help?'

How could she help? What exactly is it that I want? Go straight in.

'My name's Daniel Hove,' he replied. 'I'm Patricia Hove's brother. I believe she had some kind of relationship with your organisation. I'm trying to find out what it was.'

'Why are you asking me? Why don't you ask her yourself?'

'You obviously don't know,' he said patiently. 'My sister's dead, Ms Arendse. I'm trying to find out why she died.'

The line went quiet.

She's hung up on me.

Then the voice returned. 'I'm very sorry to hear that. But she had no real connection with us. I don't think I can tell you anything that might help you.'

The woman leant on the word 'real', rolling the initial consonant.

'I think she had an appointment with you in Cape Town, several weeks ago - more than two months ago in fact - which she obviously missed. I must talk to you, Ms Arendse.'

'Mr Hove,' the voice came back at him, sternly. 'I don't know you. I don't know who you are. I'm very sorry to hear about your sister. But there's nothing I can add to that. I'm sorry.' And then she was gone, and all Daniel could hear was the dialling tone.

He slammed the phone back on to its base. *What is it about everybody? They're all sorry, but not sorry enough to help. The only person who's been willing to talk is a teenage boy in rural Matabeleland. Everyone else has been mealy-mouthed, or downright dishonest. Right, Ms Arendse. If you won't talk to me over the phone, I'll have to come and speak to you in person. And Dr and Mrs Williams? Who on earth are you? And as for the planes flying in and out... Patricia, what did you get yourself mixed up with?*

One more call to make. He pulled over his money belt and took from it a folded piece of paper, on which he found another number. He dialled and his call was answered almost immediately.

'Henry? Is that you?... Daniel Hove here... Fine, fine. And you?... No, I've found out nothing yet. It's still a complete mystery as to what she was doing up there... Yes, yes. I'll let you know as soon as a find anything. But perhaps you can help. What do you know about the woman who owns the farm near where Patricia was found? No, not there. On the other side. The farm near the mission...'

There was a distorted answer from the other end. Daniel scrabbled for his pen.

'Sorry. Spell that again, please...'

* * *

By the time he got going again in the car he rented in Johannesburg the day was well advanced, and the drive south took the rest of it.

The seemingly endless roads stretching straight as a rule into the distance took their toll. He was forced to pull over several times on the way to avoid falling totally asleep at the wheel. By the time he stopped driving it was past early evening. He booked into a hotel in the centre of the town he had reached and collapsed onto the bed. Even a rowdy student bar immediately below his room failed to keep him awake. It was only the second full stretch of sleep he had had since the night spent in Father Barnabas' house at the mission.

He was up and ready to go at dawn the next morning and was the first to pay his bill, judging by the early morning sloth of the manager who took his money. Perhaps the only one with a bill to pay. In the light of day it looked as if the hotel's rooms were purely for the purpose of the liquor licence.

Then he was off again driving south east on the last leg.

The road signs the day before had been a potted

education in imperial history. The countryside appeared to have been subdivided by a Colonial Office cartographer working from a dog-eared copy of Debrett's. It was more of the same on his journey the next morning, the antique names of the baronetcy and the superior orders superimposed on the burnt and fractured land.

He followed the road as it wound sedately down to the coast and across an unexpected arched suspension bridge into a seaside village which sat sleeping astride a wide open river.

The previous morning, while waiting for a department store photo-counter to develop his films, Daniel had spent an hour in the public library in central Johannesburg. Sweltering in the dim stagnant air, he leafed through a two-inch thick telephone directory, looking up every Williams he could find in the dozen or more towns which shared the dialling code of the number Patricia had written down in her notes.

Methodically, he checked every number he found against the one he had dialled the previous day. He thanked goodness the surname wasn't Dlamini or Jacobs, or he would have been there all day. Eventually his persistence was rewarded. He found a number that matched, and so also a street address to suit.

It was to that address that he now drove, winding his way slowly through a genteel residential estate comprising whitewashed houses in mock Dutch farmhouse style. But not all. Further in was a much older building with a wide and welcoming encircling veranda under a Victorian corrugated roof with prim downward-curling eaves. Daniel parked alongside it and eased himself stiffly from his seat, his shirt saturated and stuck to the imitation leather and his legs aching from the drive.

A wooden front door was protected by a light mesh mosquito screen. Daniel pulled on a much-painted cast iron handle which rang a bell - a proper bell - in the interior. The inner door opened wide and a bright inquisitive elfin face, with finely drawn features and short silver hair closely sculpted to her scalp, looked out at him through the gauze.

'Mrs Williams?' he said quietly.

* * *

It was only later when Daniel asked to use their bathroom and he saw himself in the mirror that he realised why Mrs Williams had been so hesitant when she first opened the door. He looked, with his demeanour and scars and travel-creased clothing, frankly criminal with intent. It was only the appearance of Dr Williams beside her which persuaded her to let him in. Daniel's insulted reaction had obviously been clear. She was clearly embarrassed, and her almost immediate apologies were most profuse. But given what the image in the mirror looked like, Daniel couldn't really blame her.

Her husband was in his sixties, a lean man with salt and pepper hair and a closely trimmed beard. It was Daniel's surname that had persuaded him.

'My name's Daniel Hove. I'm trying to find out about my sister,' Daniel had began. 'She…'

'She came to see me several weeks ago,' Williams had finished his sentence for him. 'I was thinking about her this morning, as it happens.'

Daniel's expression must have suddenly changed, because Williams smiled. 'You seem surprised? When you mentioned your name, I thought you'd have to be connected.' He laughed. 'Yours isn't a common surname around here. Two Hoves in a matter of weeks? That would be well beyond statistical probability.'

They were both now sitting in generously upholstered garden chairs on an open porch at the back of the house, looking out through a gap in the dunes to a wide white sandy beach and the breakers and open sea beyond. There was a silver teapot on a tray on a table, best bone china and home-made biscuits displayed in a dainty silver basket. Bead-weighted gauze to protect the milk and the biscuits from a patrol of flying insects. Mrs Williams had retreated inside.

'You almost certainly don't know, but she died a couple of weeks ago,' began Daniel again once the tea had been poured. 'I found a sheet of paper in her belongings. She'd written your telephone number on it. I was wondering whether you could shed any light...'

'Oh. No. I didn't know. I'm so sorry. It must be very difficult for you,' said Williams. 'My sincere condolences. What a shame. Such a pleasant young woman. Such a shame when a student dies. So young.'

'She wasn't a student,' said Daniel. 'At least, she wasn't when she met you.'

'She wasn't? I suppose I just assumed that she was,' said Williams. 'I used to teach up in Grahamstown, before I retired. I suppose I got too used to almost everyone being either a student or a member of the department.'

'What department was that?' Daniel asked. *That was the*

town I spent last night in...

'Ichthyology,' Williams replied.

So, not a medical doctor. But perhaps the right kind of doctor, nevertheless.

Daniel put down his cup of tea and picked up the blue bag from the floor next to his chair. He opened it, and delved deep. He pulled out the shell he had found and gave it to Williams. 'Is this what she came to see you about?'

Williams smiled wryly. 'Haliotis midae. Yes. That's precisely what she came to see me about.'

* * *

'You a fan of seafood?' Williams asked, offering him the silver basket.

'Not really. Not at all, actually. Never really tried it. Don't want to. Just the thought makes me feel ill.'

Williams laughed. 'A common sentiment. But that's OK. All the more for those of us who love it. Abalone? Ever heard of abalone? Perlemoen?'

Daniel shook his head.

'OK,' said Williams, laughing. 'Marine Gastropod Molluscs 1A...'

He took the shell from Daniel's hand and weighed it in the palm of his hand. 'What you have here is a perlemoen shell. Like most sea creatures, this one has many names. I suppose the most common is abalone. There are lots of different species found all over the world. The one we have here in South Africa is Haliotis midae. The Midas Ear abalone.'

He held it up mockingly against his own ear, and then

pointed out the shape and colour on the inside of the shell.

'You can see where it got that name. The local name for it – perlemoen – is a corruption of an old Dutch word for mother of pearl.'

He caressed the shiny inside of the shell with his thumb.

'Perlemoen have become a bit of an obsession for me, I have to admit. If you'll forgive my conceit, I suppose I've become a bit of an authority. Locally, anyway. That's why your sister came to see me, I suppose. She said she was writing an article about perlemoen. I was only too happy to oblige. It's not often that the outside world takes much notice of an obscure retired academic, least of all one who is interested in shellfish.'

'As I said, I just assumed she was a student. I thought her article might appear in one of the local rags. Which is why I was thinking of her this morning. I was wondering where I might check to see my name in print.'

He laughed mockingly at his own vanity. 'If she wasn't a student, do you happen to know which publication she was working for?'

'I'm afraid I don't know much at all. I don't know whether she was working for any publication, actually. She'd just finished a diploma in art. In Cape Town. Apart from that I don't know what she was doing. That's what I am trying to find out,' said Daniel. He pointed to the shell. 'I wouldn't have thought she'd be interested in this sort of thing at all.'

Williams took a sip of tea. 'Abalone's very popular. Everyone wants to eat it – except you and a few others, of course – and there isn't enough to go around. So it's disappearing from the seas all over the world, including here. There are quotas in South Africa for the amount that can be legally harvested from the wild colonies along the coast. There are also a few commercial farms. But there is a lot of illegal harvesting. In fact, the poaching appears to be several times bigger than the legal quota. A tiny amount of the illegal catch ends up in local restaurants, but the big money is in exporting it to the far east. Your sister seemed particularly interested in this illegal trade.'

'You can find perlemoen all along the southern coast of the continent, from west of Cape Town all the way up to the middle of the Transkei, not that far from here.' He pointed to the breakers. 'I'm not sure how much of a help I was to your sister. I know a fair bit about the scientific stuff, how and where the perlemoen colonies have been devastated by poaching, that sort of thing. But I'm afraid that what I know about the illegal trade itself is no more than anyone else, really. I know it is exported from here, and I know where the perlemoen ends up. But all I know about how it gets from here to there is what I have picked up from reading the newspapers, and the occasional piece of academic research.'

'Where does it end up?' Daniel asked.

'Hong Kong, a lot of it,' said Williams. 'I must stress. All I know about *how* it gets there is from what I have read. But I do know that a huge amount of it *does* end up there.'

Daniel looked at him quizzically.

'As I said, there are restrictions in South Africa on the quantity of perlemoen that can be legally harvested and exported each season. Permits, licences, enforcement, etc. So when you export something illegally, it doesn't end up in the official records here. But there are no restrictions in Hong Kong - or the rest of China, I suppose - on how much perlemoen can be imported. It's all perfectly OK there. So the amounts of the imports, as well as their origin, are diligently recorded every month in the Hong Kong official trade statistics.'

'Those statistics show quite clearly that substantial quantities of salt-water molluscs are being imported into Hong Kong from Mozambique, Swaziland and Zimbabwe. As far as I know - and if anyone knows, I should - perlemoen aren't found naturally in Mozambique, and both Swaziland and Zimbabwe are landlocked, so they can't be from there, by definition. How can salt-water molluscs be exported from countries that have no coastline?'

'So, whatever is being exported from Swaziland and Zimbabwe must have come from somewhere else. I suppose whatever is coming from Mozambique may be genuinely from there – some other kind of mollusc, not perlemoen. But my instinct, after watching the devastation of the perlemoen colonies on our coastline, is that it is perlemoen that is being exported from all three countries. South African perlemoen.'

Daniel dug into the bag again. He pulled out one of the transparent folders, and extracted the sheaf of pages on which Patricia had made her notes. He handed them to Williams. 'Does any of this make any sense to you?'

Williams scanned through them rapidly. 'That,' he said, handing the large folded sheet of paper back to Daniel, 'means absolutely nothing to me. These, on the other hand, are just what I have been talking about. They are extracts from the Hong Kong trade data.'

'Did you give them to her?'

'Yes. She made these notes when she came to see me. I showed her some photocopies I have of the data and she copied them down. And she took that shell away with her. It was lying around in my study.'

He pointed towards the end of the house. 'She asked – for the photographs for the article, she said,' he smiled wryly again, 'so I gave it to her.'

He turned the shell over and pointed to a tiny number scratched into the uneven surface. 'A catalogue reference number. I've got a file somewhere which will detail exactly where it was collected and when.'

He pointed to one of the columns on Patricia's notes. 'These here. These are the values of each month's imports of perlemoen. In Hong Kong dollars.'

'What's a Hong Kong dollar worth?'

'Divide by 7.8. That'll give you a rough value in US dollars,' he said, and then proceeded to call out the results to Daniel, row by row, calculating them in his head. 'In a good month, anything between half a million and a million dollars. U.S. Sometimes more,' said Williams. 'Good business. And that's just the declared value, so almost certainly an under-estimate. It certainly wouldn't be an exaggeration. And of course they may be exporting to other places too.'

'So this is highly organised crime. Violent as well?'

'Very organised. It has to be. And I'm sure they aren't Buddhists. One reads now and then of poachers shooting back at police, but I would have thought that's just the tip of the iceberg. Quite dangerous too. Flying the stuff out of the country. Over the years, so one reads, several small planes have come down because they were overloaded with perlemoen, or because the load shifted in mid-air. But then everything seems to be violent these days. Try running a taxi business in a big city, for instance,' he said.

'So they can get it all the way to Hong Kong without it rotting?'

'Sure. Well packed in ice, and it'll last long enough to get to any restaurant in this country. For longer distances, maybe they would preserve it somehow. Dried, maybe. Salted, perhaps. With a bit of planning, I suppose, it could be on a table in an expensive restaurant in Hong Kong within days.'

There was a silence.

'How did your sister die?' Williams asked.

'She was murdered. She was beaten to death.' Daniel fluttered Patricia's notes. 'But why would they murder her because of a planeload of shellfish?'

Ten

A nother hard day's driving and he was again descending to the coast, this time into Cape Town. Much lusher here. Unlike any part of Africa he had been to, the road was lined with cloud-edged mountains and every turn brought another spectacular view cut suddenly short by the next dramatic twist in the road. Again, late in the evening, he found lodgings for the night and collapsed into an open-mouthed unbroken sleep.

The next morning he found the CaNRU office in an old bungalow on a bleached down-at heel suburban road to the east of the harbour. The street, a patchwork of different shades of grey, appeared to be made up entirely of repairs. The grass on the verge was unkempt and patchy, barely surviving in thin soil which was heavily seasoned with salt. Trees planted at intervals along the sides of the road all leaned in one direction, starkly marking the direction of the prevailing wind.

It wasn't blowing as Daniel got out of his rental car, but he immediately felt the heat of the sun as if it too was a prevailing wind. Looming down the street stood the mountain, silhouetted against a cobalt sky.

The bungalow's untidily rendered walls, and those of a high perimeter wall surrounding it, were painted a chemical shade of yellow, this startling colour being complemented by a roof in diesel green. A gate constructed of substantial steel bars was set on runners at one corner of the boundary wall to allow access to a short driveway. Further along was a narrow pedestrian gate of a similar hefty design.

The windows were protected by steel burglar bars in a diamond pattern picked out in scarlet, and the front door was shielded by yet another steel grill, this one painted a dark navy blue. It looked like a new-age squat in a military block-house.

Taking the hint from the elaborate security, Daniel turned back to check that the car was locked and then walked over to the smaller gate. Imbedded in the wall to the side of it was a row of buttons with slots next to each where name cards for the occupants could be inserted. Like the trees on the pavement, the row of buttons was off-vertical. CaNRU was the only name listed. Daniel pressed the button and waited for a response from a perforated steel sheet set into the plaster. There was no reply by human voice, but there was a loud buzzing as an electric lock was released.

Daniel pushed and the gate opened noisily and heavily on its hinges. He walked through the narrow entrance and let the gate swing back until he heard the lock re-engage. Then he walked up the concrete path that ran between two rectangular patches of battling lawn. He pressed the doorbell and waited.

It wasn't long before the inner wooden door opened and a diminutive young woman peered out at him. Magenta hair was cropped in spikes around her very pale face, with the occasional longer strand threaded with beads. Her clothing was many-layered and multi-coloured, and a large iridescent feather dangled from each of her ears. Daniel looked at her doubtfully. Perhaps she'd also been responsible for the colour scheme of the building.

But her smile, which almost covered the distance between the feathers, won him over. He couldn't help smiling back.

'Ellen Arendse?' he enquired.

'No. I'm Antjie,' she said cheerfully. 'You are?'

'Daniel Hove,' he answered. 'I spoke briefly to Ms Arendse on the phone three days ago. Is it possible to speak to her?'

'I'm sure you can,' she said, with a delight that surprised him. 'Please come in.'

She produced a bunch of keys from a pocket, selected an impressively long double-headed one, and turned it full circle twice in the lock of the grill. Daniel had to take a step back to allow it to open, and then he entered and waited while the doors were secured in turn behind him.

She took him through to a small office and motioned to a low chair against a wall. 'Please. Take a seat,' she said. 'Coffee?'

He accepted gratefully and she left the room, returning after an interlude with a large colourful mug. 'Ellen is busy with a call at the moment,' she said pleasantly. 'I'm sure she won't be long.'

Daniel's spirits rose. He'd expected that he'd have to plead to get in. He sipped at his coffee and looked around him.

The walls were decorated with posters, brightly coloured, polemic in nature. An oversized beaming Mandela, an unheard demand to release a pensive Aung San Suu Kyi. But most were variations on a theme. 'Put that in your white pipe and smoke it', the slogan on one shouted out in large letters, above a picture of a distorted head inhaling from one end of a broken-off bottle neck and morphing as smoke into the other end.

A second had the words Tik and Tok repeated endlessly as the background to an image of a woman with raw lesions covering her face. Yet another portrayed a wizened man holding a cigarette lighter to the bottom of a small light bulb, inhaling the fumes rising from the opened top of it. There was a slogan in Afrikaans. Daniel read it, bemused. He had no idea what it meant. He suspected that he would have been equally perplexed had it been in English.

He heard raised voices from outside the room. Shortly afterwards, the young woman put her head around the door.

'Ellen will see you now,' she said flatly, conveying more meaning with the poker-face expression she had adopted than with her words.

Daniel followed her out and up a short corridor to another office. He walked through the open door to be met by an olive-skinned, raven-haired woman with the iciest-blue eyes he had ever seen.

Here comes trouble...

Her reception was as warm as the colour of her eyes. She advanced to greet him with a businesslike handshake, brief and perfunctory. She retreated again behind her desk and Daniel sat down, facing her across it. The other woman left the room.

'I said when we spoke on the phone that there was nothing we could tell you about Patricia's death,' Ellen said firmly. 'Nothing has changed since then. I'm afraid you've wasted your time coming here.'

'I hope not. It's taken me two days' driving to get here,' said Daniel. He put his hand to his jacket pocket, pulled out the contents, and set them down on the desk in front of him.

'You said you didn't know whether I was who I said I

was.' He extracted his passport from the small pile of papers, opened it and swivelled it round so that she could read it. 'That's me. That's my name. Same as my sister's.'

She gave the passport a passing glance and then looked straight back at him, He felt as if she were trying to read his mind by drilling into his eyes. They stared at each other. Daniel was the first to blink, excusing himself from the confrontation by casting his eyes back down to his papers.

'If you're worried that someone else might know that I have contacted you, I can assure you that that is highly unlikely.' He fished in the pile and produced the creased business card. 'I found that hidden in her bag. Very well hidden. I have no reason to suppose that anyone except you and I know she had it. That's why I phoned you. Also, because she'd written a reminder in her diary that looked very much as if it was an appointment with you. That meeting would have been just over eleven weeks ago. If she had survived to make it.'

Then he went to the bottom of the pile and pulled out half-a-dozen colour photographs. He dealt them out one by one facing her in a declared poker hand on the desk. Straight or flush, he wasn't sure.

'That's how she looked when she died,' he said. 'I'm a doctor. I could describe to you in harsh medical detail what she went through, but I'll leave that to your imagination. I think you owe it to her – and me – to tell me anything you know.'

Her frosty demeanour slipped briefly. She picked up the photographs and examined them closely, and then looked again silently at Daniel. She got up. Daniel thought she was going to physically eject him from the room. Although she was considerably shorter than he was, she could have. Daniel was sure of that. But she walked past him to the door, closed it, and returned to her seat.

'No-one deserves to be treated like that,' she said quietly. She looked at the watch on her wrist. 'Look. I've got a few minutes. But that's all.'

* * *

Her eyelids closed for a moment as she composed herself.

'OK. I didn't really know Patricia at all,' she began. 'She pitched up here, out of the blue, looking for a job. She was obviously intelligent and seemed very capable, so we talked. About an hour, I suppose. Maybe not that long. She sat where you're sitting now and we talked. I am not sure why. I knew I couldn't afford to take her on. I suppose I was feeling guilty that I couldn't offer her a job. Who knows … maybe I might have been able to persuade someone that she was a worthwhile addition to the team.'

'What did you talk about?'

'I asked her about her plans, her ambitions. She asked me about what we do here.'

'Which is...?'

'What it says on the card. We're a research organisation. Our expertise is the drug problem here in the Cape. It's big business around here. Big business,' she said, emphasising the first word with an exaggerated drawl. 'We document the problems it causes. Social dysfunction, criminal behaviour, gang culture. We're trying, ultimately, to get the politicians to do something about it. Unfortunately, it isn't that easy.'

'Tell me what you told her.'

'Sure.' She paused. 'So. What kind of doctor are you?' she asked.

'Surgeon. Orthopaedic surgeon.' Daniel said. 'Recreational drugs are not my speciality.'

'No matter. You've heard of Mandrax?'

'Methaqualone. Has an effect similar to barbiturates.'

She inclined her head appreciatively. 'Very good, Mr Hove. Around here they call it *'smarties'*. And when you smoke it mixed with marijuana, they call it *'wit pyp'*. White pipe.'

Daniel nodded. From somewhere in the recesses of his brain he dredged up a memory of a late afternoon lecture years before when he'd been a student.

She went on. 'More methaqualone is abused in the western Cape than anywhere else on earth. It's been smoked for so long around here it's a national sport. When you see someone with yellowy-brown stains on their hands...' She drew a finger across the fingers and palm of her other hand. 'you know they have been smoking. It does horrible damage to your lungs, mouth, teeth, you name it. Apart from all the crime it brings with it.'

Where is this leading?

'But Mandrax is yesterday's problem. There's now a drug that's even more popular. And much more destructive. Here it's called *tik*. You probably know it as crystal meth.'

'Crystal meth's an amphetamine. A stimulant,' said Daniel, more as an aide memoire to himself than a contribution to the conversation. 'Methaqualone – Mandrax - acts like a barbiturate. The one gets you up, and the other brings you down. An over-simplification, but anyway...'

'Full marks,' she said.

Daniel was beginning to resent the teasing in her voice, but he forced himself to bury his irritation.

'Mandrax is increasingly the choice of the older addict. The *bergie* sitting in a dwaal on the pavement - he's probably a Mandrax user.'

'Bergie?'

'Tramp,' she said. 'Someone who lives rough on the berg – the mountain.'

'Ah...'

'*Tik*, on the other hand. is growing fastest among the young. They like it because of the extreme high they get. There's no mellow euphoria, like with Mandrax. *Tik* wakes you up, keeps you raring to go.' She smiled wryly. 'The hit also lasts longer. Someone once described it to me as 'more bong for your buck'. And it makes you randy, you see.' Her cold expression gave way to a brief salacious smile, and then her face hardened again. 'That's why it's such a threat. A young person gets addicted, and it's very difficult to rescue them. Mostly they're there for life. Often not a very long life, especially if they're male. But that's another story...'

'Another cup of coffee?' She got up and went over to a low filing cabinet, on the top of which stood an old dented kettle. She plugged it into a wall socket, and then glanced back at him over her shoulder. 'My personal addiction,' she said.

He smiled back feebly, and declined.

'So that's it, very briefly,' she said when she had sat down again. 'We count the numbers, estimate the damage, collect the stories. And then we write it all up, add some heart-wrenching pictures, and send it off to whoever will read it. Or, at least that's what we used to do. But it wasn't making any difference. The problem was getting worse. The days when a couple of *skollies* sold Mandrax buttons outside the off-licence to fund their own habits are gone.'

'So we made another plan. I decided that we would stop writing about the problems caused by the drug trade. Instead, we would write about the trade itself. How it works. Which gangs do what, where. Prices, logistics, gang members, Mr Bigs. Everyone and everything connected to the drug business. And then maybe we could shame the politicians and the police into doing something to stop it. Because nothing was happening. No-one was doing a damn thing.'

She took a long sip of her coffee. 'We started to talk to people. Addicts. Small time dealers. Gangsters, whoever we could get to talk. Even a few cops. We began to join the dots, draw a picture of what was going on. Doing the cops' work for them, in fact.' She sipped again. 'Do you know how they make tik, Mr Hove?'

'Haven't the faintest idea.'

'I won't bore you with the whole recipe. There are various ways to do it. The way they did it here involved cooking with phosphorous, decongestant tablets and iodine. In America, that process is called red, white and blue. Red for the phosphorous, blue for the iodine, and white for the ephedrine you extract from the decongestants. All mixed in with meths, caustic soda, spirits of salts and a few other things.'

'It stinks to high heaven, and it's extremely poisonous. Every now and then a kitchen would blow up, killing everyone in it, or burning them so badly they'd spend months travelling to the clinic and back. And there's piles of rubbish. Empty containers, pools of toxic waste. So, you can imagine, a kitchen isn't so popular with the people who live next door to it. Happy to smoke it, but not happy staying next to the factory.'

'So when the word got round that someone was going to close down the meth kitchens, it didn't take long before the word was being passed back, telling exactly where the kitchens were. I suppose it started a little over a year ago. The meth kitchens were shutting up shop. Everywhere. The small time dealers running a tiny operation out of some *pondokkie* in Gugulethu or Mitchell's Plain suddenly weren't there any more. One day they're cooking up a few grams. That night a gang breaks down the door, smashes the place up and leaves the dealer in no doubt he should take a permanent career break. If only the police could be so effective.'

'At first, everyone thought it might have been some community group or other, policing themselves. You know. Vigilantes. There's been some of that. Specially in the Muslim areas. But even though the kitchens were being closed down, it wasn't the end of the tik problem. Not by any stretch. This wasn't a vigilante operation. It was a corporate take-over, pure and simple. Tik is still there for anyone who wants it. It's just that now most of the trade is being controlled by a couple of gang lords. And the price has gone sky high.'

'At first, they had their own kitchens. Big ones in the middle of nowhere far from the Cape, where they could work full time without being bothered by the police. But even those started to become a problem. Every so often there'd be an ambitious cop who wasn't on their payroll, making it difficult to keep the production line going. So they changed their approach. They began to import crystal meth as a finished product from outside the country. In industrial quantities. Using a different, more efficient production process.'

'Because the tik is imported, there aren't any filthy kitchens advertising themselves to the police, if they ever get motivated enough to get up off their backsides. The supply is more reliable. So, more efficient production methods, lower production costs even with the longer transportation routes, more reliable supply. Equals more profit for the gangs. Globalisation, you could call it. Modern management theory applied to the drugs business.'

She leaned back in her chair. 'That's it, I suppose. We talked, in more detail of course, but I suppose that would cover it.'

She pointed to the photographs. 'Where did this happen?' she asked suddenly, as if Daniel's answer would determine whether she would continue.

'Zimbabwe. Rural Matabeleland. At least that's where her body was found. Three months ago.'

He told her about the hospital, and the doctor who'd lied. He told her about his visit to the police station, and the police inspector who'd lied. He told her about being forced off the road and beaten senseless. He pointed to the scar on his head. She made sympathetic noises. Then he told her about his return visit, his meeting with Father Barnabas, his conversation with Themba Sibanda, and his visit to the farm.

'What did you find?' she asked keenly, leaning forward.

Daniel got the distinct impression that she already knew what his answer would be. 'There was a barn that stank like a blocked public urinal. It was full of chemical equipment. Glass jars, tubing, gas bottles, drums, cans. A laboratory. Quite possibly the filthiest I have ever come across. Reeked of ammonia.'

She nodded. 'That's the other method. From what you say, it sounds like they're using a compound of ammonia as a base to make the crystal meth. That smell doesn't hang around for long, so they must have been making tik shortly before you went there.'

Daniel nodded. 'The boy said the place starts to smell, and then a plane comes a few days after that. So a plane was due there quite soon. The boy was correct. It came the day after. I saw it land and take off again. I saw a load of boxes being exchanged. Big blue boxes taken off the plane, little blue canisters loaded onto it. The boy said it was always like that. Only on Sundays. Big boxes out of the plane. Canisters in.'

Daniel dug into his pile of papers and extracted another photograph. He turned it round so she could see it. It showed the transfer operation on the airfield in full swing. 'There you go,' he said.

'Really,' she said. Daniel saw her roll her tongue around the inside of her lower lip, deep in thought as she stared at the photograph. She looked calculating and predatory. Her attractiveness had vanished. 'That's really interesting,' she concluded quietly.

Daniel dug into his jacket pocket. He pulled out the perlemoen shell. 'So what is this all about, then?' he said as he picked it up delicately with the tips of two fingers and placed it on the desk between them, next to the photograph.

She was astonished. It showed only fleetingly and she

rapidly recovered her composure, but to Daniel it was as obvious as if she had fallen off her chair.

She picked up the shell. 'Perlemoen,' she said, composed again. 'Seafood.'

'And how is that connected to crystal meth?'

'Is there a connection?' she said blankly. 'I'm not aware of one.'

She looked straight back at him, challenging him. Then, before he could even begin to answer, she glanced at her watch.

'My God. I'm so sorry,' she said. 'I'm running very late. I do need to go. It was very nice to talk to you. I'm so sorry it was in such tragic circumstances.' She stood and thrust forward her hand across the desk and took hold if his. 'I'm sorry I can't help you further.'

And before he was fully aware of it, he had been ushered from the building and was standing on the pavement outside the house, watching the steel gate trundle closed and her driving away, hand held up at the driver's window in a regal farewell.

* * *

The next morning, a Friday, Daniel drove back out to the bungalow. His journey was identical. He took the same route he had taken before. By eight-thirty he had parked the car in the same place that he had parked the previous day. He even made the same mistake he had made the day before - selecting Reverse rather than Park with the automatic gear lever. The building looked the same - bright and sulphurous in the morning sun. The mountain still dominated the view at one end of the street.

The first difference he noticed was the slip of card bearing CaNRU's name on the panel of buttons at the gate. Or rather he didn't notice it. It was missing. The previous day, CaNRU's card had been the only one on show. Now there were none.

Nevertheless, that meant nothing. Someone must be able to let him in He tried each button in turn, working down from the top. No response, no voice, no buzzing of the electric lock. Doubt immediately filled his mind. Had he mislaid a day somewhere on his travels? Was today a Saturday rather than a Friday? Was it a public holiday he wasn't aware of?

He went back to the car to wait another half an hour. The interval dragged by. Nobody entered the building, nobody left, and by five to nine he could stand it no longer. He got out and tried the buttons a second time. Again, nothing. Not really surprising, since he had seen nobody enter since he arrived. He stood leaning against the car in the sunshine, looking this way and that, then staring at the front door, willing it to open.

A few minutes later he saw the other woman, Antjie, walking briskly down the street towards him. 'Hello,' she said, surprised, as she reached him. 'I didn't know you were coming back?'

'I had some more things I needed to ask Ellen...'

'Oh. OK. I'm usually in earlier than this. Running a little late this morning... Did she not let you in?'

'I buzzed, but there was no answer. And the name card's gone.' He pointed.

She walked over to the gate and tried the button. No

response. 'Damn thing must have broken again. We're always having to get it fixed. I don't know what's happened to the card. Kids messing about, probably. Don't worry. We can get in over there.'

He followed her over to the bigger gate further along the perimeter wall. She rummaged in her bag and pulled out a bunch of keys attached to a large plastic lozenge. She pressed it, a motor began to whirr, and the gate slowly rolled open. She smiled reassuringly back at him and they walked together through the opening.

As the gate rolled shut behind them, she swung the bunch around her finger, selected the long double headed key and opened the steel security gate at the front door. Using a second key, she unlocked the wooden door behind it. They entered and she locked both doors after them.

'Ellen?' she called out, cheerily. Her call echoed down the passage.

Silence.

They walked into the reception room where Daniel had sat on his first visit. It was bare. No chairs, no table, bare walls. No rug on the floor. Mandela and the rest were gone. The only hint of the room's previous appearance was a small triangular corner of one of the posters that had torn off and was still attached to the wall.

'Shit!' she said. The word exploded from her lips, in complete contrast to the gentle unflappable demeanour Daniel had seen so far.

They both left the room and hurried up the corridor to Ellen's office. Antjie pulled out her bunch of keys and inserted one into the lock, and was visibly surprised when she found it was unlocked. That room too was completely empty. No chairs, no desk, no safe, no filing cabinet, no kettle. She walked briskly out of the door and, one after another, looked into every other room in the building. They too were empty. She opened one last door at the end of the corridor.

'Bloody hell,' she said. 'She's even taken the toilet paper.'

She rummaged in her bag and extracted her phone. She punched at the keypad and put it to her ear. A few seconds later she angrily stabbed at it again, disconnecting it. She looked back at him.

'She's cancelled her phone number,' she said to Daniel.

And then she swore with a vehemence of which Daniel wouldn't have thought she was capable. One syllable, spat out like a waterfront hooker.

'Are you going to tell me what's going on?' asked Daniel.

'Ellen Arendse isn't quite who you think she is,' she said. She paused. 'We haven't got much time. Let's go.'

'Hang on. Hang on,' Daniel protested. 'Go where?'

'I'll explain as we go,' she said. 'But we've got to get going.'

Eleven

She was on her phone from the minute they started driving, but her only communication with Daniel for a full ten minutes after they left the bungalow were directions given by way of hand signals and expressive motions of her head.

Daniel, following her instructions like an automaton, eavesdropped intently as she made a series of calls - most, it appeared, requests for information that made no sense to Daniel whatsoever. But there were three snippets which he was able to remember when he later tried to reconstruct the conversations, even if the details, almost certainly on account of his presence next to her, mostly appeared to be deliberately vague.

In one, someone called Boet was instructed to go to the beach house. There was another fragment of a discussion in which she told someone else that she was on her way to 'Diedricks' place' and to meet her there. And then a call to someone called Kobus, whose orders, to her obvious exasperation, she had to repeat twice, and with a level of detail absent from her other calls. He was sent to the deli up against the mountain, in a place whose unfamiliar syllables Daniel would have been hard pushed to repeat from memory, but which nevertheless lodged itself in a secluded part of his brain.

It sounded to Daniel as if she was deploying troops, with the authority of a field officer moving forward to engage the enemy. It was only once they had settled into the fast lane of the freeway – only once Daniel had no choice but to continue

141

driving, he recognised later - that she gave him her full attention.

'As I said, Ellen Arendse and CaNRU are not what she says they are. I know she gave you a spiel about researching the drug problem, lobbying government to get it stopped, all that rubbish. But that's not what they're about. She and CaNRU are not trying to fight the drug problem. Put simply, they are the drug problem.'

'What on earth do you mean by that?'

'She's part of the mob, Daniel. You don't mind me calling you that, do you?' She continued without waiting for a reply. 'Little Miss Meth, they call her. Funny ha ha. But she's so deep in the drugs business it isn't even remotely amusing.'

Daniel turned his head and stared in disbelief.

'Look where you're going,' she warned matter-of-factly. Daniel had allowed the car to veer from its lane.

'OK,' he said tetchily, turning his stare back to the road ahead. 'And you know all this how?'

'Drug Squad. I'm an officer with the Drug Squad.'

The car lurched again, only returning to its legal course when she leant over and grabbed the steering wheel.

'Will you *please* watch out where you're *fucking well* going!' she shouted, keeping hold of the wheel until she finally allowed Daniel to take control once more.

'OK, OK, OK,' he said, taking a deep breath. 'Carry on.'

'I'm an officer with the Drug Squad,' she said evenly, once she had satisfied herself that he could probably be trusted not to kill them both. 'I have no warrant card with me, so I can't prove it to you now. You'll just have to trust me for the time being.'

Trust?

'Ellen told you about how the production of crystal meth was moved out of the country.'

It was a statement, not a question, but Daniel answered anyway. 'Yes.'

'She didn't tell you about the link with perlemoen. Even though you asked her, in so many words.'

Hang on...

'She said there was no connection. I didn't believe her. I can put two and two together. There's definitely a link, and I could probably make a reasonable guess as to what it is. It was pretty obvious she knew something about it. But she said she was late for an appointment and it never got further than that. That's why I came back this morning. I had to find out more. But how do you know what she did and didn't tell me? Were you listening at the door?'

'Let's just say that what was said in her office wasn't as confidential as she would have liked it to be. Look. I know I owe you some kind of explanation. I'll get to the perlemoen stuff later.'

* * *

'There's a guy that we have under investigation. Big-time dealer. Big-time narcotic offences. I got the job. Find out precisely what he was doing and with who. There've been a few cases lately that didn't make it all the way through the courts. Thrown out on technicalities. Procedures not followed to the letter, that sort of thing.'

'They don't want it happening again. They want to throw the book at him and they want an open and shut case. No bits missing, no loose ends. They don't want him to hire a smart lawyer who'll get his teeth into a loophole and shake the whole case to bits.'

'By sheer chance, that's how I came across Ellen Arendse and CaNRU. A colleague in a different section tipped me off. He'd come across Ellen's name from one of his sources, said she was linked in some way to the subject we are investigating. It seemed like another bit of gossip at the time, but we weren't making much progress in any other direction, so I decided it was worth some effort to get to know more about her. I must admit she turned out to be even more intriguing than I would've thought possible.'

'I turned up on her doorstep one day and said I was looking for a job. Much like your sister, I suppose.' She stopped. Daniel saw her looking across at him. He chanced another sideways glance. 'I only met her once, but she seemed so nice. I am so sorry about what happened to her.'

She reached over and touched Daniel's hand. If it was an instinctive gesture of sympathy, which he much later doubted, Daniel didn't feel it like that. He felt her touch as keenly as if it were a charge of electricity. But he managed to control his reaction – his mouth merely twitched in acknowledgement.

She went on. 'Anyway, Ellen took me on. Why she did it I don't know. I can be persuasive, I know, but she did no checks on me at all – none that I was aware of anyway – and I started two days later. She even gave me keys to the office. In view of what I later found out, it's inexplicable. Arrogance, perhaps? Was she under some kind of pressure? I don't know.'

'I was her dog's-body. I don't mind that really, so long as

it's a means to an end, but she's bloody difficult to work for, I can tell you. I started with that house, where the CaNRU office is.' She corrected herself. 'Was.'

'As I'm sure you noticed, there were no other tenants. I thought that was a bit surprising. It turned out the lease for the entire place had been taken by a company that we'd come across before. It has connections to one of the big drug gangs. I'd say they rented the whole house to keep it solely for CaNRU. Keep everyone else out. Which is not the way you'd expect the patron of a small NGO to behave.'

'Ellen's background turned out to be much more interesting than I would have thought possible. Graduated from UCT at the top of her class. Bachelor of Commerce with Honours in Business Administration. Then an MBA at the business school. Not a mean achievement for a girl from a working-class coloured family from the Cape Flats. With her qualifications and talent she could have named her price. Any company in the country would have bent over backwards to have her. But she ends up being CEO, and, until I turned up, the only employee of a tiny NGO. Something not right there. Definitely.'

'It turns out that her family – and they aren't called Arendse, by the way. She doesn't ever appear to have been married, so it looks like it's a name she adopted sometime before she started at UCT – her family are not what she'd told everyone during her meteoric rise. She told everyone who asked that her father worked in textiles. Loom tuner was what she said he was. Mother a nurse.'

'But he's nothing of the sort. His name's Isaacs, and he's one of the Mr Bigs in the Cape drugs business, and I don't mean he makes aspirin. I don't know what her mother does, but if she's a nurse, she doesn't appear to have ever worked as one. Not under any of the names we know she has gone by, anyway.'

'Ellen's in the family business. The company that leased that building is owned by her family. I think her education was intended precisely to help them run it like a business. Organised crime rather than the organised chaos it has been for years. My theory is that after she graduated CaNRU was set up as a front to enable Ellen and her family to get close to the cops, the government, and anyone else with an interest in the narcotics trade. CaNRU was cheap to run, and the benefits to her family were immense. Information from the horse's mouth, so to speak.'

Is this some kind of racial thing? A diminutive white woman hunting down a woman of mixed race? Or is she just mad?

He examined Antjie's face to see if he could discern any outward sign that she was suffering from some sort of delusion. Or just plain lying. He could see nothing, but then he hadn't really expected to.

'You want me to believe all this?'

'I can understand you might find it difficult to believe,' she said. 'But I promise you it's all true. Every bit of it.'

Daniel thought for a moment. 'If she is who you say she is, then she was remarkably open with me about the ins and outs of the drugs trade.'

'I'll give you a hundred rand to your one if she told you anything that wasn't already common knowledge among anyone who knows anything about the subject,' Antjie replied.

A safe bet. Since you seem to know already exactly what she said to me.

146

'That's her great skill,' she went on. 'Ellen takes a bit of what she's gleaned from others, and a bit of what she knows for herself. She'll walk into any political or law enforcement office in the Cape – and further afield – oozing complete authority, authenticity and charm. Cops. Politicians. Everyone she met, almost without fail, fell over themselves to confide in her.'

'I've seen her do it myself. They told her the most confidential of things. Things that would otherwise never be divulged to anyone outside official circles. They couldn't help themselves. It was quite pathetic to watch them open up, time and time again. And in return she told them everything they knew already, but she made it sound like it was something they'd never heard before. Making them think they were geniuses. Watching her was to see a complete master at work. God, I wish I had a quarter of her talent.'

Daniel silently agreed with her. *Was it Ellen's eyes, or her manner. He could imagine just how charming she could be, if only she dropped that hard exterior. No doubt she was entirely capable of that.*

'She gave you the speech about the 'hostile takeover' of the tik production business?'

Why bother to ask. You know damn well she did…

'Yes,' he said.

'She gives that one to everyone. One of her greatest hits. But the reason she knows so much about it is because she was right at the centre when it happened. I'm reliably informed that she was the brains behind that little manoeuvre. It took her family from low-rent obscurity right into the big time. Small time dealers to kings of the castle.

They and a couple of other mobs now control the supply of crystal meth in the Cape. A sort of cosy cartel. No, not quite. An uneasy truce is probably a better description.'

'But anyway... You were about to ask her about the perlemoen. It's quite simple, really. Just think of what was going on. The drugs which provided the gangs' income were being sold here, but sourced outside the country. Income in rand, costs in foreign currency. A business risk. Currency mismatch, as any bank manager - or MBA graduate - will tell you. At first, when the volumes imported were small, the deals could be financed in rand. But the suppliers only had a limited appetite for rand, and as they imported more and more, the gangs had to start paying in something more convertible. US dollars, mostly. Or something that could be converted into something convertible.'

'As I'm sure you've discovered, there's a lot of money in poached perlemoen...'

How...? She couldn't know... she's just guessing...

'Hard currency money. After their hostile takeover of tik manufacturing, the Isaacs' gang decided to get involved in perlemoen. They integrated those two businesses. Perlemoen and drugs. It makes sense. The perlemoen sells for foreign currency, at least part of which pays for the import of crystal meth.'

'It also makes sense in a more practical way. Logistics. Whether they're bringing in the crystal meth by plane or by truck, it makes sense to use both legs of the journey – in and out – to make money, rather than having a truck or plane travelling empty one way. So they ship the perlemoen out, and get paid by a return shipment of crystal meth, and cash as well. That's it. Simple as that. It seems that, in the season, they're shipping out a dozen boxes a week. Regular as clockwork.'

A dozen...

By now they were driving through the endless conurbation that defends Cape Town's north-eastern flank from the desert beyond. Suburbs and strip malls, cloned from each other and stretched out end on end, mile after mile. And then the gradual melding of the urban and the rural. More market gardens, fewer discount second-hand car lots. The occasional vineyard, its parallel lines vanishing to almost meet in the distant mountains.

A squadron of villas sailed past them in echelon, their Cape Dutch gable ends set like sails across the wind. Walls newly replastered, grounds in resplendent bloom, windows polished to an unblemished gleam. Gentrified by refugees from the city seeking the simpler country life that only the employment of a full-time maid and a brace of gardeners will allow.

And then suddenly, within a mile or two, the countryside was drier. The properties were further apart, and the cultivated greenery and roadside grain silos had given way to vast swathes of bleached grassland punctuated by brown rocky outcrops. The edge of sheep country as the altitude rose.

Daniel broke the silence. 'And this Diedricks character? Who is this Diedricks whose place we're going to? And why are you taking me with you, now that you appear to have hijacked my car?' he asked as they drove on after stopping at a set of red traffic lights in the middle of nowhere that seemed to serve no purpose.

'In answer to your last question, you had a car handy. I

didn't. I take a taxi to work every morning. I need to get to Diedrick's place as soon as I can. You were the obvious person, the only person, to take me there.'

'The Drug Squad couldn't send a car to pick you up?'

'All otherwise engaged. But someone should be there to meet me.'

'Sorry for the inconvenience,' she said as an afterthought.

He ignored the apology and returned to his point. 'Who is this Diedricks? Where does he fit into this story?'

She was silent for a few moments. Then: 'He's the man we're looking for. Sollie Diedricks. He lives on a small farm out here. He's retired. Used to be a policeman. That's why they're so keen to nail him. They don't like former police officers branching out into this kind of business when they retire. Especially people like him...'

She gave him a meaningful look. 'Do you know what I'm saying?'

'No. Enlighten me.'

'He has a dubious past. He was allowed to retire early on a full pension not long after '94 with no questions asked about what he'd been involved in. No Truth and Reconciliation Commission for him...'

This is just totally unbelievable...

'No rocking the boat. No books, no press interviews, no talking about his past. Retire quietly and no-one will bother you. That was the deal. But he went criminal. He's become an embarrassment.'

'Especially operating across the border. That's a real problem. For some reason, some countries not too far from here start making a fuss when other people's former policemen start breaking their laws. Or rather, they use it as an excuse. A bargaining chip.'

'He and Ellen are not just linked by a bit of circumstantial gossip. He works for her family. He's their fixer. He organises things, collects the perlemoen and manages the shipping in and out of the country. Delivers the tik to them when it comes back through.'

'And my sister? What on earth does she have to do with these people?'

'I don't know, Daniel,' she said. 'Sorry. I wish I could tell you something, but I can't.'

Not for the first time, Daniel found it hard to believe her.

* * *

They left the trunk road and drove along a mean ribbon of tarmac, seeing no other cars or people until they came to a diminutive hamlet scattered on both banks of a large donga that cut through the plain. Down and across the low causeway that spanned it, more a drift than a bridge, and then Antjie's peremptory directions to Daniel resumed.

'Turn right just after the next bend,' she said, 'then down that road. His place is on the left. Some way away. Keep going till I tell you to stop. Take it slowly.'

Daniel coasted the car around the bend and then turned as she had instructed and slowed to a crawl.

'Not that slow,' she reprimanded him sharply. 'We'll have the world and its mother gawping at us.'

They cruised on. The road began to slope down gently and there were no sizeable features except for a range of hills in the distance, so as they drove quietly along they had a more or less uninterrupted view of the countryside around them. It was open veld on all sides, until Daniel made out against the background of the hills a windmill on a slim latticed tower standing proud of everything else, the steel vanes spinning in a breeze of which there was little evidence at ground level. Then, as the road bent round slightly to the left and as she had promised, a homestead came into view, sitting bucolically some distance from the road.

There was a single storey white-washed building, the simple geometric lines outlined against the dark green backdrop of a line of huge eucalyptus trees that must have been more than eighty feet high. There was a stoep running the full length of one side, and a pastel grey corrugated roof above it. An extension departed at right-angles from the house at one end. It had a door set into it facing towards them, and it looked from the road as they coasted forward like a large garage. A short distance further away, shaded by its own stand of eucalyptus, was a smaller building in the same uncomplicated style.

A lawn of the brightest green ran from the front of the main building down to a long depression in the ground that looked as if it might be concealing a stream. This ditch ran diagonally towards the road which crossed over it some distance away via a low concrete culvert.

On the near side of the gully the land was given over to pasture, or what counted as pasture in this harsh landscape. The paddock was separated from the road itself by a modest two-strand wire fence strung tautly between stout wooden posts which were almost hidden amidst a low thick hedgerow. The homestead was well-established and peaceful, as much a part of the landscape as anything natural.

'Very nice,' Daniel said, admiringly. 'If that's what a police pension buys you I'm in the wrong job.'

'That's the point. That isn't what a police pension buys you,' Antjie countered impatiently. 'He lives quietly in a backwater, away from the eyes of the world. Not much traffic comes this way. You might think it would be cheap to live out here. But he's living beyond his means. With all that land, those buildings and that stream running through it, that property must have cost a packet. Believe me. As far as I can tell there's no bond on it. So either he's borrowed the money privately, or he owns it outright. But he only runs a few merinos and a couple of horses, grows a few grapes, vegetables and fruit. Nothing that's going to make him millions.'

'He lives there on his own?'

'Sort of. Divorced, long ago. A son who's a complete slacker, so the gossip goes. There's a maid who lives on the property. You can just see her rooms from the road. They're behind the garage. And then there are the people he employs to run the farm. He has a driver, and others. They live near the village, back near where we came through. They travel to the farm each day. Unusual arrangement, but there you are.'

'Unusual...?'

'Farm jobs round here tend to come with accommodation thrown in. They will have rent to pay so he probably has to pay them over the odds. I'm not sure whether they come out of it ahead or not.'

'And that's when he pays. He's not going to win 'Best Employer in the Boland' anytime soon, from what people say. Wages paid late nearly every week, sometimes not at all.

Surly behaviour at the best of times. Violent at the worst. Apparently he's off-his-face drunk half the time. Bored, probably. Not enough to do. Over-fond of his guns, too. Not too popular with his staff.'

'So why do they work for him?' asked Daniel.

'No choice. Same old problem there's always been on the Cape farms. Jobs involve more than just wages. There's housing, usually, though not in this case, and all sorts of other things that go with them. Rations. That kind of thing. It's not so easy to move, always assuming there's another job to move to. Which there haven't been for quite some time. Farming round here's been going through a tough time.'

They were still driving slowly along the farm road. The gate to the farm came into view from behind the hedgerow. 'Drive past,' Antjie said, and Daniel overshot it and kept driving until the road bent away to the right and they were able to stop on the side of the road out of sight of the homestead.

They sat in the car. Antjie checked her watch obsessively. Eventually she swore under her breath.

'I don't know where he is. We can't sit around any longer. Let's go and have a look,' she said to Daniel, opening the passenger door.

'Hang on a moment. I'm not a police officer. Aren't there rules against that?'

'I don't know who or what is in there any more than you do...,' she said, turning to him half in and half out of the car.

Unlikely.

'And I'd appreciate your company,' she continued, sweetly.

Sure you would.

'Listen. Since Ellen appears to have disappeared, it seems to me that Diedricks is the only hope I have if I'm to find out what happened to my sister. I need to speak to him, if you ever find him.'

'Rest assured, Daniel. What happened to your sister will be part of our investigation.'

'So you'll let me speak to him? When you get hold of him?'

'Sure. Sure,' she said impatiently. 'I'll put your questions to him. But we have to find him first.'

* * *

Daniel locked the car and they began walking back along the road. A hundred yards further on, Antjie led them over to the fence and swung her legs over it. 'This way' she said. 'It'll be better if we approach from behind those trees.' She pointed to the line of tall eucalyptus looming ahead of them.

They moved cautiously over the uneven ground, changing course every few feet as they stepped around the stout tussocks of grass and avoided the hollows pock-marking the ground like shell holes. As they approached the tree line the ground levelled out.

The surface vegetation was suddenly sparser as they reached the outer limit of the eucalyptus roots, and Daniel felt very vulnerable as they walked in the open to another fence, this one of sagging wire, just before the white trunks of the trees. They both stepped over it. The windmill was creaking and squeaking above them.

Antjie led them to the back door of the main building. She turned the handle. The door was locked. Through the window next to it Daniel could see a well kitted-out kitchen. A large wood-burning range stood against the back wall, a varied selection of pots and pans hanging from hooks just above it. Wooden cabinets lined the walls.

They moved along the back of the building. As they did, there was a clear sound.

Metal scraping against metal.

Daniel looked up, but the windmill was still facing in the direction it had been, still spinning in the wind. Antjie shook her head and pointed instead in the direction of a smaller tin-roofed building further up the fence from where they had crossed it. Together they turned and walked towards it.

* * *

It was the maid's quarters. There was a small neatly cultivated patch of a garden to one side of it, leaves sprouting in tidy rows. A stovepipe chimney protruded from the roof. There was a faint distorted column of air at its tip. An old wooden chair stood up against the front wall. The single metal door next to it was shut. There was a stack of split firewood kindling, A spade and a short-handled badza rested near it against the wall.

Daniel grabbed the badza and swung it by his wrist, but he found it too unwieldy to control. He turned it upside down and, holding it by the blade, banged the end of the handle several times against the ground. The blade gave suddenly, slipping down. He was left with the handle, which he weighed in his hand, adjusting his grip until it felt comfortable.

Antjie was watching him with amused eyes, a sardonic

smile playing on her lips. Daniel glanced back at her, returning her smile with a sardonic glower of his own. Making a mental note to reassemble the badza later, he gripped the handle firmly, went up to the door and pulled it open.

The metal resisted, screeching so that it put the nerves in his neck on edge like fingernails on a blackboard, and then gave way. They entered.

The interior was dark and there was an overpowering smell of wood smoke. Two similar metal doors lead off a tiny atrium, and there was an entrance without a door from which the smoke was escaping. Two doors, one probably a bathroom. Daniel picked the door in the middle and pulled it open. It was almost pitch black inside, the murk only partially relieved around the corners of a double-thickness calico curtain pulled across a small window.

Huddled cowering into the corner on a low iron bedstead surmounted by a thin mattress was a woman. She held her hands over her face. She was whimpering quietly.

Antjie went forward and knelt before the bed, putting her hands out in reassurance. The figure recoiled, but then began to relax as Antjie touched her fingers. Slowly Antjie persuaded the woman to drop her hands. She gathered up a bedspread from the bed and arranged it around the woman's shoulders like a shawl. Eventually the whimpering stopped.

Antjie stood. Looking quickly around the room, she spotted a paraffin lamp on a low cabinet. She knelt down again and shortly had the pressure up and the wick lit.

'Three mugs of tea,' she said brusquely to Daniel, and then took the lamp over to the woman on the bed.

Daniel left the room and opened the other door. As he had suspected, it was a small bathroom. Although there was no bath, only a cement-floored shower, a toilet and a basin-less brass tap protruding from the wall.

Daniel went to the cooking alcove, too sparse and cramped to merit being called a kitchen. A small stove of blackened sooty iron stood against the wall, embers within it glowing dully below a single piece of kindling. Smoke was leaking into the room. Daniel selected a battered kettle from a shelf to one side, took it into the bathroom to fill it, and returned to place it on top of the stove.

Once brewed, Daniel returned to the maid's bedroom with three chipped enamel mugs of tea, without milk but heavily sugared. He gave one to the maid, who responded with a brief toothless grin. Four of her top front teeth were missing, leaving only the gums showing pink and glistening in the gap.

'Her English isn't very good,' said Antjie. 'In any case, she'll be much more comfortable speaking Afrikaans. I'll translate.'

Daniel leaned against the wall, cradling his mug and listening as Antjie talked quietly with the maid, and then translated her questions and the maid's answers for Daniel's benefit.

'I asked her why she's so scared, hiding in her room like this on such a beautiful day,' said Antjie. 'She said men were here early this morning in a big silver car. A Merc. They had guns. They knocked on the door of the big house, but Baas Diedricks was sleeping, she said, and they couldn't get in. So they knocked on her door and forced her to unlock the back door to the house. They went in, woke Diedricks, and then they all left, taking him with. When she saw us she thought we were coming for her.'

Antjie spoke to her again.

'I asked if she'd called the police. She hasn't. She's been too scared to do anything. She thought if she spoke to the police those men might come back to take her away.'

'Does she know who they are?' asked Daniel. 'Does she know who you are?'

'No. She doesn't know who I am. And don't tell her, please. As to the others, I was getting to that. Let's just take this slowly. The poor woman can hardly string two thoughts together at the moment.'

She spoke again.

'She didn't recognise any of them, except one. She describes him as being very large, with a scorpion tattooed on his neck. She's seen him round here before. To me, that sounds like a fair description of an Isaacs' family enforcer. I think we can take it that Ellen's people were here early this morning, and they and Diedricks left not long afterwards.'

'Does she still have the key to the house?' asked Daniel.

'She does. She locked the place up after the men had left,' said Antjie after an exchange. She spoke a few words to the maid, who fished in a pocket in her worn dress and extracted a key.

'I asked her about the other workers here. She said the driver is away and will be back late Saturday, early Sunday. She doesn't know when any of the others will be back here, so she's all on her own until after the weekend. But I think she'll be alright. She seems to be a bit calmer now.'

They left her in her room, leaving the door and curtain open. They walked back to the house and unlocked the back door.

* * *

Walking through the kitchen and across a narrow passage, they found themselves in a long sitting room with windows looking out over the stoep to the lawn and the small stream, and the road beyond. A large open fireplace with an enamelled steel heater set into it sat at the end of the room. A neat pile of logs were piled next to a set of fireplace tools hanging from a cast iron frame.

There was a wide stone mantelpiece, above which a Boer War-era Mauser rifle was secured on steel brackets fixed solidly into the brickwork. Two small mounted antelope heads bracketed the rifle on either side, black glass eyes staring into the middle distance.

A low sofa lined each of the longer walls, and a pair of armchairs facing the chimney breast completed the rectangle. Yellowing crocheted antimacassars lay over the backs of the seats. Small occasional tables, their tops water-ringed, stood to the side of each sofa and chair. Along the interior wall above one sofa a series of three gloomy prints of rural scenes hung by triangles of copper wire from a picture rail. The floor in the middle was covered by a large zebra skin mounted on thin green baize, worn through in places.

The other end of the room was taken up by a bar counter fashioned from deeply scarred and blackened railway sleepers, complete with a set of tall teetering barstools of the same material. Each had cushioned seats of spiky zebra skin to match the rug. Behind the bar, alcove shelves were set into the wall, most filled with bottles of alcohol of various shapes, with contents of diverse description. A collection of beer mugs hung from hooks above the liquor, spirit glasses on a shelf behind them. The mugs and glasses looked as if they had been accumulating grime for years.

On one side of the top of the bar counter stood a brightly coloured mannequin about a foot high. It was a white-haired bespectacled old man with a miniature plastic martini glass in one hand and a miniature plastic spirit bottle in the other. There was a button on the figure's base. Daniel pressed it. The figure's eyes began to glow a drunken red, its spiky hair bristled backwards and forwards, and its arm swung up, raising the glass to its mouth, which fell open as the jaw fell downwards.

A scratchy sound emanated from within the mannequin. Daniel couldn't make out what it was. Then the other arm rose and an arc of amber alcoholic liquid spilled from the tiny bottle onto the bar counter. This time the sound was clearer. '... and one for you,' it said.

Daniel placed the badza handle on the bar counter. He selected a glass from the shelf and placed it in front of the automaton. He pressed the button again and leaned forward as the doll's performance was repeated. This time he heard the first sound. 'One for me... ' it said. The liquid started to spill from the bottle into the glass. 'and one for you. One for me... and one for you.'

He turned to talk to Antjie. But she wasn't there.

Not again.

Then he heard the scraping sound of badly-fitting wooden drawers being pulled open. Grabbing the handle and following the noise, he walked out of the door and up the corridor. He found her in a dishevelled bedroom at the end of the house. She was methodically emptying the contents of a cupboard and a chest of drawers onto the bed, examining them in turn, and then pushing each load aside to make room for another.

'What are you looking for?' he asked.

'Anything that might help my enquiry,' she answered, distracted. 'But I'm not having much success.' She emptied the contents of the pockets of a suit jacket onto the counterpane.

Daniel left her to it, and walked back down the passage. There was another door leading off it which opened onto a second bedroom. He peered in through the door. The door of a cupboard hung open out of which burst several piles of clothes, old shoes and broken clothes hangers. A two foot high mountain of paper was piled precariously in the corner of one room, loose sheets mainly, interspersed by what looked like brightly coloured commercial pamphlets. There were boxes pushed under the bed, coated in dust.

He continued past the door to the sitting room, and through a second entrance to the kitchen, which opened onto a large dining table, also untidily covered with paper which almost buried a small portable typewriter. A plastic cruet set and a red plastic tomato sauce dispenser stood incongruously in the middle of the mess.

Another door was set into one of the kitchen walls, an interior one judging by the lack of windows on that side. Daniel turned the key jutting out of the lock and pulled it open. It led through to the extension. Daniel fumbled until he found the light switch on the inside wall and turned it on. It was a garage, as he had thought.

There was a pick-up truck parked in the centre. A large

wooden workbench was fitted along one wall, with a rusted vice bolted to the edge of it. A selection of old tools, nails and screws were rusting on top of it. Next to another wall was something covered by a sheet of canvas on which mould was growing in great patches. Daniel walked across and lifted it up. Underneath there was a motorbike with an oversized gleaming red tank, high handlebars and chunky off-road tyres. It looked almost unused, apart from a few deep gouges on one side of the gearbox cover.

Daniel turned off the light and walked back through the door. He stood staring vacantly at the kitchen cupboards, lost in thought, until he heard a phone ringing back up the corridor. He walked quickly towards the sound and found Antjie engaged in an excited conversation. She acknowledged Daniel's presence with lifted eyebrows and continued talking. He resumed his staring, this time out of the bedroom window, until she had finished.

'OK,' she said eventually, disconnecting the call. 'Let's go. I need to call on your services again, I'm afraid.'

'Where to now, Madam?' he said, sarcasm dripping.

'Enough of that,' she said. 'They've got Diedricks. Let's go.'

* * *

They were almost back at the car when Daniel realised he was still carrying the badza handle. He turned and made as if to return to the farm.

'Not now,' Antjie ordered. 'There really isn't time. Keep it as a souvenir,' she joked.

He tossed it onto the back seat of the car when they reached it.

Twelve

'So, you live in Zimbabwe?' Antjie asked, once they were on their way again.

A car sped past them on the other side of the road, but it was the only one they had seen on either side for more than a quarter of an hour.

'No. Not for a long time. I live in England.'

'Oh, yes?' she said, surprised. 'How long have you been there?'

'Ten years. More, actually,' he said.

'Long time. Why did you leave?'

'How well up are you on Zimbabwean history?' he said, glancing across at her.

She put out her hand, level, then rocked it from side to side.

'I was newly qualified at the end of 1982,' he said. 'There were other black doctors, of course, but we – me and others who qualified with me – we were the first black doctors to qualify in a large group. We were so happy to get to work after so many years of studying. We thought we had something special to contribute to the new country. Boy, were we full of ourselves.'

'I started doing shift duty in the casualty department of a hospital in Bulawayo. Hard work, but I thrived on it. I really felt I was making a difference. But that lasted only a couple of months. Maybe only a few weeks, really. Then the violence started. The start of 1983.'

He looked at her again. 'You've heard of the Fifth Brigade?'

She nodded. She no longer appeared concerned about him taking his eyes off the road.

'Those were dreadful years. Simply horrific. It was an invasion. The Fifth Brigade moved in like an occupying army. They were everywhere, with their red berets and their armoured trucks. In the city, all over the countryside.'

'Searching for armed dissidents. That's what the government said. Freedom fighters who had gone back to the bush because their party hadn't done well enough in the elections. That's what they were accused of. '

'But everyone knew that wasn't the truth. The Fifth brigade were sent in because the dissidents' party was too much of a threat. And they were from a different tribe. The government wanted a one-party state, and they were prepared to butcher an entire province to get it.'

'There was open warfare everywhere around Bulawayo, all the way from Vic Falls to Beitbridge. But most of the time only one side had guns. Defenceless civilians were tortured and killed by the thousand. The regular army and the police were also involved. The secret police - the CIO – as well. But mostly it was Fifth Brigade. They were the worst.'

'There was a cordon, to stop people coming into town, and to stop people travelling out to the countryside. Roadblocks, searches, you name it. They wanted total control of the countryside, And they didn't want people to know what was really going on out there, you see. The Fifth Brigade was running wild. They had a licence to do anything they wanted. The government was waging a war on its own people and they wanted to hide the evidence.'

'People who had been injured were forbidden to seek medical help – even from mission clinics. My parents were still out on a mission in far western Matabeleland, near the Botswana border. My mother can tell some horrible stories. She saw it from close quarters.'

'Even so, a lot of people made it. There were broken people being brought in to the hospital almost every day. Smashed limbs, burns, mental trauma - you name it. It was very difficult, because the police sometimes used to sit in casualty watching the doors, taking the names of anyone brought in. Handcuffing people to their beds. Can you believe that? Patients in hospital wards handcuffed to their beds. Sometimes they just took them away before we could treat them.'

'So even though we saw many, those who made it to hospital must have been the minority. I suppose most of them never saw a doctor or a nurse. And then there were those who wouldn't have survived even if they had made it into town. Who knows how many were killed or died of their wounds. Tens of thousands, some say.'

'You know, sometimes we treated people more than once. Someone would come in with terrible injuries. We'd treat them, against the odds – sometimes in a private house because they were too scared to come to hospital – and a few weeks later they'd be back, sometimes with the same injuries. They'd been punished for getting treated.'

'Sometimes I wondered whether someone was playing a sick game with us – torturing these people and allowing them into town so we could treat them, and then abusing them all over again when they went home. At one stage I thought it had to be someone on the hospital staff involved with that. Tipping their torturers off once they had been treated, so they could be picked up and tortured again.'

'Anyway, to cut a long story short, I was constantly debating with myself. Do I stay around to help those I could help, or do I refuse to be part of an evil system? What was happening wasn't what I'd trained to do. I took it for just over a year, going into work and hating every minute of it. '

'Then something happened which forced me to make a decision. My father disappeared. He was a teacher in a mission school, and therefore a target. He was swallowed up by the carnage. We never found out what happened to him.'

'I left. I went to England and did my exams again there. Qualified as a surgeon. Been there ever since. I'm not proud of it.'

He turned to her again, embarrassed. 'Sorry. You must think I'm crazy, ranting on like that.'

'Not at all,' she said. 'Entirely understandable.' She reached out and briefly touched his hand, again. He felt the same electric charge 'Is this what is driving you to avenge your sister?'

'Vengeance? I suppose that's what it is. Part anger, part guilt, I suppose. I just want someone to be held to account for what happened to her. And just as important, I want to find out why.'

'I can't run away again. I realised that when I got home after her funeral. I can't just leave things hanging. I wouldn't be able to live with myself. I can't come to terms with her death. If that is what grieving means, then I can't grieve. I still haven't shed a single tear for her. After how long? Somehow, I don't think I will until I've got some sort of justice for her...'

He glanced across at her again. She was chewing her lower lip, staring lost in thought, out of the passenger window.

* * *

They travelled several miles back towards the city before Antjie picked out an exit to the left. They turned off and drove through an area filled with low-roofed suburban homes with neat clipped verges. They were through the suburb within minutes. The road ran through a large area of open ground, past a business park on one side, and then back again into undeveloped land.

Then, appearing without warning from behind a low wide tumble of grey grass-tufted dunes, the shabby shacks of the squatter camps of the southern Cape Flats appeared, spread out to the horizon in all directions. It was as if a mass of multi-coloured flotsam had suddenly washed in with the tide.

Shacks constructed of variously coloured sheets of steel, wood and heavy duty plastic. Roofs of thatch, warped planking or fertiliser bags, stretched out in front of them, some tied down with blue nylon rope, others secured in place by stones. The occasional shipping container converted into living quarters.

Daniel look around him, shocked by what he saw. *Goodness knows what living in one of those would be like, steel walls radiating heat in all directions.*

The further they drove, the less colourful the slum became. Here there were pre-fabricated concrete fences, cement breeze block walls and asbestos roofing material, patched here and there by scraps of metal sheeting - all a dusty monochrome beige blending in with the colour of the poor unfertile soil. What colour there was came from hand-painted signs and gangland graffiti.

Then, again without warning, the shacks came to an end and the sea appeared above the sparse vegetation stretching down to the shore before them, glimmering in the afternoon sun.

'Left here,' she said uncertainly. 'I'm desperately trying to remember the last journey I made out here. I think it's this way.'

They continued along the coast road, dunes and sea on their right, until she pointed ahead to an interval in the low roadside barrier.

'There,' she said. 'That's it. I'm sure. Down there.'

The car bumped off the tarmac, and they drove slowly down a narrow way worn into the sand. First a single pathway, then untwining into multiple tracks, then recombining into a single trail towards the beach. The underside of the car bottomed on the dirt as they bounced unevenly forward. They continued for several minutes in this fashion until the main road was no longer visible through the back window. A small beach house came into view. There were two other vehicles already parked in front of it.

'This is it,' she said. 'Park where they're parked. Over there.'

* * *

The house stood not far from the water with the bay stretching out, deceptively tranquil, behind it. On the far horizon to one side Daniel could see a faint low smudge rising into low clouds. The mountains, ever present.

The house was weatherworn to an extreme. The walls had been scoured by the coastal wind, the edges of the bricks worn away till they resembled old rounded cobblestones. All the paint had been peeled away from the metal window frames, which looked as if they might have been salvaged from one of the rusted wrecks littering the coast. The panes of glass had been sand-blasted until they were opaque.

A dark blue panel van stood parked before the house A man sat in the driver's seat. It was parked next to a white sedan. A tall, well-built man in jeans and t-shirt stood guard at the front door of the house. He straightened up as Antjie approached.

Another man appeared in the doorway. He was huge. He dwarfed her, but he didn't dominate her. She motioned to Daniel to stop.

'Excuse me a moment,' she said, to Daniel. 'Boet,' she greeted the man in the doorway. 'Right. Where is he?'

They walked away together, talking quietly but animatedly to each other. Then they turned and walked back to the house and through the door.

Daniel began to follow them. Antjie swivelled on her heels and faced him.

'A moment longer, please,' she said.

The guard moved into his path to ensure he complied.

Daniel stood, not sure what to do next.

Then there was a shout from within. The guard stood aside, waving Daniel past him through the door.

The building comprised just four rooms, two either side of a narrow central corridor which led uninterrupted from the front door to the back. On another continent it would have been called a shotgun shack. The rooms were divided by a material so thin it barely kept apart the faded wallpaper stuck to each side of it. There was another man standing at the door to the room furthest away on the right.

Daniel walked past him.

On his back in the centre of the floor lay a man covered in newly-congealed blood. What remained of his clothing was soaked in it. His flesh had been bruised to a violent mix of colours. His eyes were swollen shut. His contorted mouth was gaping. His chest was still moving, Daniel observed, as the man painfully sucked in air through what remained of his mouth and nose. Blood was spattered on the walls near him, and the room was sweltering, which couldn't have made his laboured gasping any easier.

Another, younger man - in his late-twenties, Daniel guessed - lay up against a wall. He was bound, his feet held together tightly by a set of steel cuffs, his arms bent at an unnatural angle behind him. He was deeply tanned, and had tightly-waved peroxide blond hair that sat on his head like a badly fitted wig. He looked up at Daniel, eyes bright with fear.

At first Daniel thought that he too had been badly beaten. But then he realised that the dark delicate marks on one side of the man's face were not bruises, but intricate tattoos, like something that might have been found on the face of a Polynesian islander greeting the Bounty.

'Do what you can for them,' Antjie said, coldly, to Daniel.

There was a protest from Boet standing next to her, but Antjie spoke briefly and the protest stopped.

Daniel knelt next to the older man in the centre of the room. As gently as he could, Daniel explored his head wounds, then slowly helped him to roll onto his side. The man moved with a deep agonised groan. Daniel thrust a finger into the man's mouth to clear it of obstructions, but without medicine or equipment there was little else he could do. The man needed a hospital as soon as possible.

Daniel turned his attention to the second man. He had no obvious injuries, but still lay cowering against the wall. Daniel examined the cuffs at his ankles and then turned to Antjie.

'These are far too tight. Take them off, please.'

Another protest from Boet. Again over-ruled. The second man bent and released the manacles from around the tattooed man's ankles. He looked up at Daniel after he was done. There was fury on his face.

'And the others,' Daniel ordered.

Boet looked over his shoulder at Antjie, who nodded. The second man shoved the tattooed man face down, causing an agonised yelp. He removed another pair of cuffs from around the man's wrists. Reaching into his back pocket, he produced a pocket knife and started slicing away at a binding of thick black plastic adhesive tape which had held his arms at such an extraordinary angle behind his back.

'Any injuries?' Daniel asked him.

The man shook his head, but said nothing. He began rolling his shoulders and flexing his arms to restore the circulation, and then started to pick at the tape, wincing as he peeled it from his skin.

Daniel turned to Antjie. 'Call an ambulance. Quick.'

'I was just going to,' she said. She left the room. Boet followed her out.

Daniel spoke slowly to the man on the floor. 'Someone

will be here to help you very soon,' he said. 'Can you understand what I am saying?'

The man's head moved almost imperceptibly. His breathing was now a little easier. Rolling him onto his side must have made it easier.

Daniel rose, went to the window, and managed to force it open despite the accretions of rust that had glued the steel together. A draught of cooler air began to circulate. Daniel left the room in search of water.

He could find no plumbing inside the house, so he walked out of the back door and searched for an outside tap. Antjie was standing next to Boet, mobile phone to her ear. As she saw Daniel approaching, she flicked the phone shut.

'They'll be here as soon as they can,' she said, anticipating his question.

'They both need water,' he said.

She spoke to the guard at the door, who walked over to the van and retrieved a bottle of water from the man in the driver's seat. He handed it to Daniel.

Daniel was about to re-enter the house when there were loud shouts from the interior. Daniel, Antjie, Boet and the guard all ran inside to see, at the other end of the central corridor, two men launching themselves at the inside of the front door. It splintered open under their assault, and they burst through it to the outside.

The three of them ran into the room in which the two prisoners had been lying. Only one was still there. The older man who had been badly beaten. The younger man had left, apparently through the window, which hung crookedly from one of its corroded hinges.

The two men who had chased after him soon returned,

empty handed. 'He had a head start. He was bloody quick,' one of them said apologetically, still panting from his exertions. 'Sorry, Ma'am.'

Antjie and her lieutenant left the room again, leaving Daniel alone with the prone body on the floor. Daniel heard raised voices from outside. He ignored them, and knelt and offered the bottle to the man on the floor. Lifting up his head, he poured a little into his mouth. He replaced the cap. 'I'll be back,' he said to the man.

Daniel walked back out to the rear of the house. He walked over to where Antjie stood.

The guard came a few paces closer, but she waved him back.

'Was it your men who did that?' Daniel asked angrily.

'I don't know who did what. I don't know precisely what happened. I will find out in due course.'

'He needs to be taken to a hospital. Fast,' said Daniel.

'As I said, someone will be along shortly.'

'He needs a hospital. Not the ministrations of your thugs.'

'Diedricks will get the best treatment we can get him,' she said, flatly.

'Who was the other man?'

'I don't know.'

'And when do I get to talk to Diedricks?'

'I'm sorry, Daniel,' she said. 'This is where we part company...'

'We had a deal, Antjie,' he said, furious. 'You promised me...'

'Promise? I don't think I promised anything, did I? In any event, circumstances have changed, Daniel.'

'Changed how?'

'You've seen him. He's in no state to talk. And...'

She stopped abruptly, walked a few steps away, and then turned back to face him.

'I'm going to do you a favour, Daniel. I should really detain you along with Diedricks, but I'm going to let you go. I'm sure you realise it would be futile to try anything stupid here. I'll get Diedricks to a doctor as soon as I can. But I can't help you any further. I suggest you get in your car and leave. Now. And don't try and follow us. We'll know if you try.'

She turned her back and walked back into the house. Daniel looked around him. There was nothing he could do. Especially as the driver of the van was very casually training an automatic pistol on him through the van's side window. The pistol waved him dismissively towards the track.

Daniel did as he was bid. He got into his car, reversed around, and drove away from the house towards the main road.

Thirteen

A glorious vista lay before him. But he wasn't taking it in. Daniel sat, car pulled over into a lay-by, glaring through the windscreen over the bright white cluster of the town at the top of the bay towards the dark heights of the peninsula which stretched out behind it into the southern ocean. But he might as well have been staring into fog. His mind was fully taken up with replaying, again and again, the events of the previous twenty four hours.

You stupid, stupid, fool. You can't really have thought she would let you put any questions to Diedricks. She was just playing you along to see what she could find out from you. All she had to do was touch your arm once, and you couldn't keep your mouth shut. And as for that Ellen woman. You knew she was trouble the moment you laid eyes on her, and still you blabbed as if you'd known her for years...

He felt his forearms tightening and his fists clenching the steering wheel in fury and frustration. He slammed the steering wheel with the palms of his hands – hard, again and again - until they hurt. Then, furious energy expended, he consciously began to talk himself down.

It's your own bloody fault. You allowed those women to play you like a fiddle. One after the other. You let them do it. Especially Antjie. They turned you over, and that's why you're feeling humiliated.

You've allowed things to just happen to you. Take charge. You'll get nowhere if you allow people to take advantage like that. Think this out properly. You've got a brain. Use it. Think. Think. Figure out what you need to do. Then go and do it.

His phone rang. He answered it angrily, intensely irritated at the interruption. It was his mother. No longer grief stricken, her voice had regained its usual brusque manner.

'Daniel? That family, the Sibandas, you gave my number to? They're sitting here with me. They're in a bad way. Boy's been beaten. Sister's a nervous wreck. The mother's scared out of her mind. Apart from patching them up and giving them something to eat, what do you suggest I do with them?'

Daniel pulled a hand heavily down over the length of his face.

'Jesus,' he said heavily. 'What's happened. Tell me. Tell me everything.'

* * *

'They just pitched up at their home. Very early in the morning. Usual story,' she said.

'Who pitched up? When?'

'Police. I suppose,' she said. 'Who knows. No uniforms, in two white twincabs, no number plates. You know how they work,' she said pointedly.

'When?' he asked again. He heard her repeat the question at her end.

Her voice returned. 'Tuesday, this week,' she said.

Barely a day after I was there. Who talked? Who turned them in?

'What happened?'

'Broke down the door in the early hours. Dragged the boy and his father outside and made the rest of the family

178

watch while they beat them up. The father didn't survive. Cowards.'

Oh no... don't tell me that.

'Why were they beaten? Did they say why they were beating them?'

Again, he heard her repeating his question and listened to a muffled distant response.

'First. Not reporting your presence. Second, because they couldn't answer the questions the police asked them.'

'What questions?' he asked, fearing the reply.

'What Patricia was doing there. Why she was on that farm.'

'How did they get into town?' he asked.

'A priest arranged a lift for them. Apparently.' She checked again with her audience and then her voice returned. 'That's right. The priest at the mission helped them. He told them he couldn't risk allowing them to be treated there so he arranged for them to get into town.'

'They beat the priest as well?'

She checked once more. 'No.'

'Why not?'

'Who knows? I suppose what they did to the Sibandas will have sent the message clearly to everyone else in the district. And his reputation won't have been enhanced by him being spared, on top of not being able to treat the Sibandas at the mission. Goodness knows how their minds work. Those people. Just evil.'

As she talked, Daniel was frantically trying to decide what to do next. Then it came to him.

'Listen, he said. 'I'll call Henry. I'm sure he'll be able to give them shelter. I'll get him to call you and you can make arrangements between the two of you.'

'You sure?' she asked.

'Yes. Why not?'

'Just checking, that's all. If you think it's all right, then I'm sure it will be.'

'And you,' Daniel went on. 'Get out of town. Disappear for a while. Lay low.'

'I'll be fine,' she said. 'I can take care of my...'

'I know you can,' Daniel interrupted. 'Still...'

Bad things, they say, happen in threes.

He thought on it.

Ellen. Antjie. The Sibandas. Do the first two count as two, or is there one more to go?

He picked up his phone again and dialled Henry Mliswa's number.

* * *

It's Diedricks, he concluded, after he had sat in the car for another twenty minutes, motionless in body but agitated in mind.

Good old Mr One-for-Me and One-for-You. It has to be. It all leads back to him.

He'd thought he'd been close to talking to him. Antjie had put paid to that. But if it was Diedricks he had to speak to, then how on earth was he going to do that, now that Diedricks was enjoying the tender loving care of Antjie and her thugs?

There must be some other way. Any point going back out to the farm? Perhaps the maid might still yield something. No. The poor woman was visibly traumatised this morning. I doubt she can tell me anything more. I'll have to look elsewhere.

He started to drive back towards the centre of the city. The mountain swung back into view. It sparked something in his mind.

What was it that Antjie said? She mentioned the beach house, and Diedricks' farm. Been to both of those, and it's unlikely I'll find out anything more from either of them. But she also mentioned somewhere else. A deli. But where? Where in the city had it been? Up against the mountain? Did she mention something about the mountain?

Racking his brain, he tried to reconstruct the conversation.

He stopped at a small suburban shopping centre set just off the road and went into one of the shops. He bought himself a city map and a bottle of water. Returning to the car, he took a greedy gulp from the bottle and spread the map across his knees.

He found the mountain and then worked his way round it, identifying every suburb that lay anywhere near it. He wrote each name on a blank sheet of paper which he extracted from the blue back-pack, one name below the other in a lengthening list.

Mowbray, Rosebank, Rondebosch. Newlands, Bishopscourt, Constantia Heights. Glen Alpine. Then over the *nek* to Kenrock, Ruyterplaats, Llandudno. North again to Bakoven and Camps Bay, then Clifton, Bantry Bay and Sea Point. Nothing there that he recognised, no bell jangling in his memory.

Around the top of Signal Hill past Three Anchor Bay and Green Point. Then the suburban names became less British Imperial and more Dutch Mercantile as he paged through the older sections of the city. Schotsche Kloof, Tamboerskloof, Gardens, Oranjezicht and Vredehoek.

Pause.

Oranjezicht. There was the bell dimly tolling.

Did she say Oranjezicht? She did.

He ran the name quietly around his mouth, varying the way he said it until he stumbled upon a pronunciation which sounded like his recollection of it. The more he whispered it, the more convinced he became. He dredged up a dim memory of naively questioning himself at the time as whether there were citrus trees in Oranjezicht. No matter. That was it. He was sure. He looked on the map at the streets in Oranjezicht.

Not many. There can't be many delicatessens there either. Surely?

* * *

With the map still on his knees, Daniel drove around the mountain. He laboriously pushed his way through the rush hour traffic and then worked upwards towards the lower slopes. Up through the gently rising streets of Gardens, past the tree-sheltered cottages on each side of the road. Plenty of shops here. A few delicatessens.

Perhaps she wasn't being precise? Not Oranjezicht exactly, but in the general area...

He dismissed that thought for the time being and kept going.

The further he drove, the steeper the ascent became. Fewer cottages, more Victorian villas and contemporary houses crammed cheek by jowl. The more substantial the dwellings, the less commercial the area became. The trees lining the avenues became more exotic, more tropical. Fewer oaks, more palm trees.

The road split, the lanes separated by a long thin grassy island, well watered and green in the bright sunshine. Daniel hadn't seen a shop for some distance. He saw an incongruous patch of blue to one side. He consulted his map.

The reservoir. It must be.

He drove past it and then began threading his way back and forth through the cross streets, climbing higher each time he turned. And then there it was.

A short parade of shops facing up towards the mountain top ran from the street corner half way down one block. There was a convenience store with an entrance on the corner underneath a ornate curlicued Dutch gable, windows and door fully exposed to the relentless sun. Adjacent, a rectangular cantilevered construction of brick and concrete which overhung the pavement and extended further down the street.

Large printed canvas blinds dropped down vertically from the outer edge of this veranda roof, one for each establishment sitting protected in the shade behind it.

Between two other shops stood a delicatessen. A florist on one side. A boutique, fashionably empty, on the other. The delicatessen had large glass windows either side of a glass-paned door. Daniel could see the bottom two-thirds of them.

This has to be it.

There weren't many roads left for Daniel to drive up, and he doubted there were any more shops further up the mountain. In fact, looking at it from this side, it appeared that there weren't many more buildings of any kind much further up in this suburb. One more street, as far as he could see, and then the ground rose steeply and undeveloped towards the grey and rocky, almost vertical, slopes of the mountain behind.

He pulled into a parking bay across the road and sat back.

Now what do I do?

The decision was made for him.

Fourteen

Daniel saw the door of the delicatessen open. In the shade thrown by the blind, what caught his attention first was the slight shudder of the reflection in the door's lower pane of glass as the door swung closed after a figure which stepped out onto the darkened pavement. The figure was only visible from the waist down. The torso-less figure walked, semi-hidden, a few paces and then stooped as it stepped out from under the blind into the road.

As the figure's head emerged into the sunlight, Daniel recognised it immediately. The facial tattoos which he had mistaken for bruises. The matted yellow hair. It was the younger man from the beach house. No doubt about it.

Daniel opened the door of the car, stepped out, and then, with a sudden recollection, ducked back inside to grab the badza handle from where he had thrown it onto the back seat. The movement attracted a glance from the tattooed man across the street. His eyes widened in alarm as he recognised Daniel.

Then he was gone.

Daniel saw the reflection in the glass door vibrating again as the door closed. He ran across the road, jerked the door open and burst into the shop.

As he exploded into the interior he almost demolished a pyramid of expensive-looking wine bottles facing the door. Swerving at the last moment, he careered into a narrow gap between a long shelf filled with fruit which gleamed as if it had been polished, and a glass-fronted counter with cured hams and sausages and partially-sliced wheels of cheese enticingly displayed.

He hurtled towards the counter. The cashier behind it, a young dark-haired man, saw Daniel's badza handle and stiffened. One of his hands disappeared out of view. Daniel leapt towards him and smashed the handle onto the counter. The counter-top cracked, and the sound ricocheted shockingly loudly around the shop.

'No you don't,' Daniel shouted. 'Away from there. Into that corner. On your knees.'

The cashier complied rapidly, as if this kind of behaviour wasn't unusual among his customers. Daniel moved behind the counter and sank down onto his haunches, all the time keeping his eyes on the man cowering in the corner. He stole a quick glance at the shelf beneath the countertop. A small alarm button stuck down from the underside.

'D'you press this?' he barked.

The cashier shook his head vigorously. Daniel pulled the button's casing away from its mounting, bending the small screws securing the plastic to the underside of the countertop as he levered them out of the wood. He prised up one of the wires entering the back of the switch and ripped it away.

He glanced further into the cavity. There was something lying towards the back in the shadows of the shelf. He shoved his hand in and extracted a large heavy revolver, worn almost white at its chamfered edges. It was greasy with gun oil. He looked up at the cashier.

It was this, not the switch, you were after...

He stuck the gun into the back of his waistband. He felt a little stupid as the barrel sagged between his buttocks.

'The man who just came in here. Tattoos on his face.

Where is he?' Daniel barked again, and the cashier backed further into the corner, struck dumb.

Daniel looked around. There was a door further back behind the counter.

'Come here,' he ordered. The cashier remained rooted to the corner. Daniel waved the handle at him. He rose slowly to his feet and approached Daniel in trepidation.

'What's behind that door?' asked Daniel.

'S- storeroom,' he stammered.

'There a door to the outside through there?'

The man nodded.

'Open?'

The man shook his head.

Daniel motioned him to come even closer. He whispered into his ear. 'I want you to open this door and then walk through in front of me. No games. No funny business. Understand?'

The cashier nodded again, fear all over his face. Daniel put his finger to his lips. The cashier put his hand on the door handle, hesitating. Eventually he pushed it down and the door swung open in front of him.

Daniel prodded him in the small of his back with the end of the badza handle. He stepped through the doorway, with Daniel two steps behind him.

Daniel watched with curious detachment as the cashier was floored by a man who launched himself out from behind the wall. The cashier screamed. The man grunted and swore loudly as he wrestled the cashier over onto his back. There was a knife, stubby and dull, in the man's right hand. As he rolled him over, the man saw the cashier's face. He suddenly bent his head round to look behind him.

Daniel reacted with an instinct that he didn't know he possessed.

The badza handle curved down and up. The man raised his arm in self-protection and the handle struck him flat on his wrist. He screamed in agony, and the knife spun away to the corner of the storeroom.

Daniel took a step back and turned on the light switch near the door. The tattoos on one side of the man's face became visible as the darkness in the storeroom was dispelled. Daniel pushed him with his cudgel. 'Over against that wall! Both of you. Apart! Not together.'

The two men, both now sitting on the floor and staring fixedly at Daniel, shuffled away like crabs to the back wall. The tattooed man nursed his wrist in his hand, massaging it tentatively.

Daniel looked around the room. Against one wall, set apart from cases of wine and boxes of produce and tinned goods stacked up on top of each other, were two cylindrical blue plastic containers, about two feet high. Of the type Daniel had last seen being loaded onto the plane on the Matabeleland farm.

'Getting warmer,' he muttered to himself.

''Skuus?' asked the cashier.

Daniel ignored him and walked over to the other man.

'Sollie Diedricks,' he said. 'Where've they taken him?'

* * *

'Fucking bastard. Like, you've totally fucked up my hand, man.' The tattooed man spat between Daniel's feet, and went back to manipulating his wrist. These were the first words Daniel had heard him say, and despite the expletives he was softer spoken than Daniel had expected.

'And I suppose you weren't planning to harm anybody with that knife?' Daniel said, moving a step back as the man spat again. 'Anyway, it's just bruised. It'll be better in a couple of days.'

'How the fuck would you know, man?'

'I'm a doctor. If it was broken you wouldn't be able to move it. Your wrist will heal by itself, I promise you. Just take it easy for a few days. More importantly – where's Sollie Diedricks?'

'Ask your chinas.'

'Chinas?' Daniel asked, jabbing at one of the man's shoes with the badza handle.

'Your fucking mates at the beach house, man. The cops. Ask your mates the boere.'

'They're police. I'm not.'

'Bullshit, man.'

The man briefly stopped rubbing his wrist and wiped a greasy lock of yellow hair away from his eyes. He stared at Daniel and resumed his massage.

'Fucking bullshit,' he said again.

'If I was a policeman,' asked Daniel, 'I wouldn't be asking you where Diedricks is. But I'm asking you now. Where've they taken him?'

The man kept staring at him. Daniel could almost see his brain working.

'I don't know what you want, man,' he said eventually. 'But I don't know where they've taken him. I swear.'

'OK,' said Daniel. 'Up you get.'

'Not you,' he said, turning to the cashier who had also

started to move. 'You stay where you are. Ten minutes. If I see you come out before that...'

The man slumped back down against the wall.

The tattooed man stumbled unsteadily to his feet. Daniel stepped aside, motioned him to the door and then followed him out. They walked to the front of the shop, Daniel behind.

'We're going to walk over the road to the car you saw me get out of. In case you're thinking of running away again…' Daniel extracted the revolver from the waist band in the small of his back and pointed it at him. 'You drive.'

'How can I drive with my hand all fucked up like this, man?'

'It's automatic. You won't have to change gears. You'll just have to use your left hand for everything. Get into the driver's seat. I'm going to get in right behind you. No bullshit. I warn you.'

He emphasised the point with the barrel of the revolver, and then tucked it back under his shirt, this time in front.

* * *

Where to go during the Friday afternoon rush hour?

Daniel guided their progress from the rear seat and took them down against the flow of traffic into the city centre. Following the municipal signs, he directed the tattooed man to an ugly brown parking garage near the foreshore. They thudded onto the ramp and began the climb from floor to floor, tyres squealing mutedly against the polished concrete. Two storeys below the top Daniel pointed over the tattooed man's shoulder to one end. There were no cars left parked on that floor.

A bit of seclusion where we can have a quiet chat.

They parked. Daniel made the tattooed man pass him the car keys. He pressed the button on the fob and the locks on all the doors slid down. He pulled out the revolver and held it up so that the man in the driver's seat could see it in the rear view mirror. Then he pushed himself back in the middle of the rear seat.

'OK,' said Daniel, looking at the reflection of the other man's eyes in the rear view mirror. They were green, and the whites surrounding the green were bloodshot. 'What were you doing at the beach house?'

'I lost some diving stuff, man. A mask – a kif one. A ankle strap. I thought I might have left it there. I went to look but when I got there, there was all hell going on...'

'What hell was going on?'

'Massive fight, man. Cops shooting. South Side Kids shooting. Lead flying everywhere.'

'South Side Kids?'

'Isaacs gang, man. Skebengas.'

'How do you know it was them?'

'South Side Kids, man. Tattoos on their necks. Scorpions,' he said, as if this should be common knowledge even to strangers in town. He indicated a place on his own neck with a grubby finger.

'Cops and robbers, man. Real cops and robbers. Like on the box.' The man's face broke into a mask of nervous laughter. 'A vrou also. Screaming her fucking head off, swearing at the cops.'

'D'you see her? What did she look like?'

'Dunno. Didn't see her. Just heard her going off on one.'

Ellen. Had to be.

'Which gang d'you belong to?' he asked.

The man looked at him, bemused.

'Those tattoos on your face...'

'No, man. Not a gang. They's s'posed to give you good karma in the waves. I had a stukkie who liked that kind of thing. Women, hay...'

The tattooed man laughed again.

He looked round at Daniel. With exaggerated delicacy he slowly extended his fingers and extracted a green- and gold-coloured plastic tobacco pouch from his shirt pocket.

'Skyf?' he asked.

'What?'

'Smoke, man? Cigarette?'

'No. Thanks.'

The man opened the packet, pulled out Rizzla papers and began rolling himself a cigarette with an efficiency born of long practice. He seemed no longer to be overly troubled by the blow to his wrist.

He lit up, filling the car with thick smoke. It had an acrid quality to it, and Daniel wasn't sure it was pure tobacco. He held the cigarette pinched between thumb and forefinger, burning end facing down like a truant schoolboy smoking at a street corner. He blew a nervous smoke ring and watched as it collided with the windscreen.

'How did you end up in that house with the cops?'

'They caught me, man. The South Side Kids fucked off. I was behind a dune. The cops saw me and caught me. They chucked me in that room with Sollie.'

'How do you know Diedricks?'

'Diedricks?' There was a pause. 'I done some work for

him before.'

'What kind of work?'

'Diving.'

'You dived for him? That's all?'

'Just the diving, man. I swear. I surf and I dive. But no-one pays for surfing, man. I dive to surf, man.' The man looked face on into the mirror and forced another smile.

'Perlemoen?' asked Daniel, ignoring the joke.

'No, man. Not perlemoen. I swear.'

'Perlemoen,' said Daniel, this time as a statement of fact. 'And Diedricks? Who beat him up like that?'

'When they chucked me in that room, Sollie was already fucked, man. He was covered in blood and shit when I got there. You saw. They beat the shit out of him, man. I thought I was next for the high jump.'

'Who beat him? The Isaacs gang? The cops?'

'I didn't see who did it, man. But it had to be the cops.'

'Why did they do it?'

'Dunno, man.'

Daniel looked straight at the mirror again and caught the other man's gaze. He prodded his shoulder with the barrel of the pistol.

'I swear, man. I don't know why. Maybe he wouldn't go peaceful, like.'

'They were asking him questions, weren't they? They were still beating him when you got there, and they were still asking him questions.'

'OK. So they was asking questions. But I don't know what for. Then you came with that other meisie. That cop.'

'Then what?'

'You took the cuffs off me. You opened the window, and

then you all left. I took the gap.' He said it as if it was an obvious progression that happened every day.

'What did Diedricks tell you?'

'Nothing, man. I swear. Sollie could hardly breathe. How could he talk? You saw, man.' He was staring at Daniel, eyes pleading.

Daniel persisted. 'Nothing? You know Diedricks. You say you worked for him. And now you say you said nothing to each other? Not one word? You just got up and ran?'

The tattooed man's brain was working again.

Daniel pressed him again, angrily. 'What did he say?'

The man was quiet. And then: 'After you came with that meisie. You walked out and the other cops were somewhere else. He said she was a cop and they were going to take him away. That's all he said, man. I swear.'

'He knew who she was?'

'Right, man. He knew who she was.'

'What else? What else did he say?'

There was no response. Daniel poked the pistol barrel into the hollow behind the man's jaw. It worked.

'He told me to run, man. He told me the address and he told me to run.'

The tattooed man's voice was now sounding less constricted. Daniel spoke more gently to encourage him.

'What address? The address of the shop?'

'Ja. He told me to go to the shop. But the address was for another place. He said the cops were going to take him there. He told me to go to that shop and tell them the address where they gonna take him. I swear, man. I swear that's all he said.'

'And you told them? At the shop? You told that cashier in

the shop?'

'Ja, man. I did. I told him.'

Daniel took a swallow from the bottle of water, and then offered it across. The tattooed man took it gingerly over his shoulder with his right hand, and then transferred it to his left before drinking from it.

'How's your wrist? Better?' Daniel enquired.

The man nodded. He wiped his lips dry with the back of his hand, wiped the mouth of the bottle with the palm of his hand, and returned the bottle to Daniel. He inhaled deeply from his cigarette.

'Tell me about Diedricks,' said Daniel.

'He's a china,' he said, shrugging his shoulders. 'I work for him sometimes. Sometimes we have a dop together.'

Daniel maintained his gaze.

'He's my mate,' the tattooed man insisted. 'I been diving for him a long time.'

'Who owns that shop?'

'People Sollie knows. People he does business with.'

'Isaacs' people?'

The man nodded.

'Why did he want you to talk to that guy in the shop?'

'So they can get him away from the cops.'

'They can do that?'

'Sure, man. Why not. The boere aren't so strong like they used to be. They don't want the cops talking to him, man. And...'

'And what?'

'What those cops did. That's, like, war, man. Yussus – those cops in the South Side Kids' yard. That's war, man.'

'What do you mean?'

195

'That place on the beach. That whole place round there is Sollie's people's. It's in their yard, man. That's their territory. The cops can't just come there like that, man. That's war. They have to get Sollie back. Like, it's their honour. They have to get him back. Soon as they can.'

'Where's this place he thinks the cops will take him?'

'Just near that shop, man. Few streets away round the mountain.'

'Right. Let's go and have a look.'

'No man, you don't wanna go there. It'll be war up there. I promise you.'

But Daniel wasn't in a mood to be dissuaded.

Fifteen

They drove back up the mountainside as the sun disappeared into the ocean behind them, and parked on the side of a street facing up towards the mountain.

Standing formidably before them across the intersection in the watery light from the street lamps was a long whitewashed stuccoed wall that Daniel guessed must have been more than fifteen feet high, and not an inch less than three feet thick.

Set into two enormous gateposts were a pair of high solid wooden gates, reinforced with broad flat steel braces six inches wide. A security camera kept watch over the entrance from a tall mast planted behind the wall.

If there's going to be a war, they'll have to bring a tank.

The property was part of the way up a secluded residential road at the top of a mountainside suburb. There were similar walls along the street, although none with quite the bulk of the one in front of them. Daniel had seen a pair of cement griffins with wings outstretched atop one set of gates as they drove up from the city. The gateposts in front of them were furnished more conservatively by large carriage lamps, but the effect was just as intimidating. The lamps flooded the entrance with pools of bright white light.

They sat in silence, Daniel still behind the tattooed man, and kept watch on the gate. A car approached sedately, but it slid quietly past without stopping, leaving the street empty again. The tattooed man dragged carefully on another hand-rolled cigarette until he was holding the last few millimetres pinched between two fingernails. He stubbed it out in the overflowing ashtray Then he rolled himself a replacement and smoked that one too down to the last few wisps of tobacco.

Daniel could hear nothing through the window he had partially opened to relieve the stuffiness inside the car. No traffic noise, no nothing.

He speculated about the local property prices. *This kind of silence doesn't come cheap.*

Just past eight o'clock, after they had been sitting there for well over an hour, a bulky panel van drove up and turned into the entrance. In the strong light thrown by the gatepost lamps he couldn't have been sure of its precise colour. But it was dark, and it could well have been the same blue van as he had last seen at the beach house. The van stopped. There were two men sat in the front of it. Daniel saw the man in the passenger seat put a mobile phone to his ear.

Speaking to someone inside to get the gates opened.

Indeed. The gates began to swing slowly inwards and the van inched forward with them.

As it did, Daniel and the tattooed man saw four balaclava-ed figures slip in through the gates after the van. Just where they had come from Daniel couldn't fathom.

'Told you, bru,' said the voice from the front seat, as if resigned to his fate. 'War.'

He leaned back over his seat and sent the glowing remains of his cigarette butt arcing accurately through the gap at the top of Daniel's window with a flick of his fingers. Daniel swore at him under his breath, before winding the window right down so he could hear more easily.

There's more than one way to fight a war.

Daniel watched two of the dark figures, one at each gatepost, pushing wooden wedges into the hinges of the gates. As they did, the two other men were pulling the two occupants of the van onto the driveway. Guns were rammed against their heads, and joined now by the two wedge-men, they were frog-marched quickly out of Daniel's sight towards the house.

Daniel heard a very heated exchange being briefly conducted, all out of sight behind the wall. Staccato shouts in quick exchange. Then silence.

No sound. No movement.

Time appeared to stop.

The men re-appeared. The first two were running in step with one of the occupants of the van held firmly between them, his legs flailing. The other two were lifting a slumped body – one by the shoulders and one by the feet.

Diedricks.

They ran in a small phalanx down the street, to be met by a large pick-up truck with a fibre-glass canopy covering the back coming straight towards them, its engine revving. The door at the rear of the canopy was flung up from within, the tailgate dropped and the four men bundled their booty and themselves inside it. The pick-up drove off at speed.

The driveway began to fill with men from inside the house.

'Down,' Daniel ordered, and they both ducked as low as they could.

Daniel raised his head slowly after an interval, to see the driveway emptying and two men freeing the gates and allowing them to close again.

'Told you,' said the tattooed man. 'Lucky we didn't get

caught in the middle.'

He lit another cigarette. His voice was calmer now, much more relaxed. The drags on his cigarette were shallower.

'Where're they going to take him?' Daniel asked.

'Sollie's people's place down on the Flats.' he said.

* * *

'OK,' said Daniel. 'What else did Diedricks say to you at the beach house?'

The tattooed man stared back at him in the mirror. 'Nothing man. I swear. Just what I told you already.'

'You seem very sure you know where they've taken him. Did Diedricks tell you where they'd go?'

Silence.

Then: 'OK, man. Sollie told me. He told me the cops would probably bring him here. So he asked me to go to the shop. He knew his people could get him out of here. If they did, he knew they would take him back to the Flats. He said he was hundred per cent about that.'

'When will they let him go? Can we pick him up tonight?'

'I don't think they'll let him go,' said the tattooed man. 'They don't want the cops to get hold of him again. They'll just keep him there. He can't go home, man. It's not safe. And the mess he's in... He needs a doctor.'

There was another brief interlude.

'Hey, bru! You's a doctor. You can treat him,' he said, as if the notion had just occurred to him.

'Somehow, I don't think they'd be happy to have me there. You think I'm a cop. From the look of those people we just watched at that house, they'd shoot first and ask whether I was a cop later.'

'Na,' said the tattooed man. 'You ain't a cop.'

'Oh, yes? What's changed your mind?'

'If you were a cop you'd have helped your mates at that gate just now. You got a gun. You could have slotted one of those guys in the masks. Easy. Or you could've handed me to the cops, bru.'

Daniel felt in his lap, and was reassured to find the pistol was still there. *As for 'slotting' one of those guys...* Daniel wasn't sure he was competent enough to hit the side of the mountain rising into the dark in front of them.

He looked up to find the man smiling at him in the rear view mirror. 'So why do you want to speak to Sollie?'

'Long story. I want to know about this business of his. The perlemoen and drugs. I think he can answer some questions I have.'

'Drugs?'

'Don't give me that bullshit. You know damn well what Diedricks does for a living.'

The man gave a slight shrug.

'So maybe you'll help me get him out? He needs help man. He needs a doctor.' He took a deep drag on his latest cigarette, and looked hopefully at Daniel in the mirror.

'Is that what Sollie asked you to do? Get him out of this place on the Flats?'

The man nodded.

'Why did he want you to get these people to help him in the first place if he doesn't think they're going to let him go?'

'I couldn't get him out of that cops' house, man. Not in a million years. They could. But maybe I can get him out of the place on the Flats.'

'How are you going to do that? Those men we just saw look like they're not to be messed with.'

'They won't be there. They're protection for someone big. Maybe that woman who was swearing like a hoer. She doesn't stay where they're taking Sollie, so they won't be there either. Anyway, we'll have a look when we get there,' he replied. 'Stay cool, bru. We'll make a plan.'

Sixteen

Thinking back on it later, Daniel couldn't remember exactly who of the two of them had suggested they drive out onto the Cape Flats there and then.

Clockwise round the mountain they went, past brightly-lit restaurants and clubs, roadside bars spilling out onto the pavements in the balmy evening warmth. The circular towers on the university campus flashed past, twinkling like huge twin lighthouses against the dark mountain behind.

Daniel heard the crescendo of a large jet descending overhead. Then he saw the signs for the airport. But they continued driving, returning to the semi-darkness. The tattooed man changed lanes and they turned off the highway.

Daniel was beginning to worry. *Where is he taking me? Have I been done over again?*

The road was now very uneven beneath them. They kept weaving, this way and that, around corners, dodging obstacles. Potholes, mostly, but they weren't missing all of them. The shacks either side of the road were unlit, silhouetted in black against the dark blue sky. The air carried a strong taste of wood smoke.

'Pity 'bout the car, bru,' said the tattooed man.

'What's wrong with it?' asked Daniel, a little offended.

'Bit larney for here. Not beaten up enough. Sticks out. But it's dark. Maybe people won't notice.' He laughed. 'Maybe they won't notice me also. Whities is a rare species round here. You got no problem, bru. Just don't open your mouth...' He laughed again.

For the first time, Daniel found one of the tattooed man's remarks vaguely funny. He smiled.

Eventually they stopped. The tattooed man pointed out through the windscreen down the unlit street.

'There,' he said. 'That big wall on the left. That's it.'

Daniel saw two high prefabricated concrete walls set back from the road. Where they met they formed an acute-angled corner which pointed up the road towards them.

'How are you going to get inside that place?'

'Let's go and have a kyk.'

The tattooed man drove down the street, the car lurching over the rocks and ruts. They drove past one side of the wall, which stretched for more than fifty yards on their left. A gateway was set into it about half way along. The gates were made of steel sheets, crudely constructed, severely scratched and much dented. They appeared to be secured with a heavy chain wound through apertures cut raggedly through the steel and padlocked on the inside. Several strands of barbed wire were stretched haphazardly across the top of them.

The stretch of the wall came to an end and turned away from the street at right angles. The remaining street frontage from there to the next street corner was taken up with the low shacks and rude dwellings of the kind they had seen when they first arrived. They turned left at the corner, drove slowly up the intersecting street, and turned left again at the next intersection. More shacks, more hovels lining both sides of the road. Then left again, driving steadily as they completed the circumnavigation.

Halfway down this last stretch of road the concrete wall reappeared from amid the tumble of wood and iron sheeting. They followed it down to the sharp corner. If this irregular intersection of streets covered an area about the size of a city block, Daniel calculated, then the area bounded by the concrete wall must take up about a quarter of it. Compared with the tiny patches of land taken up by each individual shack around it, this was a substantial compound.

'That's it?' said Daniel from the back seat. 'That wall goes all the way around?'

The tattooed man nodded.

'No guards outside? Cameras? Anything?'

'Don't think so. Didn't see any. Not on the outside.'

'So the only way to get in is from these two streets. Where the wall is?'

'No. I think there's a way round the back.'

'But what about all those shacks?'

'Sollie says no-one lives next to the wall. They've all been moved out, man. That's where there's gotta be a way in.'

* * *

It's not pleasant making Molotov cocktails inside a car - even just a couple of handfuls of them. The petrol spills when you're filling the bottles. The motor oil, which you add to make the contents slightly more sticky - a bit more like napalm - gets everywhere. The fumes fill the car no matter how many windows you open. And when you're working with a chain-smoker tempers tend to flare.

They could've used Daniel's hotel room, were it not for his veto. Every outdoor venue they considered seemed suddenly to fill with day-trippers bent on observing their every movement. So the three of them had stopped on the side of the road and, in the dark, had manufactured the means by which, the tattooed man kept assuring Daniel, they would spirit Sollie Diedricks away from his unwanted hosts.

It was Saturday night. The tattooed man had spent the previous night on the floor of Daniel's hotel bathroom, while Daniel dozed outside across the closed bathroom door. He wasn't about to let him get away, and he was still there in the morning. But he had evidently slept much better than Daniel had.

The morning had been taken up with a search for more ammunition for the revolver, which Daniel was getting used to carrying. The tattooed man knew a man who knew a man, he said, and, sure enough, he secured a box of cartridges of the correct calibre, and a heavy plastic bag containing more.

'Fuck me,' he had said. 'That's a moerse cannon you'se got there. You'll have to hold it vas, really vas. Or your wrist'll be fucked like mine,' he said. He waved his right arm mockingly at Daniel. 'Where d'you find it?'

Daniel told him, and the tattooed face creased into uncontrollable laughter.

'They'se gonna get a taste of their own medicine. Woo hoo. Bullets like that'll blow their fucking doors down!'

Calibre .455, Daniel read on the chafed waxed-cardboard box in which some of the cartridges were packed. Webley Patents, he managed to decipher from worn letters stamped into the steel body of the pistol itself.

Daniel put himself through several trial runs, unloading and reloading the revolver at speed, but his attempts were ham-fisted, and he had severe doubts as to whether he could do it for real.

And then the tattooed man dropped a bombshell. They

would need another pair of hands, he said. Daniel had been adamant. No way could there be a third person. He could feel what little control he had left over this suicidal escapade slipping away just at the mention of it. But he was eventually forced to agree with the logic. They couldn't do the job without someone else. So the two of them had been joined by a tall coloured man, another of the tattooed man's connections. He had mischievous eyes and a derisive smile, and he didn't even attempt to conceal his contempt for Daniel's meagre paramilitary skills.

The plan was simple, and infallible, the tattooed man had insisted. After the arrest and rescue of Diedricks, and what they saw as the invasion of their territory, the occupants of the compound would be on a hair-trigger, fully expecting a confrontation and eager to exact revenge.

'They're expecting a fight. So that's what we'll give them,' he had explained. 'And while they're busy in front, I can get Sollie out round the back. Sure as shit,' he promised.

You mean while your mate and I are busy in front. But he kept the thought to himself.

And so the three of them sat in Daniel's rented car late at night on the side of a quiet road in a deserted industrial estate. Daniel having second and subsequent thoughts in the driver's seat, the tattooed man next to him, and the third man in the back seat with a dozen petrol bombs lying on the seat beside him. Waiting for the auspicious moment which the tattooed man said he would announce.

Which Daniel hoped would be sooner rather than later, because the tattooed man was just hanging out for a smoke. As he kept telling them. Repeatedly.

* * *

It was past midnight when they drove back into the slum. The tattooed man sat next to Daniel, giving him directions as they returned to the scene of their reconnaissance of the previous day. They drove past the corner where the two walls met in a point, past the steel gates, and turned into the intersecting street behind the compound.

After a short distance the tattooed man told Daniel to stop. He got out of the car and pulled a thick dark woollen cap down low over his forehead, carefully tucking in his hair. The effect was startling. In the shadows and at a distance of a few yards, the whiteness of his skin was not apparent. The tattoos looked like streaks of camouflage cream.

He walked round to Daniel's side, stooped down and huskily repeated what he had said several times that evening. 'First bottle, five minutes time. I need five or six minutes after the first bottle. Ten minutes, that's all. Wait for me. Just here. In ten minutes.' And then he was gone. The last view they had was of him squeezing himself between two ramshackle dwellings and disappearing into the labyrinth.

The tall man started to arrange the petrol-filled bottles on the vacant seat next to Daniel, leaning over the seat and pushing them close together into a rectangle of shiny missiles. And then they drove off, the tall man counting off the minutes as they moved.

Slowly they followed the roads around.

There were a few people still abroad. Individuals walking alone mostly, a trio of maudlin drunks singing out of tune.

They'll disappear as soon as the fun starts, the tattooed man had promised. No-one will want to be involved, and the nearest cops are miles away.

Nevertheless, Daniel had insisted on covering the number plates with sheets of paper, taped on tightly but easy to remove when necessary.

Daniel felt a tightness at the top of his stomach. He could almost hear his heart racing. And then the tall man was counting them in.

'Now,' he said. 'Lights out. Keep going. Round the corner. Stop just near the gate, keep the engine ticking over. I'll light the first two. You light the rest and hand them out to me.'

He sounded doubtful.

Daniel coasted to a halt. The tyres crunched loudly on the verge as the engine noise subsided. Too loudly, Daniel was sure, but then he didn't yet fully appreciate how loud things were about to get.

Handbrake on. Gear lever to neutral. He picked up the tattooed man's lighter, grabbed two bottles from the seat, lit them and shoved them out of the window.

The tall man was already out, standing next to the car, and a few seconds later Daniel saw two flaming wicks drawing spirals against the darkness as they curved high over the concrete wall.

Daniel lit the wick on a third bottle and handed it out through the window. And another, and another, and another. Within a matter of seconds, it seemed, almost all the bottles had been tossed over the gate and the wall to the compound within. Daniel heard the repeated smashing of glass and the dull whoomph as the fuel mixture ignited.

By now there were muddled shouts coming from within the compound, noise and confusion as the occupants tried to put out the fires. Shots cracked out, and Daniel ducked his head involuntarily.

There was a clatter at the gate. Daniel jerked his head back up to look.

The chain, doubled over through the apertures in the steel, was moving violently. Someone must be trying to unlock it from within. He was about to shout out a warning to the tall man, but he was already well ahead of Daniel.

'Gun! Use the fucking gun!' he demanded.

The words were shouted very loudly through the window. Daniel grabbed the revolver from his lap, stepped out of the door and levelled it across the roof of the car.

Half a dozen shots straight at the gate as close as he could get to the middle. Daniel counted the reports, and the immediate dull clangs as the bullets punched through the steel. ... Five. Six. Somewhere in the midst of them there was a scream.

Is this what makes young men go willingly to war? This kind of power...?

Daniel leant down into the car and ripped the top off the box of cartridges.

As he did so, the tall man demanded the remaining bottles, unlit. There were three on the seat next to Daniel. He handed them out behind him, two together, followed shortly afterwards by the last one. Daniel heard several bumps overhead as the tall man stood the bottles on the roof of the car.

Daniel returned his attention to reloading the pistol, going methodically through the drill.

Lock release, Break the pistol open. Make sure the spent cartridges go into the passenger foot well, not onto the floor in front of the driver's seat. Six new cartridges from the box. Into the cylinder. One. Two, Three, Four, Five. Six. Barrel back up until it locks.

Back out, across the roof of the car. Six shots through the gate. Holes punched easily through the steel like a pencil through paper.

Back into the car.

Repeat the exercise.

Another six. Reload.

And another six. Reload.

Then the tall man starting throwing the remaining petrol bombs. Two went over, one after the other, spiralling over the wall and exploding inside.

The tall man threw the last one straight at the steel gates. It smashed against them, and a sheet of fire spread, dripping down over the steel, reducing further the chances of anyone trying to leave the compound by that exit.

That'll make them think twice before they try to open the gate again.

As he watched, Daniel appreciated just what the tattooed man had meant when he said they couldn't do without him. This guy, so tall and with windmill arms that seemed to go on forever, could throw a petrol bomb very accurately a very long way.

Then the tall man was back inside the car, yelling for Daniel to go.

Gear lever into drive, handbrake off, foot down.

Daniel drove light-less down the street to where the concrete wall turned and disappeared into the maze of shacks. They slid to a halt again on the tall man's command. He was immediately out of the car, having grabbed the revolver from Daniel's crotch, and was firing into the compound over the corner in the wall. He reloaded the pistol himself. Another dozen detonations reverberated in Daniel's ear.

Then they were off once more to the darkened intersection, left turn and a short way up the street, where Daniel stopped.

'One minute,' said the tall man from the back seat. He leaned across and opened the other door a fraction, and stayed there, ready to push it fully open with the ball of his foot.

Five minutes? We were there five minutes? It seemed like thirty minutes, and at the same time thirty seconds.

His pulse was racing, and the knot in his stomach tightened. Daniel looked over towards the shacks. He couldn't see a thing.

'OK. He's now late,' said the tall man.

Time late, not dead late, let's hope.

Still they waited. And then suddenly there was a huge explosion and the sky lit up. An orange fireball shot vertically into the sky, drenching everything in a brief fiery glow.

'Fuckin' A,' said the tall man gleefully, thumping Daniel's shoulder in delight. 'Petrol tank. We must've smacked a car.'

And then the tattooed man appeared from the darkness of the shacks. He was carrying a limp body in a fireman's lift, bent under the weight as he staggered towards the car.

The tall man kicked open the back door. He leant

forward, took hold of Diedricks' shoulders, and pulled his slumped body onto the back seat as the tattooed man fed him in by his legs. Two doors were slammed shut.

This time it was the tattooed man shouting directions as Daniel drove them away.

His foot was flat on the accelerator, and he was praying as hard as he could that the gear box would change down and the car would speed up. After the chaos of the night and amidst their frenetic withdrawal, Daniel was absurdly struck by one more thing that he had learned that night.

Never use an automatic as a getaway car. It's too taxing on the nerves.

He almost didn't notice the convoy of cars, trucks and a fire-tender with lights flashing and sirens blazing which passed them going in the other direction on the opposite side of the carriageway.

Seventeen

Diedricks opened his eyes – a painful, almost impossible procedure given the livid bruises that masked them and his grossly swollen cheeks and brows. Once open, his reaction was immediate. He tried desperately to lift himself up from the bed, but the pain was too great and he sank back defeated. He tried to cry out through his swollen lips, but the sound that emerged was very weak, made to appear even more distressingly inadequate by the size of the frame from which it escaped.

'Andries,' he croaked. It was as if even his voice had been beaten to a pulp. The trigger for his alarm was standing over him.

* * *

They had driven back towards the city, to a block of flats whose walls of flaking plaster appeared to be supported only by rusting window frames. Daniel and the tattooed man, taking one arm each, heaved Diedricks up a filthy stairwell to a flat on the top floor. There was a worn-through doormat outside a door which, from its multiple and multi-coloured repairs, looked as if it had been regularly forced.

And everywhere the pungent, languid aroma of freshly smoked weed, which didn't quite mask the underlying stench of unwashed clothes. It was like a damp changing room at a bottom-division football club.

Leaving Daniel propping Diedricks up, the tattooed man unlocked the door. It opened only partially and with much resistance, finally triggering an ear-rending crash within. An angry shout echoed up the stairwell from the floor below.

They squeezed Diedricks and themselves through the narrow gap and were faced with an unconquerable barrier of surfboards which had been toppled by the door as it opened. The tattooed man swore.

A thick coating of wax on the decks of each board had coagulated into scar tissue-like bumps into which crusted beach sand was embedded. With faded once-garish colours lying below the crazed top coat of glass fibre, the boards looked to Daniel as if they were beyond gainful use. But the tattooed man fastidiously checked each one as he returned them to an upright position, running his hands almost lovingly over the rails of each, searching for new dents, carefully testing the solidity of the anchorage of the fins.

'No space, man,' he said apologetically.

There was indeed no space. The flat was tiny. A short passage, a bathroom off it, and a bed-sitting room at the end with a two-plate stove and sink in one corner. There was a stained and threadbare armchair against one wall, a low divan-like bed against another, and a pile of wetsuits and assorted bleached clothing piled up on the screeded concrete floor between them.

Through a large window and the lifting gloom Daniel had a bird's eye view of a car-breaker's yard. The two of them shouldered Diedricks to the bed and laid him out on it.

He looked like a corpse.

* * *

An array of medications stood stacked together on the

floor. The chemist in the 24-hour pharmacy had raised both of his eyebrows in knowing arcs when Daniel had bought them in the early hours of the morning.

Daniel, kneeling next to Diedricks, was about to start swabbing away the dried blood from his face and body, but his patient was having none of it.

'Andries,' he croaked again, turning his head towards the passage.

Andries, up to this point tagged in Daniel's brain only as the tattooed man, was in the bathroom.

So that's his name. Strange how you can go through all sorts of things together and still not know what a man is called.

He added his voice to Diedricks'. 'Come and talk to him. Get him to calm down.'

Andries emerged dripping wet, a thin towel wrapped not quite all the way around his waist.

Diedricks partially extended a battered arm towards him. Andries bent over his punished head, listening intently to the gasping whispers escaping from his mouth.

'No. No. He's OK, man. Promise you. He's fokol to do with them,' he said, once Diedricks had fallen silent. 'Moenie worry nie. He's a doctor. Let him sort you out.'

He straightened himself up. 'He thought you's a cop. He'll be OK now. You see.' He returned to the bathroom.

Diedricks sank back. It was clear Andries hadn't fully persuaded him. His eyes were riveted on Daniel as he returned to his task, as if expecting that he might administer the *coup de grace* at any moment.

It was quickly apparent that Diedricks had not been beaten further since Daniel had first seen him on the floor of the beach house. He was still filthy, but he had received some medical attention. The wounds to his head had been cleaned up, the most grievous stitched.

Daniel gently eased him onto his side. The particularly bad lacerations on his back, stained purple with antiseptic, had also been sewn closed.

Antjie's orders? Maybe not.

Then Daniel thought back to the rudimentary fort from which they had extracted Diedricks earlier that morning. He doubted whether there was any first aid worth the label available there.

Must have been her.

'What did they hit you with?' asked Daniel, examining the network of welts that crossed his flesh.

'Sjambok. Boots. Fists.' The words were just discernible.

Daniel winced. 'They check for broken bones?'

'Ja,' Diedricks rasped almost silently. 'None.'

Diedricks' words were now escaping over saliva leaking from the corners of his lips. Daniel wiped them dry.

'You're lucky. Bruises like that...' He pointed to Diedricks' blue- and purple-patched torso. 'You'd expect some damage to the ribs at the very least. Kidneys... Anyway...'

Daniel checked each line of sutures. They were neatly tied, no excessive inflammation, no unexpected swelling. Although given Diedricks' bruising, it was difficult to be sure...

Anyway. Probably no need to worry about them for the next day or so.

He placed a pillow under Diedricks' feet to elevate his legs. It was too late for ice, and the bruising was too extensive to wrap him in bandages. Rest would be the best therapy. The only therapy, unless he could somehow get Diedricks to a hospital. But how do you do that when the countryside is alive with people looking for your patient, not necessarily with his best interests in mind?

He resumed washing him down, gently wiping away the dirt and blood which had dried together in great caked splashes.

'So Andries does some diving for you,' Daniel said, as if by way of conversation, as he swabbed Diedricks' skin with lint drenched in antiseptic.

He was being generous with the liquid, the smell of which now overrode that of both the marijuana and the sweat. But there was no reply from Diedricks, who showed no sign that he felt any pain as the antiseptic channelled freely through the nerve-endings of his raw exposed wounds.

'What's his surname?' said Daniel, trying again.

'Andries?' he heard Diedricks croak. 'Andries. Diedricks. Andries. Jacobus. Diedricks.' The words came out singly, his lips still not fully under his control.

'Related?' asked Daniel.

'My son!' Diedricks spluttered, puzzled. 'Who did he say he was?'

'He didn't. The subject never came up.'

Well, well. Diedricks' wayward son is closer to his father than people thought. AJ the surfer and Sollie the cop. Mealtimes in the Diedricks household must have been a joy.

'You are?' croaked Diedricks.

'Daniel Hove.'

'What are you?' He was still staring fixedly at Daniel.

'A doctor.'

218

'Police doctor?'

'No. Andries already explained that to you.'

Diedricks mumbled doubtfully. 'What do you want?' he said eventually.

'I'm looking for some answers.'

'Answers to what?'

'I want to know about your business. Your export-import business.'

* * *

Diedricks sank back and turned his head with great concentration to one side as if examining the wall for defects. From down the passage came the sound of bad plumbing belching and spluttering.

'Dunno what you're saying,' he said to the wall. 'No business... retired.' His pronunciation was improving.

Daniel put down the lint and the bottle of antiseptic and leant backwards on his haunches, pulling the blue back-pack towards him.

Here we go again. How many times do I have to do this?

He picked out the photographs and the perlemoen shell. Selecting a photograph, he held it between the tips of two fingers where Diedricks could see it clearly.

'That's the plane you use. Note the registration mark. It's on a small airfield in the south of Zimbabwe. They're off-loading blue and white boxes from that plane, full of these.'

Daniel gently placed the perlemoen shell onto Diedricks' chest. Diedricks' eyes glanced down quickly at it and then resumed staring at the wall.

'Don't know nothing. Fokol to do with me,' he wheezed,

and was then seized by a coughing fit that would have had him hunched up in pain had he been able to contort himself that far.

Daniel eased the pillow from under Diedricks' head, doubled it up, and used it to prop up his head and shoulders. He produced a second picture, this time of the bakkie driving off the airstrip, suspension fully compressed under the weight of boxes and people.

'The boxes were taken away.'

Another picture. 'And they loaded these blue plastic drums in their place.'

Diedricks said nothing.

Yet another picture held up in Diedricks' face, this time of the plane taking off. 'Then the plane flew back south over the border, and those blue drums were brought down to Cape Town. I know that because I saw some of them the day before yesterday in that delicatessen in Oranjezicht. Where you told Andries to go. Those blue drums were filled with drugs.'

'You're dreaming, man. It's you who's on drugs.'

'No I'm not. Not in the least,' said Daniel, evenly and quietly.

Best if this is kept between you and me for the time being.

'On Friday morning some members of a gang called the South Side Kids – I think that's what they're called – fetched you from your farmhouse. I'm told that they're a gang you are involved with. You went with them to that beach house, where we first saw each other. There you were beaten up, by the police it appears, although I'm not sure whether they were the only ones. Maybe the South Side Kids were disturbed before they could really get started on you.'

'Crap,' said Diedricks, dribbling a stream of saliva as he spoke.

'Then the police took you away to a house in a very exclusive estate at the foot of the mountain. But you were released from that luxurious little prison rather impressively by the South Side Kids. Andries and I watched it happen.'

Daniel let his words sink in for a moment.

'What I can't understand is why you're so popular. Backwards and forwards and backwards and forwards. Why is everyone so keen to have the pleasure of your company?'

'My business is my business,' said Diedricks. 'Nothing to do with you.'

'Ah!' Progress!' said Daniel, sarcastically. 'Now we both agree you *do* have a business.'

He picked up the lint and antiseptic and resumed sponging down Diedricks' torso.

'Let's go on from there...'

'My friend,' hissed Diedricks, meaning exactly the opposite. 'You don't know what you're getting yourself into.' He looked narrowly up at Daniel through his black-bruised eyes. 'What the cops did to me is nothing. They can do a helluva lot worse.'

'I'm sure they can. I've had similar treatment, from people in a similar line of work to the ones who beat you up,' said Daniel. 'Broke my leg, as it happens.'

He gestured in the direction of his shin.

'I've also seen at first-hand what they can do. You're right. They can do a lot worse. My sister was killed, horribly, on that farm where the plane landed. It was done by your friends up there.'

'I know nothing about your sister,' Diedricks said.

'Whatever happened to her is fokol to do with me. And this is all fokol all to do with you. I don't have to tell you anything about anything.'

The bathroom door was still closed. Andries seemed intent on draining whatever supply of water remained.

Here we go. Either I'm correct in my deductions, or I'm about to find out this is just a blind alley I'm going up.

'I think you ought to think again,' Daniel said. 'Why were you so keen to get away from your business partners? The ones who so caringly sprang you from that police house and took you to that fort on the Cape Flats.'

'Would you like to stay in that slum?'

'Depends.' said Daniel. 'Depends on whether it was safer inside that compound or not.'

'What does that mean?'

'It means what I said before. It isn't just the police who want to speak to you. I think you're very worried that your business partners might work out what you've been doing. If they knew for sure, they'd definitely want to have a few words with you. And the rest.'

'Knew what?'

'You've been short-changing them. Fingers in the till, Sollie.'

'Now you're really talking out your arse,' Diedricks spat the words back at him.

'I don't think so,' said Daniel. He picked up one of the photos. 'Eight blue and white cool boxes were offloaded from that plane. I counted them myself. I was told that it's the same number every time the plane comes in. Eight boxes a week, in the season. But I was told that twelve boxes are shipped north from here every week. Where do the other four go to, Sollie?'

'I said before. What's the matter with you? Don't you listen? You don't know what you're talking about.'

'I think I do. It's not quite One-for-you and One-for-me, like that little man on the bar counter at your house.'

Diedricks stared at him in fury.

'More like Two-for-you, One-for-me. But that's more than thirty per cent, Sollie. Thirty per cent comes to a lot of money. You're skimming a hell of a lot off the top, Sollie. Taking all the cream and a good part of the milk. I think they might want to talk to you about that. If I told them where you are...'

'So now you threaten me? What are you? A doctor? Or a blackmailer? How much do you want?'

'I'm not asking for money. As I said right at the beginning, I want some answers.'

'And if I talk to you? What then? For me. And for you.' Diedricks stared at Daniel. 'What then, meneer? You haven't thought this through.'

'It's more a case of what happens if you don't talk to me,' said Daniel. 'You've already got the cops looking for you. Ellen's people also, I'm sure. If you don't talk to me, these photos and a short summary of my suspicions will find their way to that delicatessen, and also to the police. Together with directions to where they can find you. Then they can fight it out amongst themselves to see who gets to you first.'

Diedricks' head fell back onto the pillow. It seemed to Daniel that he might have decided to stop talking altogether.

Then: 'What do you want to know?'

'Everything, Sollie. Every bloody thing.'

Daniel heard the bathroom door opening, and Andries

emerged, dressed and pulling a comb painfully through his matted hair.

'See,' he said to his father. 'I told you he'd sort you out.'

* * *

Andries was feeding his father soup, holding the cup near his chin as Diedricks sucked noisily through a straw. Daniel nursed a cup of coffee and watched with undisguised distaste as Diedricks drank.

'Ready when you are,' he said impatiently.

'OK, man. OK,' Diedricks croaked, concentrating on trying to lick traces of soup from his distorted lips. 'Just let me finish.'

He made an effort to wipe his mouth with a napkin. Daniel could see he found it painful to even lift up his arm, although there had been a remarkable recovery in his power of speech.

'OK,' he said again, wearily.

He sighed, took a difficult breath and began. 'I have business partners here and I have a business partner over the border. I collect together the shellfish here and send it up there. It gets shipped to wherever they send it.'

'Hong Kong,' said Daniel.

'Believe so,' said Diedricks.

'You know so,' said Daniel.

Diedricks shrugged, as far as he was able.

'They pay for it how?'

'Hard currency, in cash. Goods.'

'Not goods. Drugs,' said Daniel. 'Crystal meth, to be accurate. I know - I've seen where they make it. You're not telling me anything I don't know already. Tell me something I don't know, Sollie.'

· 'What more is there? It's a simple business. All I do is logistics. My partners here pay me a percentage of the cash they get for the shipment. I only arrange the transport of those blue canisters back to here. I don't sell them or deal in them or take any commission on them. I have nothing more to do with them once they are in Cape Town.'

'Tell that to the judge,' said Daniel. 'But the percentage they pay you obviously isn't big enough.'

'A man has to live.'

'Where do you sell the rest? The third you keep for yourself.'

'Depends where I can get the best price. Swaziland. Mozambique, maybe.'

'Tell me why they killed my sister on that farm up there.'

Andries stirred in the corner. Daniel glanced quickly around, but there was no further sound or movement, so he returned his attention to Diedricks, who was spitting with anger.

'I didn't know they'd killed anyone. I don't know your sister. I don't know what happened to her. How many bloody times do I have to tell you?'

* * *

Daniel again bent down to the back-pack. He pulled out a sheet of paper, his notes of his telephone conversation with Henry Mliswa.

'This Nyarai Simango.' he said. 'The one that owns that farm where the plane landed. She your business partner?'

'You're well informed, Hove.'

'Tell me about her.'

'She calls herself Nyarai Simango. She owns that farm, but she doesn't do so much farming, from the look of it. It was in a hell of a mess the last time I saw it. But that's up to her. I'm only interested in shellfish.'

'Calls herself?'

'You Zimbabwean, Hove? You sound like one.'

'Yes.'

'Then you know that names up there are ten cents a dozen. Everyone has more than one name. Depends who they're talking to.'

'Not me,' said Daniel. 'I'm just plain old Daniel Hove.'

'Then you're a rare specimen. Nyarai Simango is how I've always known her, but that isn't the only name she's ever been known by.'

'You met her how? From when you were a policeman?'

Diedricks coughed violently.

'What kind of policeman were you? Secret policeman? Spy?'

'What you think I am? Some James Bond or something? Where d'you get that nonsense?'

'The woman from the Drug Squad, as it happens. She told me you were a retired policeman. But what kind of policeman needs to be given immunity from the TRC? Seem to me that means you were some kind of secret policeman.'

'Drug Squad? What woman?'

'Antjie. The woman I was with at the beach house. Or does she also have another name?'

'Antjie? That what she told you?' Diedricks collapsed again, this time into derisive phlegm-filled laughter. 'She really tell you that?' he repeated, in mock amazement. 'She's been filling your head with kak, man. Drug Squad, my arse.'

'She's not from the Drug Squad? Where is she from, then?'

'That little bitch?' Diedricks said furiously. 'I knew her from before. She's from the same part of the police as me.' He paused. 'And where do *you* know her from? How did *you* get mixed up with her?'

'You're supposed to be answering the questions, not asking them. But I'll tell you. I met her through your business partner this end. Did you know she was working in Ellen's office?'

'Antjie?'

'The one. She was working for Ellen as her assistant.'

Diedricks didn't reply. This time his amazement was genuine. He looked up at Daniel, shock on his face, and then he swore.

'God! That stupid bitch. That stupid bloody idiot bitch.'

* * *

'Ellen,' said Daniel. 'Why did she want you to meet her at the beach house?'

'She said something had happened. We need to make a plan, she said. She said someone had come to her office who knew too much. A cop, she was sure. But she wasn't sure what kind of cop. That was you, wasn't it? She thought you was a cop from that side. From Zimbabwe.'

It was Daniel's turn to scoff in disbelief.

'And all the time, you say, she was paying Antjie while the little bitch spied on her?' Diedricks asked. Again he spat out the word. 'Idiot.'

Daniel nodded. 'What plan did she suggest?'

'She wanted me to give her all the documents for safe-keeping.'

'You couldn't have been very happy to hear that. What did you say?'

'Never got that far. Antjie's little bunch of friends arrived and the discussion ended. Ellen was out of there so fast I could hardly believe it. Screaming at the top of her voice as she went.'

'And she mentioned nothing to you about my sister? You see, I went into great detail telling Ellen what happened to my sister.'

Diedricks said nothing.

'As I thought,' said Daniel. 'You *do* know something about what happened.'

'All I know is what Ellen told me. She told me about your sister. But I don't know *why* she died. Neither does Ellen.'

'Her people. They do anything to you before they left?'

Diedricks shrugged.

'Well?' Daniel prompted him.

'No,' Diedricks replied. 'Nothing.'

'And when they got you to that place on the Flats? What happened there?'

'Nothing there either. They said they were going to keep me there until things had died down. She wanted to talk to me again, they said. But she was lying low for a while. Meantime, they just put me in a room and let me sleep.'

'So she'll still be looking for you?'

'Of course, man. Of course she'll still be bloody looking for me.'

* * *

'Well, Sollie. Where were we?' said Daniel after a pause during which he made himself another cup of coffee. 'Tell me about your career as a secret policeman.'

'Not secret. Security,' said Diedricks, taking offense. 'I worked for state security. I went to work in a suit, to the same office every day. Not much secret about it. I was in the business of information, that's all. No guns, no invisible ink, no sexy women. Sexy women would've been nice. But there weren't any. Unless you think that little bitch is sexy. I don't.'

'She said you should have been hauled in front of the Truth and Reconciliation Commission, but you were given immunity.'

'Ja, well, I already told you she tells lies like she can't help it.' He took a deep breath, as if he was bored of explaining it. 'As a country, we had to know what was going on up north. Nothing wrong with that. My job was to find out. With other people, of course.'

He paused.

'Early '80s when I started. You know what I'm talking about, Hove?'

Daniel nodded. 'Gukurahundi.'

'That's it,' said Diedricks. 'The wind that separates the wheat from the chaff.'

'Not quite.'

'Huh?'

'It means 'clearing away the chaff'. Sorghum, millet chaff. Not wheat. It's also used to describe the rains that wash away the chaff after threshing. So, the rain that clears the chaff.'

'OK. You taught me something. Great one for poetry, your man up there. Fancy words for mass murder. For genocide.'

He stared back at Daniel, challenging him to disagree.

'They would say you - the South Africans - provoked it. You all stirred up trouble in Matabeleland and they had to use force to quell it.'

Diedricks scoffed. 'You mean destabilisation? All that stuff? Sure, there was some of that. But that was others. Not me, you understand? That wasn't what I did. I told you, I collected information.'

'Destabilisation? Is that what you call it? Talk about fancy words. Arming bands of thugs so they could terrorise the countryside. Then watching from the sidelines as the government did the same?'

'Nonsense,' he said dismissively. 'That was never so big a deal as your man up there claims it was. The pot was already boiling over. All we did was chuck an extra log on the fire. You people would have found a reason to kill each other whatever we did.'

'My people? It wasn't 'my people' who committed those atrocities. And he – that 'man up there' - he's not my man,' said Daniel. 'Never was.'

'No?' said Diedricks.

He looked Daniel up and down. Despite his impotent recumbent position, he might have been measuring him up for a suit. Or a coffin.

'Perhaps not.'

* * *

Andries sat quietly in the corner, glancing occasionally up at Daniel, then at his father, then back again, but listening intently to everything that passed between them. Daniel wasn't sure whether he was silent because it was all new to him, or because he had heard all it before. There was nothing in Diedricks senior's demeanour either way, but then he wasn't currently capable of making full use of his complete store of facial expressions.

Diedricks took up his story again.

'So. It was early '80s. '81 or '82. '82, I think. She was an officer in the army up there. Captain in Intelligence. I used to speak to her from time to time. We'd meet and talk, and she was paid a small sum of money for her trouble. People should talk more, Hove. Then they wouldn't misunderstand each other so much.'

'Why did she talk to you? You were the enemy. How did you persuade her to starting talking to you?'

'Persuade her!' Diedricks guffawed, but the laughter didn't last long before transforming itself into another retching convulsion.

Daniel took the glass of water and tipped it gently against his lips. Diedricks sipped and sank back.

'She came to us,' he said, almost swallowing the last syllable as he tried to control the tremors in his throat. He paused to allow himself to calm down. 'She wasn't the only one. We were beating them off. Every couple of weeks another one of your compatriots would try to sell us their services.'

'Why?'

'Money, mostly. They were being paid peanuts in an

increasingly worthless currency. Also, people rebel. That's what happens when you run an outfit like the Party up there. A few chefs at the top with all the power, everyone else underneath with nothing. That's why she did it, I think.'

'She'd made a name for herself when she was in Mozambique,' he went on after a pause for breath. 'She worked in internal security for the Party while they were in exile. Dangerous business. You can make a lot of enemies doing that job. But you also learn a lot about people. Things other people will pay for.'

He attempted a grin but it came out as something else, quite grotesque.

'She got home full of religion for your workers' paradise, but she found herself at the bottom of the pile. Others with less talent were getting very rich, very quick, simply because there was a powerful relative somewhere in their family. If I was her, I would also want to stick up a finger to the people treating me like shit. Behind my back, of course.'

'You didn't think all these volunteers were being planted on you?'

'Of course we thought that,' he said sniffily. 'Some of them were. But sometimes you gotta take a risk. We tried her out, and she turned out to be a real gem. She was in just the right place for us. She was in Matabeleland. She was high-ranking enough to see the orders coming down from the top. But not so high that she didn't know what was happening on the ground. In detail. From personal experience. What she gave us was hundred per cent correct almost hundred per cent of the time. Good stuff. So if she was playing double, she was doing it better than anyone ever did it before or since.'

'We met more and more often. For a stretch of about a year, we met every two weeks. Saw her more often than I saw my wife. My dearly beloved ex-wife...'

Diedricks glanced across at Andries. A strange wheeze emerged from the back of his throat, and he stopped talking again. Daniel supposed it was a sort of strangled guffaw.

'Where did you meet?' he said impatiently.

'Zambian border. Vic Falls. Sometimes on one side, sometimes the other. Weekends, most of the time. Lovely up there. Sometimes I got in a spot of fishing also. You a fisherman?'

'No.'

'You should try it. Might calm you down.'

Daniel let the insult pass. 'She was paid how?'

'Cash at the beginning. Later, when she got more used to us, we paid into a bank account here.'

'And this went on for how long?'

''82, '94. What's that? Twelve, thirteen years? She left the army, but she was still very useful. By then she had at last begun to climb through the ranks of the Party. Ditched her principles. She had quite senior positions by the end. She knew all sorts of people. I stayed as her liaison.'

'Why did she leave the army?'

'She finally opened her eyes. Saw the workers' paradise was doomed from the start, and she might as well jump on the money-go-round like everyone else. But she stayed in the Party and began to play by their rules. She appeared to be the most loyal comrade they ever could have wanted. But she was talking to us all the time. That's what I meant about sticking a finger up. I suppose she could look at the people at the top, and know she knew something they didn't. By then it definitely wasn't about the money. She was making much more from her businesses. But she kept talking to us. To me.'

'Then the powers that be - the new powers that be - decided that we shouldn't be spying on our brothers and sisters across the Limpopo. The arrangement with her was terminated. Not long after that I was given my marching orders. Cleaning out the stables for the new masters. Early retirement, full pension.'

'And then?'

'Even a full pension's not so great. I needed to find something to do. I got hold of her. Just for old times' sake, and we found out we could be useful to each other. We went into business.'

He looked up at Daniel.

'That's it, Hove. Simple as that. All of it. From the beginning to the end.'

Daniel put down his coffee cup. 'We're not finished just yet. I'm still puzzled.'

Diedricks' expression changed slightly. Daniel realised he was rolling his eyes in exasperation.

'Antjie. She said they wanted to arrest you because your smuggling had become an embarrassment to the government. She said you were breaking the terms of your early retirement. She said they want to shut down this cross-border trade in perlemoen and drugs. But if she isn't from the Drugs Squad, then why's she interested in you?'

'You really think she gives a shit about smuggling?' Diedricks barked hoarsely. 'Half her colleagues are doing exactly the same. I wouldn't be surprised if they're doing deals right now out of that house up the mountain. Maybe she's doing it herself. Who knows?'

'How did you know they would take you there?'

'Some things don't change. We used that place before I retired. It was confiscated from a Frenchman who tried to play a double deal with the old government. Oil or something. Sanctions busting.'

He stopped, and started again. 'Smuggling? That's not why she wanted me. Not a chance.'

'Then why?'

'They want to re-open that channel. They must have realised they made a big mistake not watching what's going on up there. They want to start speaking to Nyarai again.'

'Why do they need you to do it? Couldn't they do it themselves?'

'Sure they could. But it would go much easier if they had an introduction. Perhaps you don't realise how delicate things are up there.'

'Tell me...'

Daniel has meant it rhetorically, but Diedricks took it as a request.

'When you get as high in the Party like she is, things get very complicated. Even as high as she is she needs protection. You have to be in a faction. If you don't, anyone can just eat you up. You can't stand in the middle. Even being protected by a faction, she has to watch her back the whole time. For example, that policeman in the district police camp. He only acts in her interests because someone higher up ordered him to do it.'

Oh yes?

'Mpofu?' he said.

'Could be. I don't take too much interest in those kind of

235

details these days. This is all just what she has mentioned from time to time, one friend talking to another.'

Lying bastard.

'So she's allowed to smuggle shellfish across the border? I bet that plane has never filed a flight plan, let alone been cleared by Customs. Or declared to the taxman.'

'Stop being so naive, Hove. You're beginning to make me angry, being so childish. For the big men – and women - at the top there is no such thing as the law. Anything is possible if you know the right people. The only crime is disloyalty - to your faction or the Party. That business is one of the rewards for her loyalty. They can take it away just like that...' He tried to click his fingers but failed. 'And there are plenty of people who'd kill to have it.'

'Which faction is hers?'

'That's not important. The point is what faction she isn't part of. Near the top of it is a very senior man in the CIO. A real secret policeman,' he said.

Daniel looked at him, saying nothing.

Diedricks stared back.

'Go on,' said Daniel. 'Who?'

'Mutambiro,' Diedricks said. A look of what could have been construed as glee moved his bruised features. 'Ja, meneer,' he said. 'You know...'

Daniel did know. Few people didn't in that part of the world. His notoriety preceded him by a very long distance. Bonnyface Mutambiro. Confidante to the powerful. Fearless by repute, although how much was mythological was uncertain. Ruthless, without doubt, in the direct experience of many. Gatherer and guardian of the presidential secrets.

How many times had Daniel seen his face on television

news, in newspaper pictures? Never in the front row but, no name mentioned, often at the back, invariably staring straight at the camera. Unblinking, confident, staring down the cameraman, daring him to keep him in his viewfinder.

Diedricks interrupted Daniels thoughts. 'You see? I was right, wasn't I. You just haven't thought this through. I'll give you this advice for free. I'm telling you. You don't want to get yourself mixed up in this. These people play for keeps. They'll suck you in and spit you out, Hove...'

Daniel ignored him. 'You were saying...,' he said. 'About Nyarai's business...'

'Ja, well. You can imagine what would happen if Mutambiro found out what Nyarai was doing all those years. It would give him the perfect excuse to shut her down, and there is nothing – sweet piss all - her political friends could do to stop him. He'll stop at nothing. He didn't get that far up the greasy pole by being nice. He'll flatten her. Believe me.'

Diedricks took another series of deep breaths.

'Antjie and her bosses don't want to scare her off if they can help it, so they wanted me to make the contact. Discretely. In a way that Nyarai would trust. An introduction - that's what they wanted.'

'But look at you,' Daniel protested. 'She'd hardly be reassured if she saw you looking like this.'

Diedricks looked at him scathingly. 'I didn't look like this when they first asked me. But I told Antjies' halfnaaitjies to fuck off, so they beat the shit out of me.' He shrugged philosophically. 'They'll find a way to do it without me.'

'So why? Why bother to beat you up?'

'Bother? It's no bother to them. They enjoy it, man.'

It doesn't ring true. Daniel stared at Diedricks, trying to gauge from his battered features how far he could believe him. He decided he couldn't.

'They beat you just for the hell of it? Is that what you're telling me? Or rather, because you wouldn't provide an introduction for them?'

'Ja.'

'I don't believe you. It doesn't make sense. Why involve you if they can do it themselves. If I was them I wouldn't want you anywhere near.'

'Ja, well. You aren't them. You don't know...'

'What did they really want, Sollie? Stop messing with me. Tell me, What were they after?'

Diedricks paused again. Daniel let him pause, but the silence continued past the point he was prepared to let it.

'I'm losing patience fast, Sollie. Stop fucking me around...'

'Wait, for fuck sakes,' Diedricks shot back. 'I'm just catching my breath, man.'

He paused again, and then, after noisily attempting to clear his throat, resumed.

'OK. Nyarai didn't trust the new people when they took over. So when I left, she asked me to make sure her file was destroyed. I was happy to help.'

'What's she scared of? Being tried for war crimes?'

'You still don't understand, do you? You thick or something?'

This time Diedricks managed to convey his deep irritation clearly through his bruised face.

'It's fucking obvious, Hove. You're talking about justice. But this isn't about justice. It's about power. Nobody up there is worried about what they did in the '80s because your man at the top gave them all immunity. All nice and legal. They think they'll be in power forever, so why worry? But talking to us. To South Africa. That's a serious thing. That could get you into deep kak if anyone found out. Nyarai thought Antjie's bosses might get too friendly with her own government. She didn't trust them to keep their mouths shut about what had happened in the past. Before...'

'So what did you tell them? At the beach house?'

'They was convinced the file still exists. So I had I to tell them something. I had to stop them before they went too far.'

A sort of smirk passed over Diedricks' features. 'But she can look all she wants. It isn't there. I burned it a long time ago.'

Bullshit.

* * *

'This Simango woman. She never asked you about my sister? Never mentioned her to you?'

'Never,' said Diedricks, meeting Daniel's gaze a little too steadily. 'Anyway, I haven't seen her for ages. That's not how the business works. She doesn't run it day to day. She has a manager who does that.'

'How does it work then, Sollie? How does she get hold of you if she needs to? How do you contact her?'

Diedricks retched. Daniel held the glass of water to his lips again.

'From that side, usually a message with the cash on the plane, requesting a meeting.'

'And from this side?'

'Same thing in the other direction. But most times, a notice in the personal ads of the Bulawayo newspaper. In the Friday paper,' Diedricks replied. 'Whichever way, a meeting two Friday's later. Depending.'

'Depending on what?'

'In the old days it was only through a message in the Friday paper. There was no planes, so no messages on a Sunday. When the planes started, the arrangements had to be for the same day. So: Friday message in the paper, meeting fourteen days later. Sunday message, meeting twelve days later. Whichever, the same Friday for the meeting.'

'Seems like a long time to wait. What if you had to contact her urgently?'

'It wasn't an urgent kind of relationship. I suppose we could have made other arrangements, if we had to. But in all those years we never needed to.'

'But she has contacted you, hasn't she. Very recently. She wants a meeting with you, to discuss my sister, so she sent a message with the plane. Last week.'

Diedricks nodded. 'She sent a message but I don't know what it's about.'

'Meeting when? Next Friday?'

'Ja.'

'And Antjie knows about this? You told her?'

Diedricks shrugged. 'I had to tell them things...'

'So Antjie will be there instead of you. How would you warn Nyarai about this? Now?'

'Can't. Today's plane's has already gone. There's no other way to contact her, except through a meeting arranged like that. I'd have to go there as well, and...' He waved vaguely at his injuries.

'So there'll be a meeting five days from today. Will she pitch up?'

'Of course, man. Definitely. She asked for the meeting...'

'Where exactly?'

'Vic Falls Hotel. The old one.'

'And...?'

'And what?'

'How does it work at the hotel? It's a big place. Where at the hotel is the meeting?'

'The person from our side books a room. A message is left telling her which room to go to.'

'Antjie knows that?'

'Ja.'

'How does she get that message?'

'It's left in a place on the flagpole in the front of the hotel. The one looking out over the river. Nyarai knows where.'

Daniel paused.

Here comes another flyer. Let's hope I'm not barking up the wrong tree.

'So, Sollie. You're in it up to your eyebrows. You've got two women trying to find you, and whichever one gets hold of you first will have your balls.'

'I'll survive.'

'You might. But I still haven't got any closer to finding out why my sister was murdered on that farm. Was it because she found out that the woman who owns that farm was a South African spy? But how could she possibly have found out about such a thing? So why? Why was she murdered?'

241

'How many times have I told you?' He shouted the words at Daniel one by one. 'I. Don't. Fucking. Know. Get off my fucking back.'

'I don't believe you, Sollie.'

'That's your bloody problem.'

'No, Sollie. You don't seem to understand. It's your problem. Let me put it as clearly as I can. I have heard nothing from you so far to stop me sending those photos and this address all around Cape Town.'

There was a loud explosion from Andries in the corner. 'Leave him alone, man. He's sick. He can't tell you anything more.'

Daniel turned to him.

'Shut up,' he said. 'The sooner he talks the easier it will be for everyone. For a start, he can tell me where that file is.'

'I told you. I burnt it.'

'I don't believe you, Sollie. I don't think you destroyed that file at all. I've been through your house. From what I saw there, you don't strike me as the kind of person who destroys anything. There are papers, bits of other stuff, years old, of no apparent use or value to anyone, piled in every corner we looked. If you keep that kind of rubbish, then I think a valuable file like that is still sitting around somewhere.'

Diedricks glared at him, his eyes wide. Very wide. Andries failed to hide a wry smile in the corner.

'Where is it, Sollie?' Daniel shouted. 'Tell me where it is.'

Diedricks appeared to hesitate before he answered, and Daniel almost cheered out loud.

Whatever he says now, that file is still around somewhere. I knew it. I was absolutely right.

242

And then he saw that Diedricks hadn't been hesitating at all. He had collapsed. He was slumped back flat on the bed, his head to one side, and Daniel wasn't even sure he was still breathing.

* * *

Andries was shouting at him at the top of his voice. 'What the fuck have you done to him? You've fucking killed him. You bastard. You fucking bastard.'

'Shut up.' Daniel turned to him, pulling the revolver from his waistband as he did. 'Shut up and don't say another word. I can't help your father with you screaming at me. If you want to help, go and fill that kettle with hot water from the bathroom. If there's any left.'

Andries removed himself silently. Daniel heard a tap running. He shouted after him. 'And bring a towel or a face cloth or something.'

Daniel turned back to Diedricks. He found a pulse. He was still alive. But the beat was very weak and very fast. If he leant close to Diedricks' battered face he could make out that he was still breathing. But, like his pulse, the breathing was shallow and rapid. And he was getting cold.

Daniel pulled the pillow from behind Diedricks' head and let his head subside onto the mattress. He had thought Diedricks had passed the danger point for the onset of shock. It must have been his increasingly agitated state that brought it on.

What had they been taught? Do no harm. And it wasn't just Deidricks who'd been harmed.

Daniel felt ashamed.

Andries was back. Daniel took the cloth, dipped it in the water, and applied it to Diedricks' hands and feet and face. He did it again and again, attempting to warm them up. Eventually he pulled the blanket over Diedricks, tucking it in firmly at each side, enveloping him in it. There was another blanket on the floor at the foot of the bed. Daniel spread it out over the first and tucked it in as well.

Andries was staring intently at his father. 'He's sick, man. Do something.'

'He's suffering from shock,' Daniel replied. 'He'll recover. I'm sure of it. But we need to get him to a hospital. D'you know where we can take him? Where they won't ask too many questions.'

'I know a clinic,' said Andries. 'But after that you leave us alone. Everything that has happened to him has been because of you. I never want to see your face again, man. Ever. I fucking mean it.'

Eighteen

In silence they carried Diedricks to the car, swaddled in the blankets, and laid him out on the back seat like a cocoon. Then they both sat in self-conscious silence while Andries drove them back around the mountain through a dilapidated suburb to a clinic run by a medical charity. It was only Sunday morning, and the place already looked like a sanitarium in the bowels of a Roman amphitheatre.

Daniel was stunned. It was a long time since he had worked in a casualty department, and even then it had been nothing like this. Almost unbelievably, compared with some of the patients in the queue to be seen, Diedricks' exterior injuries were not extreme. But his state of shock caused the triage nurse to catapult him to the front of the queue. He was seen by a second nurse shortly afterwards, and taken through to one of a very few in-patient beds in a tiny ward at the back of the clinic.

Expecting to leave Andries there with his father, Daniel made to leave. But as he walked out of the door he felt a touch on his shoulder and found Andries at his side.

'Sorry, man,' he said contritely, as he stared at Daniel from beneath his lowered eyelids. 'I was wrong to shout. Sorry, man.' he repeated quietly.

Daniel reached out and gripped his shoulder, accepting the apology. He walked on.

Andries walked briskly next to him. He spoke again. 'Can I catch a ride? There aren't so many buses out here.'

'What about your father? Aren't you going to wait with him?'

'I'll come back. They said they's going to keep him till tomorrow, at least. And he's not talking...'

Daniel nodded, if for no other reason than it would be useful to have a guide out of this place. They sat in silence again, this time with Daniel driving. Directions from the passenger seat were all that passed between them until Andries spoke again.

'What you gonna do now?' he said.

'Go home, I suppose. I don't know what more I can do here.'

'Ja. Shame, man.'

Daniel made no reply.

Andries tried again. 'Your sister,' he said. 'What was she called?'

'Patricia,' said Daniel, looking across at his passenger, alerted by something in his tone.

'Ja. Trisha.'

Daniel pulled sharply over to the side of the road and stopped the car.

'You knew her?' he demanded.

'Ja. A bit,' he said.

'For crying out loud! OK. Out with it,' he said angrily.

'She was on the beach,' said Andries. 'Must have been last year. Ja, Must have been. Last year I was surfing a lot on the False Bay side and she was on the beach at Muizenberg. She was at the Tech, right?'

Daniel nodded.

'Saw her on the beach quite often, when I was there. She was a friend. Easy to talk to. Funny.'

'When did you last see her?'

'Shit, man. Long time. Three months, maybe?'

'That fits,' Daniel said. 'But how were you friends? Was she mixed up in all this smuggling stuff before she met you, or what...?'

'Hey, man. I didn't push her into this...'

'No. No. I didn't mean that,' Daniel said, backtracking. 'Just tell me what happened. Do you know? You must know. You must.'

But Daniel knew what he would say before he said it.

'Her old man,' he said. 'She wanted to know what happened to her old man.'

* * *

'We was just talking. On the beach one day. I remember. The wind was wrong and the surf was kak so we was just parking off, talking. Just talking about our families. She said her old man had died, but no-one knew what happened to him. That true?'

'Yes.'

'No body? Nothing?'

'Nothing.'

'So maybe he's alive?'

'No. He's dead. We're sure of that. But we don't know where he's buried, or how he died. Not exactly, anyway. Makes things difficult.'

'How?'

'You can't get it out of your mind. Sometimes you think maybe he's still alive, even though you know deep down that he isn't. When you can't be exactly sure, then a million things are possible. And you go through them all till you think you're going mad.'

'Ja. Sorry, man.'

'Not your fault.'

'No. But anyway...'

'So you told her about Sollie? What he did?'

'Ja. We was talking, like I said. I knew my old man had something to do with what went on up there. Like, over the border. What he was telling you just now. I told her about it. She wanted to talk to him. Ask him what he knew. I told her I thought it was a bad idea. You seen him, man. He still thinks in the old way, man. You know,' he paused, as if uncertain to continue. 'Black people... Nothing personal, man...'

'He doesn't like black people?'

'No. No. It's not that he doesn't like them. Difficult to explain. Maybe he just doesn't know how to be friends with them.'

'To be honest,' said Daniel. 'I don't think Sollie knows how to be friends with anyone.'

'Also true,' said Andries. Daniel could see him mulling the notion over in his mind.

'So that was it? You just talked?'

'No. I knew Sollie kept some papers, so one day we went and looked at them.'

'Papers? Is this the file Sollie was talking about at your flat? The file he took with him when he retired?'

'I don't know when he took it. I don't know if it's the file he was telling you about. But your sister read it, from one end to the other. I didn't really see her after that. Not at the beach. Nowhere. She must have gone looking for him.'

'Looking for who?'

'Her old man. Your old man. She said what was in the file

told her where he was, man.'

'How did she get involved with Ellen – Sollie's business partner.?'

'That I don't know, man. Seriously...'

'So Sollie didn't burn the file? He said he did, but he didn't?'

'Ja, man. Probably. It's like you said back there. He never throws anything away. Mostly he leaves things lying around. But some things he hides...'

'And you know where he hid it?'

'Hey, bru. That's what I'm trying to tell you.'

'Why have you taken so long to tell me all this?' said Daniel angrily.

'Sollie...'

'Sollie what?'

'Just Sollie...'

'He thinks you believe he destroyed it?'

'Something like that. And...'

'And what?'

'If he knew I knew he would have gone mal, man...'

Daniel looked at him askance.

It's because she's black. That's it, isn't it. He didn't know about her, and you were scared of how he would react if he found out.

'So where is it?' he demanded.

'At the farm.'

'But they will have torn that place to pieces. Either Ellen or Antjie. One of the two. Maybe both.'

'Sure, man. But they'll never find it.'

'So you'll show me where it is?'

'For sure. If you want.'

'I want. You bet I want.'

'For her, also,' said Andries.

'Yes. For her as well.'

* * *

Daniel's possessions, few in number and shoved into the back-pack and a smaller grip, were now sitting in the back of the car. Daniel still had the badza handle, which was lying next to them. And he'd kept the pistol. The weight of it reassured him. As did his newly acquired experience of the damage it could do. He reached to his waist to check it was still there as Andries drove them out on the familiar route to the hinterland.

All the way he treated Daniel to another seminar on paramilitary tactics that Daniel still found ill-fitting in someone who otherwise appeared to prefer the gentler contest between wave and board. Even after the attack on the gangland fort.

The Cape Dutch villas sailed past again. They were driving fast. 'We need to be there before the sun goes,' Andries had said. The traffic lights in the middle of nowhere were red again, and as before, with no intersecting roads, there was no cross traffic to benefit. They stopped and then travelled on until they turned off and drove through the village and down and across the causeway. And then, instead of turning right towards the farm they carried on straight.

Daniel tapped Andries on the shoulder, pointing this out. But Andries kept on driving.

'We're going round the other side,' he reminded Daniel. 'Trust me, bru.'

As they drove they drew closer to the range of hills on the far boundary of the farm. Suddenly, as they entered the shadow of hills with the sun sinking rapidly behind the skyline, it became quite dark.

Andries kept going and then slowed and turned off onto a track that left the road at an angle. A few yards further on he stopped completely, and there they sat as the shadows grew until all that was still visible of the sunset was a thin strip of light at the hilltop.

'That way they'll be staring into the light if they're looking out for us,' Daniel remembered Andries telling him. It was meant to reassure him. It didn't.

They got out. Andries locked the car and tossed the keys across to Daniel, who dropped the catch and had to scrabble for them in the scrubby grass. Andries led them to the stream bed, barely flowing, and they walked slowly down towards the farmhouse. The ditch deepened until it and the low bushes along its banks almost completely concealed them from their surroundings. They were able to get quite close to the house before the land began to level out again and the ditch became progressively shallower.

Andries halted them at a bend in the course of the stream. They squatted low and surveyed the house. The light was failing quite rapidly now. Even the top of the windmill no longer reflected the last rays of the sun from beyond the hills, and the creak from its vanes subsided and then stopped as the stillness of dusk descended. Still they remained, looking out at the gloomy stoep and the darkened sitting room behind it.

They heard a sharp bang – a door slamming shut, it sounded like. There was an interval and then a figure appeared from behind the house, walking away down the driveway towards the lower road.

Cop? Or robber? For all the difference that makes.

Daniel didn't recognise him. He nudged Andries. Andries shrugged back.

They remained where they were, looking out over no-man's land as if from a trench.

After what seemed an eternity, Andries moved them on, putting the vegetation ringing the lawn between them and the lower road. He led them along the outside edge of the stoep towards a door in the garage extension. Pulling a key from his pocket, he unlocked it and pulled it open.

They entered in silence.

The place had been searched. The doors of the truck were open and the canvas cover had been removed from the motorbike. The contents of several boxes had been spilled onto the floor. Andries moved over to the workbench, and after rummaging through a mess of tools abandoned on top of it, he extracted a ring spanner marked with a short splash of red paint, which he waved triumphantly at Daniel in the gloom.

He moved swiftly around the truck to the motorbike. He found a catch on the side of the frame, pressed it and swung up the seat on its hinges. Inside was a set of keys which he inserted into the ignition between the handlebars. He unscrewed the cap on the petrol tank and jerked the bike around by its handlebars. Satisfied with the sloshing he heard, he replaced the cap.

He leant over the machine to turn the fuel tap, and then pushed it heavily around the car until it faced the door by which they had entered. The front wheel touched the door itself, the stand propping it in the at-ease position, ready to spring to attention.

'Just in case,' he mouthed, repeating what he had already told Daniel in the car.

And then Daniel and he walked through the unlocked interior door into the main part of the house. Andries had pressed him persistently as they had driven out. Had he locked the door again on his previous visit, or could they rely on him having left it unsecured? Daniel heaved a heavy interior sigh of relief that his memory hadn't failed him.

Straight through the kitchen in tandem – drawers and cupboards standing open, contents scattered in chaos on the countertop - to the sitting room. Sofas upended, pictures removed from the wall, although the Mauser still hung proudly above the fireplace. Presumably because it looked an unlikely hiding place for a file. Likewise the two diminutive duiker's heads which looked disdainfully down over the disorder with their glass eyes.

Andries squatted down below the bar counter, just behind the silver-haired mannequin which had been knocked over on the counter top. He felt for a nut recessed under the furrowed timber of the railway sleeper, placed the ring spanner around it, and after an initial exertion began moving it round. Almost a complete half-turn each time, then disengaging the spanner, swinging it back, turning again.

He did this almost a dozen times before the nut loosened sufficiently for him to move it manually – using the tips of his fingers at first, and then with a final spin from the inside of his index finger until it fell and bounced across the floor with a clatter that seemed loud enough to wake the district.

Daniel's nerves juddered.

But the wood refused to yield. Andries struck at it with the heels of both hands, but still it didn't move. Cursing, he walked swiftly back through to the kitchen, and returned with a thick-bladed knife which he speared into a fine crack on the edge of the counter. He worked it back and forwards, up and down, and finally the crack began to widen.

Inserting the ends of his thumbs he widened it further until a thin section of the underside of the sleeper came away in his hands. Lying on top of it, as he held it out to Daniel like an offertory plate, was a manila folder, corners dog-eared, edges ragged and disintegrating, with a green diagonal stripe across one corner. It was held closed by a broad rubber band across the middle.

Daniel stared at it, mesmerised.

He picked it up, felt its weight – it was about half an inch thick – and then froze as they both heard the unambiguous double-tap of a footfall on concrete.

Close by.

* * *

There was a series of three stop-motion images which Daniel was later to play back repeatedly in his mind.

He looked up at the long window which ran the length of the sitting room, separating it from the stoep. A large figure stood in silhouette, looking straight at them, levelling the barrel of an automatic pistol directly, Daniel was convinced, at his head. He would have remained utterly sure of this even if he had known that Andries also believed with total conviction that the barrel was aimed at his own skull.

The second frame was of the two of them standing rooted to the ground watching the flash from the muzzle showing bright and star-like against the darkness of the sky.

And third, both of them coming-to in amazement that neither of them had been hit.

From then on it was pandemonium.

They were through the sitting room door almost instantly, just before the room reverberated from another explosion. Then they were skidding over the floor, across the kitchen and through the second door into the garage. Andries was astride the motorbike within moments, stamping down the kick-start. The engine took first time.

Daniel flung a leg over the pillion and grabbed around Andries' waist with both arms. The file was tucked under his shirt. How he had had the presence of mind to do that, he would never fully understand.

The bike burst through the door, pushing it so violently that it crashed back and then bounced forward again to hit Daniel on the side of his leg as they went past. In the rush of adrenalin he didn't feel it.

But someone else did. As Daniel glanced over his shoulder, he saw the automatic-wielding figure from the stoep hunched over, holding his nose with both hands. He must have collided with the door just as it flew open.

It seemed that the bike was across the lawn in an instant, and then down into the stream bed and off, away, with shouts of fury and further gunshots following their flight. A second, possibly a third man must have joined the first.

There was a shout from Andries in front of him. Daniel couldn't make out the words, so he pushed forward as far as he could. 'Shoot, man!' he heard Andries shout again. 'Use the fucking gun!'

Again! When will I get the hang of this?

Daniel felt down into his groin. It was still there. He pulled it out, turned half backwards as they leapt further up the watercourse, and loosed off two shots in the approximate direction of their pursuers. He congratulated himself that his wrist was still intact, and let off two more. He heard a pane of glass shattering. Goodness knows which one.

This had the temporary effect of subduing any further shots from behind them. When they resumed, Daniel - the newly seasoned firearms expert - confidently told himself that they were more for form than in any realistic expectation of being effective.

They were now some distance from the farm house, and speeding further away, the engine revving and slowing as they alternately flew and grounded in their progress up the increasingly boulder-strewn gully.

Andries abandoned the protection of the ditch. He gunned the bike up and over the lip of the stream onto the open pasture. The bike landed heavily, suspension bottoming and sending a jarring thump up through Daniel's spine. But it was easier after that. The flatter ground allowed greater speed and a slightly easier ride. And before Daniel was really aware of it, Andries had ridden them right up to the road and off again along it to where the car was parked.

'OK, bru,' he said breathlessly. 'That way.' He pointed up the road. 'Keep going straight and you'll get to the main road. Keep your lights off till you're there. Then go like fuck until they won't be able to find you. Cheers, man. See you.'

Daniel was about to say something. Anything. To wish

him well, to wish his father well, to thank him in some fashion. But Andries had revved the engine again and was gone in the other direction, dust kicking up from behind the back wheel, riding arch-backed and bareheaded into the dusk.

Nineteen

Daniel drove steadily until dawn, when a rapidly emptying fuel tank and increasing hunger brought him into the forecourt of an open-all-hours petrol station on the side of the road. He filled up, avoided buying a pastry of apparently the same vintage as those he had shared with the tramp in Musina a week previously, and returned to the car. He sat devouring a chocolate bar, an excessively large packet of crisps and a styrofoam cup of stewed and super-heated coffee, pondering his future movements.

I need to sit down and read that file.

In fact, it wasn't a need so much as a craving he had been desperate to satisfy since driving away from the farm, hoping that his lack of headlights wasn't going to lead him into an axle-bending pothole.

What was it that Patricia found in it? And I desperately need some sleep.

Twice earlier that morning he had found himself believing he could drive while closing just one eye. But at the same time he knew he had to put as much distance as he could between himself and the farmhouse.

Goodness knows who had shot at them as they rode away. It could have been Antjie's men or Ellen's. Whichever it was, Daniel was glad that he wasn't one of them. He wouldn't in the least relish the prospect of explaining to either of those women how the fugitives they had been waiting for had got away. Again.

Better to take the main road north and hope to hide in all the other traffic? Or take the back roads and avoid the large towns until I've put some distance behind me?

He considered one option and then the other, and then reached into the plastic recess near the gearstick, selected a coin and tossed it.

Back roads it is, then.

He started the car, turned wearily out of the forecourt, and resumed his journey north.

* * *

He reached the Orange River at midday at a small town called Prieska. The semi-desert on the approach to the town gave way to a thick band of vegetation either side of the water. Daniel crossed it on a low concrete bridge. The river was in full flood and isolated clumps of trees were being bent downstream by the flow. But despite the water and the greenery, it was unbearably hot. Daniel sped up as he left the town and pressed on.

Hamlet by dorp he felt his way northwards until he chanced upon Kuruman, which, as a mission child, felt an apt place to stop. He was now within striking distance of Johannesburg. And he was dead tired.

But he kept on going, and only after another hour-and-a-half's driving further on did he allow himself to pull over into a small town on the western side of the road.

Following a sign, he turned off the main road and cruised the surrounding streets until he found a small scruffy motel.

What is it? The fourth or the fifth different address since I started south from Musina?

He'd lost count.

* * *

The rooms were set out in pairs in a horseshoe of small semi-detached chalets which curved within a corner bounded by the intersection of two quiet suburban roads. Daniel found his way to a fly-blown office behind a gauze-screened swing door at one end of the line. The thick coiled spring on the side of it screeched as he pulled it open. Inside sat a white woman, late middle-aged, with a face that appeared never to have suffered a smile. Her hair, peroxided beyond redemption, had been pulled back so tightly into a ponytail that it had distorted the skin around her eyes, which looked as if they had the capacity to maim at a thousand yards.

She chewed gum open-mouthed as Daniel completed the register which she pushed at him across the reception counter. It allowed him a gratuitous view of her dentist's artistry.

He enquired after prices. She pointed mutely to a tariff card stuck onto the wall beside her with curling sticky tape so brown with old age that it looked little different from the ancient tight coil of flypaper suspended from the ceiling.

He counted out the notes on the counter and she swept them up, opened a drawer, and locked them away. She rose and left the office. There was not a word of invitation or explanation. Daniel, slightly perplexed, followed her.

She began to walk down the driveway which ran along the inside arc of the line of chalets. She wore a pair of Bermuda shorts too brief for modesty, and a multicoloured shirt which hung draped over a substantial bosom and a belly of similar cantilevered proportions. Her feet were wedged into a pair of fluorescent green fluffy mules two sizes too small. As if winding herself forward along some hidden clockwork railway, she swung the room key slowly and deliberately around a stubby many-ringed index finger as she picked her over-delicate way along the path.

'No visitors,' she said abruptly, as if she had suddenly noticed that he had a troupe of freeloading guests hidden in his car. They were the first recognisable words she had spoken to Daniel since he had arrived. She was standing at the door to his room, holding out the key at arm's length. 'No food in the room,' she continued. 'Unnerstan'?'

She stared at Daniel to ensure he had. He could see the chewing gum held temporarily motionless between her teeth.

He was too tired to react. She dropped the key into his hand, reluctant to make any direct contact, even remotely through the medium of steel and wood. He opened the door and squeezed sideways past her, smiling as sweetly as he could before quietly closing the door on her glare.

Inside, he walked to the window and parted the grubby curtains. He could see both roads where they met at the corner. As he had driven in he had noticed that the gaps between each pair of neighbouring chalets were filled with well established bougainvillea bushes, all in flower and covered by a mass of dark red and purple blooms. His car would not be visible from either road.

Satisfied, he closed the curtains and went to the bathroom to wash away the grime of the previous twenty four hours.

* * *

He sat down on the bed and pulled the manila file towards him, Reclining wearily against the headboard, he began to read.

'Date: 18 June 1982,' he read on a short memo at the front of the file.

'Subject: Nyarai Simango.'

'Above-named referred DST, CSI, SADF to NIS. IA 24 May 1982.'

'II NIS Messina 5 June 1982. Recommendation: further screening.'

'Processed NIS Pta. Initial contact Livingstone 12 June 1982. Engaged 16 June 1982.'

The second page was similarly brief.

'Biography: Born 17 May 1958, near Mt Darwin, Mashonaland. Parents peasant farmers: Baptismal name Mary. Given name Chidiwa. One brother.

Adorable. Her name means adorable. Is she? To her parents, I suppose.

'Educated 1964-1973, St Joseph's Mission, Mt Darwin District. 1974: Left school to join ZANLA in Zambia. Went with ZANLA to Mozambique. Employed cooking/portering duties. 1976: Appointed Party internal security staff. Commissioned Captain ZNA Intelligence Corps, May 1980. Attended Staff College 1981. Acting Major June 1988. Resigned commission ZNA May 1990.'

There was a photograph stapled to the top left hand side of the page. It showed a woman with a strikingly angular face, a strong jaw line bisected by a dead-level pair of compressed lips. She was expressionless, neutral. Her head was uncovered, revealing hair that was neatly braided. She stared out from the photograph from below dark prominent brows.

Daniel scrutinised the photograph but could discern little from it. The face looked younger than someone in her late-30s, but older than he imagined she would have looked aged 24 when she was first 'engaged'. He turned the page.

'Date: 13 June 1982.'

'Subject: Meeting with NS, Livingstone, 12 June 1982.'

'Initial deployment of elements 5 Brigade ZNA, Matabeleland South.'

There followed a detailed description, in military terminology with which Daniel was unfamiliar, of the forthcoming deployment of an army unit, the name of which was only too familiar to him. It sent an involuntary shudder across his shoulders. A training exercise, it appeared to be, and she had known about it in advance. There was a scribbled note at the foot of the page indicating that the actual deployment took place three weeks after the date of the meeting.

Daniel leafed forward through the file. There was a succession of further memoranda along similar lines, referring to subsequent meetings and detailing activities in Matabeleland which must have been eagerly dissected at the time, judging by the length and detail with which the conversations were recorded.

As Diedricks had joked, the meetings increased in frequency until they were dated about a fortnight apart, give or take, and appeared mostly to have been held in Livingstone, on the Zambian side of the Victoria Falls border. Although, as Daniel paged further into the file, he noticed that the hotel on the other side of the border was more frequently the venue.

A sign of increasing complacency, perhaps, to meet so openly. Perhaps not. Perhaps it was easier to explain away meetings there than a constant crossing of borders, for one party at least.

Who knows how these decisions are arrived at...

He paged on through the minutes of meetings during the first months of 1983. Detailed descriptions of the rampage of the Fifth Brigade through the northern part of Matabeleland, moving across the countryside like beaters on a grouse moor, driving civilians before them by the tens and hundreds towards collective mass beatings and random executions.

Time and again, atrocities were recorded in numbing repetition. Vivid memories were waking in Daniel's mind, of the kind he had been diligent in forgetting over the intervening years. He was caught between a desperate repulsion and the mesmerising horror conjured up by the blankness of the prose.

He paged forward, giving each new sheet of paper a cursory examination. There was nothing further that caught his eye until the reports began to be dated from the start of the subsequent year. 1984.

* * *

FOOD EMBARGO, one page was titled.

This appeared to be a précis of several of her reports, rather than the near-verbatim transcripts of individual meetings in the first part of the file. Daniel read the first paragraph.

'February to April 1984. 24 hour curfew imposed in

Matabeleland South. Entire civilian population (est. 450 000) restricted to within 50m of their own dwellings. All forms of transport forbidden. No movement of food allowed into the curfew area. No food allowed to circulate. Stores closed. Drought relief stopped, despite a fourth consecutive drought year. Population reduced to eating grass, insects and wild fruit...'

Daniel closed his eyes, and breathed in deeply. After a few moments he flipped further through the file.

Another page, this one headed by one single word:

BHALAGWE

Daniel closed his eyes again and then turned the file upside down onto the bed beside him.

He rose and walked to the window. Parting the curtains, he looked out. Although the afternoon was very well advanced, there was still inviting sunlight.

He returned to the bed and picked up the file. He marked his place by folding over the corner of the page, closed the folder, and then slid it carefully into the back-pack. He looked at the rest of his meagre travelling possessions.

Leave? Take?

He was tempted to leave them where they were and sort them out when he returned.

Don't be lazy. Pack it up and take it.

He packed everything into the second bag, swung the back-pack over his shoulder, turned off the light and left the room. He turned, locked it after himself and walked to his car.

Who knows, I might just be able to find a secluded spot where I can resume reading. But first I need to settle my stomach. And my mind.

* * *

There wasn't very much choice of shops. In fact no choice at all. He found himself leaving yet another corner shop with a large soggy packet of limp fat-soaked chips and a bottle of milk. He wasn't looking forward to the meal. But it was better than one of the alternatives - a diminutive fowl of indeterminate species which was rotating sadly on a rotisserie in the window.

He got back into his car and drove aimlessly for a few minutes, searching for somewhere where he could stop and resume his reading. But the light was disappearing quickly, and eventually he turned and drove back in the direction of the motel. There at least, he thought, he could sit comfortably, even if his reading material was offensive.

He drove up one of the streets alongside the motel, and as he went slowly past he glanced over to the chalet in which his room was situated. His neck prickled with alarm. In the mellow light of dusk, it was difficult to be definite, but Daniel could have sworn that there was a light on in his room.

Did I leave the light on? I'm sure I didn't...

He reversed, and stopped a little further back up the street, where he still had a view of the window.

The curtain moved.

That bloody curtain moved. I looked out, but I never opened the window, so it can't be the wind. Is it the manageress in there, tidying up? No. She's not the type. Snooping, maybe? Unlikely. A maid? Not at this time of the evening, surely. Considering the state of the room when I walked in, it would be the first time a maid has visited in weeks...

He reversed the car still further away and sat watching the street ahead of him. The entrance to the motel was close. He went through the possibilities.

If there's someone in the room – I'm as sure of that as I can be - they won't have arrived on foot. So when they leave, they'll leave via the entrance. Which means it's a 50-50 chance, on the best construction, that they will turn towards me...

They won't be there long. There's nothing to find. And – dammit – there's nothing left in the room to indicate I might return. The one time that laziness might have been better.

No point hanging around. Best to take advantage of their temporary stop-over in my room, and put as much distance as I can between them and me.

He turned the ignition and drove as fast as he could without attracting attention to the main road, turned on to it, and pushed on further north.

Twenty

It had to be the security police, or drug squad, or whatever they were, he decided a few miles up the road.

Who else could have tracked me down to that dusty motel in that one-corner-shop town? It had to have been the car that gave me away. But did they follow me, or did they take a call from the motel's manageress

He relived his journey from Cape Town to the farm, and then from the farm onwards, again and again in his mind, but he couldn't fix on anything.

However they did it, that's in the past. I have to press on. I have to duck beneath their sight and disappear.

Both Antjie and Ellen knew I crossed the border near Beitbridge. So stay clear of there. No more 'travelling light' over the Limpopo. I can't even play a decent game of office politics at St Botolph's, never mind a bout of double-bluff for keeps. And since it's Antjie on my heels – it has to be her - the stakes have risen. She's far more capable of tracking me down than Ellen could ever wish to be...

He'd need to change the car. Then he'd need to take the different car across a border. He was increasingly sure of that. But if they had traced him this far, they could easily stop him from crossing openly through any border post. So he would have to do it without them knowing. And it's one thing crossing the border line. It would be stupid to be caught later without the right papers. So he had to find a town big enough to host a rental company that would let him take their car across the frontier.

He did the arithmetic.

Two and a half, maybe three hours to Johannesburg, if I keep clear of the speed traps. Surely I can lose myself more easily somewhere around there than out here in the boondocks. But if not Beitbridge, where do I cross?

Somewhere along the line he had to fit in time to read the rest of the file. And also get some sleep. Finding his eyes starting to wander from the road again, he opened the window. He let his face be blasted by the gathering coolness of the darkening air outside.

It was mid evening and pitch black as he approached the outer fringes of Johannesburg from the south west. Or it would have been pitch black were it not for the extended line in the distance on the right hand side of the road glowing an acidic industrial orange against the horizon. He turned north and kept driving until the road entered a ravine formed by vast mine dumps, spectral tiered ziggurats on either side of the road. Then the light from the street lamps changed from yellow to white and the surroundings from razor-wired compounds to suburban bungalows in the outskirts of Krugersdorp.

He saw a roadside sign advertising one of a chain of business hotels. Having located it, he drove past it for five minutes. He abandoned the car near the pavement of a side street. He locked it, and was about to lay the keys on top of a front tyre, a small gesture of convenience for the hire company when they eventually found it. But he changed his mind.

Act as if you're coming back.

He opened the back-pack and pulled out Patricia's jersey, and a couple of sheets of paper. He left them prominently on display on the top of the dashboard.

Taking the keys with him, he walked back in the direction he had come from until he reached the hotel.

He booked in, hoping that this time he might get a full night's rest.

* * *

He woke mid-morning, twelve hours later, toasted into consciousness by shafts of strong sunlight streaming in through the window. He sat staring at the wall for a few moments, then pulled the back-pack towards him, pulled out the manila folder, and, turning to the dog-eared page, resumed his reading.

BHALAGWE

Just the word provoked a physical reaction. He had never been to the place, but Daniel felt the skin on his forearms prickling again, the muscles at the back of his thighs tightening. His throat constricted slightly and he thought he was about to gag. He swallowed, composed himself, and read on.

'The base of a battalion of 1 Brigade ZNA (1:7) until mid-1982. Elements 1:7 Bn were accused of disloyalty. The base was shut down by force (July? 1982). Thereafter it has been used as a detention and processing centre for dissident sympathisers.'

Disloyalty? Those soldiers weren't guilty of disloyalty. They were guilty of being from the wrong tribe. Everyone knew that. And detention and processing? Abduction and torture, that's what it was. Nothing but weasel words. Weasel words to hide the truth.

No. Not correct. Not hiding the truth at all. No-one – neither those who spoke them nor those who heard them - believed those words. But by using them, the powerful were underlining their total control: 'We can say whatever we want, and there's nothing at all you can do about it.'

Daniel thought back to those long months working at the hospital. The severely injured and maimed, some who would have had to crawl in had they not been carried in by relatives. All terrified of being picked up again, warned by their tormentors that to seek treatment for their wounds was to risk death.

Civilians with broken limbs, violated genitals, burst eardrums, blinded eyes. And those countless people, unable to walk or even sit properly, who'd been beaten repeatedly on the buttocks until their flesh was a pulp. Just like Patricia. And when prompted for details, more and more often just one word was whispered: Bhalagwe.

He read on.

'Bhalagwe is the central camp. There are sub-camps at Sun Yet Sen, Plumtree, Sitiza, Silobela and other places in the west. Detainees are processed by 5 Bde from their districts to the sub-camps, and then on to Bhalagwe. They are routinely beaten on their way to the sub-camps, again at the sub-camps, and then on arrival and afterwards at Bhalagwe. The sub-camps and Bhalagwe are administered by CIO and 5 Bde.'

The words on the paper were more conversational now, less bureaucratic.

Was this Diedricks' writing relaxing into something less formal? Or were they her words, this Simango woman's, transcribed verbatim?

He flipped back to her photograph, but he could glean nothing from it.

Daniel thought back to the image that had formed in his mind when he had first started reading the file.

When was that?

He sorted his movements in his mind.

The day before – Monday - in that dirty motel in that god-forsaken town.

Beaters. Drivers on a shoot, pushing the targets before them. That had been in the north of the province. Now the beaters had moved south, and were doing it again. But it was no longer random. There was a system. They were driving their captives before them into a process, sub-camp to centre, Sun Yet Sen and elsewhere to Bhalagwe.

The words echoed from Daniel's childhood.

Sitiza, Silobela, Plumtree. Far off districts, but someone always knew someone, however remote they were. Distant mission stations, exotic names for lonely settlements. Sun Yet Sen? How did that name travel so far to be dropped into the Matabeleland bush, the given name of a hamlet next to an isolated mine called something entirely different. And what about Brunapeg, Empandeni and Embakwe? They had also had their share of trouble, but they weren't mentioned here. Or were they just included in 'other places in the west of the country'?

'On arrival, detainees are segregated by district, and occupation, and sex. All documents on their persons are taken from them. Then they are interrogated, with regular beatings. There are deaths, every day and every night. The bodies were buried in the camp at first, by burial parties of detainees. But later those bodies were removed, and now they are taken away immediately after death. Not buried at

Bhalagwe. Some are buried in mass graves elsewhere. Some have been thrown into disused mines. Up to 10 000 individuals in total could have been processed through Bhalagwe.'

Daniel turned the page. He glanced at it, and then turned to the next one, and again, and again. Page after photocopied page. The originals had been printed with faint horizontal lines, as if from a primary school exercise book. Vertical columns had been imprecisely ruled by hand. The columns were filled with family names, then first names, then districts, then ID numbers for some, but not all. And dates. At the end of each row was a date.

What were these names? Were they those that had entered the camp, or those that didn't leave alive?

Daniel flipped through the photocopied pages, counting them.

Twenty five names to a page. If there had been anywhere near 10 000 individuals brought to Bhalagwe, then the names on these pages wouldn't account for more than a fraction of them. So were there pages missing, or were these the lot? And the dates? Dates of entry? Dates of exit? Or dates of death?

Daniel began to search through them. Since the dates were consecutive, there was no alphabetic order to the names. He had to read each line. On the fourth page he found what he had expected and feared.

'Hove, Gilbert,' the handwriting spelled out. 'Bulilimamangwe District' There was an ID number.

Was that his? No easy way for him to check. But the date. '15 March 1984.' That fitted. And how many Gilbert Hove's could there be?

Daniel remembered it as clearly as if it had happened the

week before. 1984 had been a leap year. At the hospital he'd been the butt of much teasing that a nurse in obstetrics he had been dating was going to propose on the 29th February. But whether that had been her plan or not, it didn't happen. His mother had phoned in tears the day before and told him that his father had gone missing.

So this must be what Patricia found. Finally, confirmation of what we suspected had happened to him. Confirmation of sorts, anyway. Last known whereabouts, if not more than that.

He paged further until he reached the end of the photocopied lists. There were a few more transcripts of meetings with the Simango woman, and, then, four pages stapled together.

All maps, detailed maps with small circles, hand-drawn with red marker pen at various positions. Daniel looked at them in turn, paging backwards and forwards.

The pages are adjoining. Or rather they should be..

He let them fall back like playing cards in one half of a casino shuffle until he was at the front of the folder. He undid the fastenings, removed the pages before the maps, and placed them carefully on the floor next to the bed. He extracted the four map pages, put the folder with the remaining contents aside, and using his fingernail bent open the staple holding them together at one corner. Then he laid them next to each other on the bed beside him, moving the pages until the features and gridlines met at each edge. They formed a rectangle, two pages in a row above the other two.

He peered at them intently. They portrayed the area south of Gwanda which he had twice visited. The road to the border ran from top left to bottom right. The intersection with the bisecting dirt road was clear. So was St Cuthberts mission, on the left hand map in the bottom row.

He picked up that map, which seemed to contain more red markings than the others, and examined it more closely. Many, though not all, of the red circles were at places which were also marked with the same tiny symbol.

He checked the bottom of the map. There was a partial list of symbols there. But he knew before he looked. The tiny marks on the map were the symbols for mines. Hammer and pick, crossed. Mine shafts. The red circles, most of them, were marking mine shafts.

Something was niggling in the back of his mind, a connection he was struggling to make.

There was a pattern. A familiar pattern. An arrangement, rather.

There was something in the placing of lines and symbols on the maps that he recognised. He grabbed the blue back-pack and fished out the leather document case.

He pulled it open and shuffled through its contents until he found the sheet that had mystified everyone, the sheet with the crosses and the oblique lines. He unfolded it and held it over the maps. The sheet of paper was too opaque to see through. He went to the window and held the sheet and one of the maps – the one showing St Cuthberts - up to the light. He shifted one over the other, seeking a match. And then he had it.

The crosses on Patricia's sheet of paper, and the circles on the map beneath it, began to coincide. A diagonal line on Patricia's sheet of paper ran exactly over the road marked on the map below it. The line she had drawn bisecting it coincided with the other bisecting road on the map.

There were two crosses north of the main road, matching

the mine symbols on the map beneath. It suddenly made sense. She had traced the necessary details - enough detail to navigate by, using the minimum of information - from the map to her sheet of paper.

To part of her piece of paper...

Daniel picked up one of the other maps – the other sheet from the bottom row.

Daniel looked again at her marks.

Three more crosses south of the line...

Daniel looked at the second map. The three southern circles to which her crosses corresponded were grouped roughly together, beyond another boundary line which ran parallel, more or less, with the bottom edge of the map, and which was also reflected on her tracing.

It was the boundary between the communal lands and the farm. It marked the fence along which he – and she, presumably - had walked, and through which he – and she - had ducked. The division between us and them, as described by Father Barnabas. The boundary over which her body had been unceremoniously dumped.

She copied down the circles on the maps, most for mine shafts and others for what purpose? Who knows...?

He knew. He went back to the pages of text. 'Some were buried in mass graves elsewhere. Some were thrown into disused mines.'

These red circles marked the positions of mass graves, in mine shafts and elsewhere. She had copied them. She had made a graphic list of mass graves. Three of them were on that farm. Daniel himself had walked close to one of them. The boy Themba had warned him against stumbling into others.

Was one of them the last resting place of Gilbert Hove?

* * *

Daniel sat on the bed with his back against the wall, staring into space.

Was that why Patricia was murdered? Because she found out where the bodies were buried? That doesn't make sense. As Diedricks said, everyone connected with those crimes was given immunity. They aren't considered criminals. Not in the Party, not in law. They probably aren't even troubled by their own consciences. So why?

He sat thinking. And then he had it.

It wasn't what she knew. It's how she knew it.

They hadn't seen her drawings, her tracings from the maps. Those had been hidden in the cleft in the rock with everything else. But Simango must have suspected.

Did they pick her up near one of these graves? Had she been killed as Simango tried to find out how she knew what she knew? Or when she found out how she knew?

No wonder Diedricks is so sure Simango will be at the hotel. She must be desperate to ask him about this file. The file he told her he had destroyed.

Daniel picked up the folder and went over to the window. The light was better and he stood there reading.

The pages were now taken up with political discussions. He leafed through them. Profiles of individuals in the party, discussions of policy, gossip, rumour and analysis.

How many cabinet ministers, speculated a two-page treatment, were being encouraged to toe the party line by the threat of the withdrawal of their regular state-sponsored cocktail of anti-retrovirals?

Another piece of gossip reported that one party loyalist, a policeman on the make who Daniel remembered from years before as having a particularly vicious reputation, listed his pastimes in the force's magazine as bird-watching and golf.

A report from Harare's overactive rumour mill considered the identity of the man currently filling the role of First Boyfriend to the presidential spouse.

How such knowledge furthered the strategic advantage of a neighbouring state, Daniel couldn't fathom. And he could find no further mention of events in Matabeleland. It was as if the whole subject had been forgotten, as if it had never happened.

He reached the end of the file. Almost the end. Right at the back was an envelope made of stout brown card, secured shut with a piece of thin twine wound around a fibre disk riveted to the flap. It was clipped into the file, so he removed all the pages on top of it and then the envelope itself.

Once freed, he opened it and withdrew a few pages stapled together. They had been typed on a manual typewriter, the lines of slightly unsteady words seeming somehow archaic and outdated, so remote in time as to be worthless.

But the further Daniel read, the more transfixed he became. And then, attached to the final page, a photograph. Faded colours. Smaller than the picture of Nyarai Simango at the beginning of the file, and taken without the subjects, a group of five men, being aware of being photographed. But most of the figures in the picture were incidental to its purpose.

On that final sheet of paper, typed just below where the

photograph was fixed, one individual was identified by name. It was the figure just to the left of centre, and as he read the name Daniel's mouth fell open in horror. He swore and then looked again at the picture. There was no error, no room for doubt.

He shouted, the force of it surprising him. He swung round, his fists punching into the cupboard door as hard as he could swing them. Then he found himself at rest, his forehead against the wood supporting his weight. He was breathing hard, his fists were smarting. If he had been asked, Daniel would have been hard-pressed to say how much of what he felt then was anger, how much frustration, and how much a gathering sense, if not of triumph, then of the direction to it.

He picked up his phone and called his mother.

Twenty One

D aniel walked, ill-at-ease, down a wide gallery clad in marble and plastic-coated brass, back taut with tension, convinced he was about to feel the cold grip of an official hand on his shoulder. The mall was thronged with shoppers and he scanned each group as they passed him, trying to identify which of them were about to arrest him.

He had started out from his hotel earlier that afternoon. Like a criminal drawn back to the scene of his crime, he had found himself returning to the street where he had abandoned the car the night before. He could see from some distance that it was still parked where he had left it. Not stolen. Not towed away. He could also see, parked on the other side of the street and facing away from him, another car. Inside it, he could clearly see three men. Three men, he thought. Two men? Probably innocent. Three men? What on earth could three men be doing here except on some kind of mission?

And then a fourth man walked out from behind the car he had abandoned, crossed the street, and joined the three others. Daniel was immediately chilled. He had turned and walked away, and kept walking until he found this shopping mall, which itself did little to settle his nerves.

Perhaps it'll be mall security who'll detain me?

The bright yellow plastic handgrips of a substantial pair of boltcutters were sticking out of the top of the blue backpack slung over his shoulder. They felt to Daniel like a beacon designed solely to attract the attention of the centre's bouncers. It wasn't the boltcutters themselves that were the particular cause of his jitters. He could easily prove that he had just bought them in a hardware shop further back down this particular walkway. And he was confident he could persuade them he wasn't planning an assault on a jeweller's window.

But only a slightly more diligent investigation would have revealed the revolver and ammunition sitting heavily at the bottom of his bag. He was acutely aware of the weight bouncing against his back: unlicensed, inexplicable, and easily proven to have been used in at least two recent incidents of public violence - one of them almost certainly against officers of the state.

He could think of little else in the print shop on the tier below the one along which he was now walking. He had stood nervously wondering which would have been worse – to have the revolver unearthed in such a public place, or to have the sales assistant start reading the pile of documents he had asked her to copy.

He had thought hard several times about abandoning the weapon and ammunition. He couldn't stop himself thinking about abandoning them. But each time he'd decided to stick to his plan. He would keep them until the task he had set himself was finished.

When it's done. If it's done. Not until then...

He did the same in the print shop, promising to get rid of it as soon as he was able. But neither of his imagined catastrophes took place. He'd walked out of the shop with two copies of Diedricks' file stuffed with the original into the bag, on top of the pistol and bullets.

His next stop before the hardware shop had been a stationers', where he purchased two very large strong padded envelopes, and a smaller plain one. There was a small cafe nearby where he had ordered coffee, and used the table to assemble his packages.

He placed one of the copies of the file into the plain envelope and sealed it. He then slid that envelope into one of the padded bags, and addressed it to the solicitor who had handled his divorce. He inserted a note asking the lawyer to hold the inner envelope for him until he returned. And instructions as to how to dispose of its contents should he not return by the end of the month.

Safety harness. And now the bait. At least, the first part of it...

Into the other envelope he fed the original version of the file. On top of it he placed the final rendering of a two page memo which he had composed from several drafts in his hotel room. In it he had set down the details, as they were burned into his memory, of the pre-arranged meeting on the following Friday at the hotel in Victoria Falls.

The following Friday? Three days...

On the outside of the envelope he wrote an address in large block capitals. He didn't know whether the address was strictly accurate, but he was sure it would get there, and from there to the addressee. The question was, would it get to him in time?

And now he had to find a courier to deliver the envelopes for him. With some relief he escaped to the outside of the mall, the doors closing with a bang on the disagreeable atmosphere he left behind, which appeared to consist entirely of some gaseous form of sugar. It took him half an hour of walking before he found what he was looking for.

He gave a false name on the paperwork, and had to bite his tongue when the clerk, like the priest at a wedding, recited the impediments to shipment before he sealed the envelopes. 'Are you aware of any firearms, explosives, or banned goods of any kind in this consignment ...?' The clerk pointed absently at a poster listing the contraband items.

Close, but not close enough, Daniel thought, as the clerk stamped it and gave him the bill for a small fortune. He could feel the weight in the small of his back even more intensely.

Finally, the last item on the afternoon's shopping list.

On the edge of town, a few streets further on from the courier - secluded, Daniel was relieved to find - was a car rental company. He glanced nervously at the sun before he entered. He wouldn't have the luxury of hanging around. He would need to get on his way, and minimise the chance of his tracks being picked up again. He could almost feel them getting closer. He had to move quickly.

There was a woman at the counter when he entered, and he had to wait, each minute ticking agonisingly by. He sauntered over, as composedly as he could manage, to a set of shelves against a wall. He casually perused the contents - as casually as was possible given his total alertness as to progress at the counter. He picked up a tourist guide to the countryside to the west of him. The maps were very detailed. He flicked from page to page. Surprisingly detailed. They confirmed what he remembered. Behind him he heard the salesman thank the woman.

He turned, smiling broadly, and went to the counter. This is where the whole thing collapses, he thought. This is definitely where they grab me.

'I want to rent a 4x4,' he said. 'To travel across the border. Can I do that?'

I'm stammering. I must be. Mumbling. They'll say no. And then what? Try and use the abandoned car again, and make it dead easy for them to follow me? Assuming I can even get near it again...

If he had been stammering, the salesman was too polite to betray he had noticed. 'Certainly, sir,' he said. 'Where do you wish to travel to?'

The process took no time at all. Paperwork completed, signed and stamped. Only one hitch. He couldn't pay in cash. Or rather, he didn't have enough to pay for it all. Which meant he had to use his credit card. Which meant he had to use his real name. Which meant he would have to move fast.

He settled himself into the truck, a sturdy vehicle he was confident would be able to travel off-road. Boltcutters on the floor, backpack on the seat beside him, map wedged into the dashboard in front of him. Badza handle on the...? Left in the other car. Probably for the best. And a manual gearbox.

He turned the ignition, pulled down the sun-visor, and headed towards the setting sun.

* * *

Three hours driving later he pulled over, consulted his map, and then headed north. Another hour and a half, his speed reduced as the road narrowed and the light disappeared, and he was approaching the border with Botswana. He kept looking to his right, until he saw the fence change from the standard three-strand cattle fence to the much more substantial game barrier – three times as high and ten times stronger, square mesh reinforced with huge tubular steel supports and braces, a row of large stones marking where it was dug into the earth.

There he slowed still further, coasting easily through the night, tyres ringing on the tarmac.

Just before the final approach to the border-post he stopped at an intersection. He peered at the signboard, checked the map again, swung the wheel. Right turn. The game fence turned with him. Ahead, dark black against the horizon, a conical-shaped hill.

They had come here on honeymoon. Several secluded days in a lodge not far way. Cost a fortune, more than they could really afford. They had been driven along this road, and he remembered the hill.

He drove towards it, keeping his speed down. The road was flanked on each side by wide swathes of crumbly gravel littered with small stones. The light from his headlights transformed it into a lunar scene. Once or twice he saw tiny buildings, dimly lit, on the left hand side of the road. On the other side of the border. To the right, thick bushveld behind the game fence.

The road veered slightly to the right. The hill disappeared to his left. He was suddenly alarmed. And then another hill swung into view in front of him. Another conical hill, a carbon copy of the first. He remembered - the same thing had happened before. The road was now running close alongside the border. Game fence to the right, then the road, and to his left the border itself. The only things marking it were a few strands of wire that wouldn't have delayed a mouse. He kept going, still aiming at the hill ahead of him.

He drew closer to it. The road began to swing further to the right, describing an enormous circle as it skirted the foot of the sharply rising ground to his left. Half way around he saw the thatched covered entrance to the game park. A spotlight hidden in the rafters shone down from within it, making the structure appear to glow.

He drove past it and continued until the road completed its half circle around the conical hill. A few hundred yards further on he pulled over onto the side of the road, turned his lights off, and sat, adjusting his eyesight to the dark and his ears to the soft night noises of the African bush.

* * *

He sat for half an hour. Half an hour that felt like half a day. No traffic passed in either direction. There were still lights that he could see flickering on the Botswana side, but much fewer than there had been when he stopped.

It was now past midnight. He eased open the door. The interior light came on. He hurriedly pulled the door closed again and spent several minutes working out how to stop it happening again. He warily opened the door a second time. This time the light stayed off.

He stepped out and walked across the gravel to the fence, semi-hidden among low thorn bushes and dry sproutings of grass. He gazed over it. Some places were more heavily vegetated than others. But he was sure he could get the truck through the more sparsely covered gaps through the bush.

He returned to the truck, brought out the boltcutters and walked over to the nearest steel fence post. He paused.

Another point of no return. Another entry on the charge sheet.

He cut the top strand, clipping it as easily as if he was pruning a hedge. It sprang away, more or less silently. He severed the next two strands. They bounced away after the first. Then the final, bottom strand. It parted neatly. The fence post fell back.

No sirens, no searchlights, no barking dogs, no shots.

Nothing.

Just the chirp and rustle and muted clatter of insects and small mammals going about their nocturnal business.

He walked over to the wires where they lay twisted in released tension several feet away and dragged them clear. Then he was back in the truck and gently feeling his way, driving lightless again, across the frontier, disappearing quickly from the sight of anyone who might pass along the road behind him.

. The steering wheel seemed to have a life of its own. He could only set a general direction, and then it was jerking his hands this way and that. He winced occasionally as he imagined the effect on the paintwork of the thorn branches scraping along the bodywork as he forced the truck through tight openings in the scrub. Once or twice the tyres failed to grip. But he kept the revs low, and kept pushing the vehicle forward, the dark form of the hill to his left.

And just as he was beginning to despair, he came across the road he had hoped would be there. More a wide path, really, but better than what he been fighting through. He turned left on to it and immediately felt a sense of achievement. He was on his way. He was over the border. And now he needed to get a move on. A real move on.

* * *

He was sixth in line at the next borderpost that morning,

waiting for the gates to open. He was more nervous now than he had been cutting the fence five hours before. He went through his papers again. The insurance was valid. The ownership papers for the truck were valid. The rental agreement was valid. But his passport wasn't. Or at least it didn't have an entry stamp. As far as his passport showed, he hadn't entered Botswana.

Do they check for that? Can't remember. Not if my life depended on it. And what else don't I have? There must be some paper or other that I would have had if I had entered by the normal route.

A guard swung open the gate. The cars filed through and parked. By the time Daniel got inside, there were a dozen or more people in front of him. The queue edged forward.

Please. An official with a hangover. Please, oh please. Someone whose brain is still addled, not thinking straight.

Another two to go.

Another one.

He approached the counter, documents greasy from the sweat of his fingers. He looked up. The official was looking straight at him, clear-eyed, fully *compos mentis*.

Couldn't be more alert if he was on amphetamines. On tik. Let's hope he hasn't got a dose of paranoia. He doesn't look like a junkie. Oh Jesus, here we go...

The official leafed through the rental documents. He made a note on a pad of paper beside him, thick blue ballpoint letters on cheap porous paper. Daniel craned to see the writing.

Makes no sense. What does it mean?

Flap. Flap. Flap. Flap.

Page-flipping. Same old page-flipping. He's looking for the entry stamp. Shit. He's looking for that bloody stamp.

The official reversed direction. Flap. Flap. Flap.

He's DEFINITELY looking for it. He thinks he missed it the first time. But he won't find it. What do I bloody well say now?

Two official fingers held the passport open. One page had already been used. The other was blank. The official's other hand reached across in front of him.

Thump.

His rubber stamp came down neatly on the blank page. He filled in the date with his blue ball-point. Then a reference number. Then he tore the top sheet off the pad at his side, stamped it and handed it to Daniel, stuck like a bookmark in his passport. Daniel gripped it tightly in his hand.

He must have rooted himself to the ground, because the official stared at him disdainfully and pointed over Daniel's shoulder.

'Over there,' the bored voice muttered at him from across the counter. 'Customs.'

As he walked away, Daniel opened his passport and glanced at the slip of paper. The writing, incomprehensible when Daniel had tried to read it upside down, was the truck's registration number. It was the gate pass.

* * *

Daniel joined the second queue.

Whatever happens, they mustn't search the truck. It'll only take them two minutes and then it'll be jail for a very long time. No talking your way out of what they'll find.

The second official, elbow resting wearily on his counter,

beckoned him forward with a contemptuous wave of his hand. He too flapped his way through Daniel's passport until he found the first official's stamp. He endorsed it, and then looked dully at Daniel.

Daniel looked uncomprehendingly back at him.

The official clicked his fingers. 'Pass,' he demanded, irritated.

Daniel handed it over, smiling apologetically. It was stamped and returned to him. And that was that. He couldn't quite believe it. He was through. Or he would be as soon as he could get past the boom.

He joined the queue of cars at the checkpoint. Slowly they edged forward. Daniel reached the front. He held the pass at arm's length through his window. The guard peered forward, checking the number plate against the pass and then raised the boom to let him through. Daniel followed the exit onto the road and then followed its arrow-straight path to the border itself.

A short single-span bridge crossed the river, its brilliant white water-starved sand reflecting the glare of the early morning sun straight into his eyes. Then another stretch of tar through no-man's land, before he reached the border post on the Zimbabwe side.

Daniel felt his anxiety levels rising again.

Is my name on a list? Will they search the truck? Will they this, would they that, what if...?

For the genuine commercial traveller it is an annoying, tedious occupational hazard. For the bona fide tourist it is irksome bureaucracy larded up with licensed daylight robbery. Daniel, being neither, spent the next hour in a state of enhanced nervous tension.

First immigration.

His visa, single entry, valid for five days, was issued with little hindrance, except for the exorbitant cost and the time it took for the immigration officer to take his cash away and return with the correct notes in change. And all while those in the queue behind him looked at him accusingly. Too late, Daniel saw the notice above the hatch. He should have tendered the exact amount.

Then he took his turn in a succession of other queues. Third party insurance to be purchased, road tax to be paid, a contribution – compulsory - to an environmental enhancement fund.

I bet that the only environment that enhances is the one immediately surrounding some minister or other.

This to be forked-out for, that to be surrendered, and each time his passport and papers were scrutinised in detail.

What am I hiding? Guilty, even if innocent.

By the time he collected the last stamp and left the building clutching a sheaf of papers, his nerves were shredded and it was an hour and a half later. He would have been ranting at the unplanned-for raid on his finances and the offences against his dignity had he not been overwhelming relieved to be walking out of the door without wearing handcuffs. There was that, at least.

Another hour to go.

Twenty Two

T he wall surrounding the property stood out from the others lining both sides of the road.

Alone among them, it confidently displayed no advertisement of a subscription to an armed-response security service. There was no enamelled sign tacked to the gate, as on several others Daniel had driven past, warning in three languages and a comic-book sketch of the presence of a many-fanged attack dog. Unlike the neighbouring walls, there were no trees with overhanging branches by which the casual housebreaker might gain access.

The wall was also distinguished by its lack of embellishment, unusual in this suburb. No tawdry colour scheme, no wrought-iron flourishes, no rustic picket fences pre-cast in concrete.

It was topped by a slim tube of fresh-from-the-factory razor wire, the unpaid bill for which the suppliers had finally decided it would be imprudent to pursue. Just behind the coil, the tensioned strands of a motion-detection alarm were supported by delicate upright wands – an extravagance none of the surrounding householders had risen to. The invoices for this had also been discarded, unopened.

There was a gate engineered with little finesse from rampart-thick wooden planks supported on a heavy steel frame, built to roll back behind the adjacent stretch of wall on the command of a remote control. There was no street number to be seen. It was what it was, built to deter enquiries and intrusion.

If you don't know who lives here, it's none of your business. Move on.

Daniel wiped his brow.

He had covered the last stretch from the border in record time. The full heat of the day had by then yet to build, so the driving was bearable as long as he kept the window open. He had driven into Bulawayo through the smut-encrusted industrial sites, fences and telephone lines festooned here and there with greying plastic bags like Christmas bunting. The roads were busy, the pavements filled with pedestrians. It felt good to be back. Or it did until he had driven south of the city and found his way to this fortification. Now, having stopped, the heat was having an effect. Daniel looked along the length of the wall.

Andries would have had a plan by now. Over it. Under it. Around it.

He considered the rocks from which it was constructed. They were huge, bound together by shape and cement to make a barrier two feet thick and ten feet high. He remembered the wall around the Cape Town mansion.

Probably not through it.

He checked the paper on which he had written the address, and then craned his neck sideways towards the entrance to the property next door. The numbers differed by two digits.

This has to be it.

There was a button on a steel post to the side of the culvert over the storm-water drain. He engaged a gear and turned off the road. Leaning out of the window he pressed it, and waited.

And waited. There was no intercom. He could hear

nothing that indicated any response from beyond the gate.

CaNRU, here we go again.

He pressed the button once more. This time there was an impatient grunt from within. The gate rumbled back a few inches and a butcher's slab of a man in shiny shoes, a shinier suit and reflective Ray-Bans stepped through the gap.

He walked over to the truck. His full heavily-pitted cheeks glistened with sweat below the sunglasses. The sheer bulk of his chest forced his arms to curl away from his torso. His shoulder muscles bypassed his neck completely to merge directly with his head. As a result, the yellowing buttoned-up collar of his shirt was strained horizontally just below his ears.

He stared down at Daniel. Daniel looked back up at him over the top of his glasses. 'Is the doctor in?' he asked.

'Wait,' the man appeared to say. He turned his back on Daniel, pulling a mobile phone from his pocket as he moved away. As he stood with the phone pressed to his ear, Daniel could see the fabric of his suit being stretched by the bulge of muscles on his upper arm. The conversation was brief. But not brief enough to prevent something in Daniel's memory from being stirred.

The man turned back, his face, or that part of it which Daniel could see, still frozen, impassive. He pointed his arm at the gate. It rumbled back noisily. He grunted, swaying his head slightly in the direction of the entrance. Daniel drove slowly behind him as the man walked ponderously up the driveway. He could have been the chief mourner in a funeral cortege.

* * *

Daniel sat on the edge of a leather armchair staring, unblinkingly, out at the view. The house stood on a low ridge above a wide valley thick with trees. Just below the top of the opposite slope he could see another large residence partly visible behind lichen-stained granite boulders, ochre on grey. He supposed there were equally large houses to either side of him, but he couldn't see them. They had all been well hidden behind rocky cascades and abundant foliage, natural and strategically placed, to create the illusion of seclusion.

The armchair was one of a circle of chairs and sofas set in a circle around a large low square table on an open terrace. The terrace sat partly beneath one corner of the high-beamed thatched roof which covered the house. Sliding doors of polished hardwood and gleaming plate glass joined it to spacious sitting rooms within. A drinks' cabinet occupied one corner of the terrace, from which Daniel's interim host had produced a dripping glass of ice cold beer, before disappearing back into the house, leaving Daniel to wait alone for his employer's return.

It was an alluring view. A second narrow terrace just below where he sat was covered with a plumped-up lawn, closely-trimmed, brilliant green. This vibrant band of colour led in turn on to the greys, browns and occasional splashes of olive drab of the indigenous bush spread out below a cloudless powder blue sky.

Despite the dark shadow thrown by the thatch, the bright light of the sun appeared to be totally diffused, coming simultaneously from everywhere and nowhere in particular.

Daniel looked up at the wall next to him. Hung from it was a large semi-abstract painting in oils of Matabeleland granite boulders entwined by the gnarled roots of a native fig. The hue of blue showing through the branches of the painted tree precisely matched the sky above. Like the view in front of him, it was a scene of perfect contentment. Except for the single strand of contorted barbed wire sketched across the bottom of the canvas.

He felt a tremor work through his hands.

* * *

There was a sudden grind of rollers as the wood and glass door behind Daniel trundled back. He turned towards it.

Henry Mliswa emerged from within and advanced towards him, arms outstretched in an extravagant welcome. 'Daniel!' he exclaimed jovially. 'What a surprise. How are you? You should have told me you were in town.'

He looked Daniel up and down. 'You're looking well. How's the leg? Fully healed?' Without waiting for an answer, he pointed a plump stubby finger towards Daniel's empty glass. 'Another?'

Daniel shook his head.

Mliswa walked over to the cabinet in the corner, poured himself a drink, and then rejoined Daniel, standing next to him.

Uncomfortably close.

'Quite a view,' he said, waving a hand expansively as if he owned it all. He looked at Daniel: 'Wonderful, isn't it,' he prompted.

Daniel nodded mutely. He had picked up the blue backpack and was unclipping the cover.

'And what do you think of this?' said Mliswa, waving behind him. 'Nice place, hey?' He paused to allow Daniel to respond.

'Very nice,' Daniel agreed absently, engrossed with what he was doing. The contents of the back-pack had become jumbled. Eventually he freed the photocopied file and pulled it out.

He straightened himself up.

'Where are the Sibandas?' he asked firmly.

Mliswa turned to face him.

'They're fine,' he said.

He was his old ebullient self. Daniel remembered clearly how his cheeriness and optimism had made him so popular.

'Just fine. I've been looking after them, as you asked.'

'Where are they, Henry? Here?'

'No, no. Not here. They're at my other place. In Gwanda.'

'All three of them?'

'Yes. Of course...'

Liar.

'I want you to bring them here, Henry. Let them go.'

'Daniel!' he said, taking mock offense. 'You make it sound as if they're in prison. Anyway, we can't do that. It wouldn't be safe for them. And it really wouldn't be convenient to bring them here.'

'I'm serious, Henry. I want them brought here and let go.'

'I just told you...'

'I don't give a damn what you told me, Henry. Bring them here. This afternoon.'

Daniel paused.

Calm down. Cool down.

'I asked you to protect them. But it's you they need to be

protected from.'

'What's got into you, Daniel? What on earth are you talking about?' The ebullience had evaporated.

Daniel thrust the copy of Diedrick's file towards him. 'Read that. Then you'll understand exactly what I'm talking about.'

Mliswa snatched the file from Daniel. He walked over to the sliding doors and shouted through the opening – Daniel couldn't make out what - before pulling them closed. He shot an angry glance at Daniel, and fell back heavily onto one of his vast leather sofas.

Daniel looked out over the valley, affecting an intense interest in the middle distance. He mentally braced himself.

Mliswa opened the file and read the first page. He turned to the second page and read that as well. Then he threw the file down dramatically beside him and exploded.

'This is just rubbish! You can't expect me to believe this crap.'

Daniel turned to him. 'It's not rubbish. Henry. It may well be a surprise to you, but it isn't rubbish, I promise you.'

Mliswa picked up the file again and read several pages at random. He let a few more escape one by one from under his thumb, examining them briefly as they flipped past, then slapped the cover closed.

'Bullshit,' he spluttered again. 'Complete fucking bullshit.'

Daniel ignored him. 'She's your sister, isn't she? Nyarai Simango is your sister. And however you look at it, she's a traitor. She was talking to the enemy.'

'Not true. Not a single word of it.' He shook the file at Daniel. 'This is a pack of lies. Where did you get it? Or did you cook it up yourself?'

'It's genuine, I promise you. Patricia got it from the house of the South African... ah... policeman who was your sister's handler for all those years.'

'You believe that? This is fiction. It's been fabricated. It's designed to cause trouble. Are you so stupid you can't see that?'

'Actually, I do believe it. It makes sense of all sorts of things.'

'What things?'

'You, for instance.'

'What do you mean, me?'

'In the last part of the file there. Read it.'

Mliswa didn't move. The file remained closed on his lap.

Daniel went on regardless. 'We always thought there was some bastard at the hospital turning people in. We talked about it often. Even you. Remember? People who'd been beaten. They were treated at the hospital, they left, and then some of them would turn up again, shit beaten out of them for the second time. Punished for seeking treatment for the first beating. Come to think of it, you and I spoke about it not so long ago when you were sorting out my leg. It was you, wasn't it? You were that bastard.'

Daniel saw Mliswa's fist clenching.

'I'm warning you, Daniel. Be very careful what you say.'

You don't realise quite how careful I'm being.

'How did it work, Henry? Did you just take their names and addresses and pass them on to your sister? Is that how it went? And then she sent out the goons to find these people so they could give them another good kicking? Or did you go and help them out? Perhaps you offered a little professional advice on how to inflict the precise amount of damage. Although I doubt there would be much you could teach those people. There's a pretty compromising picture at the back of the file. I really do suggest you look at it. It's in the brown envelope'

This time Mliswa opened the folder. He tore out the envelope, opened it, and inspected the photograph within.

'Who's that you're standing with?' Daniel asked. 'They all look very military to me. And there, on the right. That's someone we both know very well. That's Mpofu, isn't it? That shit Mpofu.'

'This proves absolutely nothing. Nothing at all.'

'I'd say it's pretty damning evidence. Not good company for a doctor to be seen in. Where was it taken, Henry? Bhalagwe? Or one of the other feeder camps? And think about this for a moment. How do you think that picture got into that file?'

Mliswa heaved himself to his feet. 'All right. Have it your way. I warned you.' He moved towards the doors.

Not yet, Henry. We're not finished.

'Did you enjoy it, Henry? Did you get a kick out of it?'

Mliswa turned on him. 'It was a duty. Something you wouldn't understand. It's not about enjoyment. It's about doing what has to be done.'

He looked contemptuously at Daniel. His voice rose.

'Why are you getting so worked up about them anyway? It was years ago. Ancient history. They were just cockroaches. They had to be crushed. You know what cockroaches are like. If you don't get them right under your heel and stamp...'

'My father? Was he a cockroach?' Daniel kept his voice as

even as he could.

'What's your father got to do with anything?'

'It's in the file, Henry. Everything is in that file. His name's in there. He was butchered at Bhalagwe. The people you turned in were sent there as well, weren't they? Some of them managed to crawl back into town to be treated a second time. But how many others didn't survive, Henry. How many did you send to their deaths. You would have known, from talking to me, what my father thought of what was going on. He was very outspoken. Dangerous too, being a teacher. Might infect the youth with his subversive ideas. Did you turn him in as well?'

'I had nothing to do...'

'But you did have something do with all the others.'

'I stand by what we did.'

He was now boiling over with anger, flecks of saliva spraying from his lips.

'I'm guilty of nothing. Those people had to be dealt with. Otherwise the fucking whites would have been back. If we didn't do what we did, the whole war would have been a waste. We would be back where we were before. I wouldn't be a doctor and neither would you. You'd be cleaning toilets for a white madam somewhere.'

'What kind of logic is that? You protect the country against the whites by killing thousands of black people? It doesn't make any sense, Henry. Have you any idea how stupid it sounds?'

'They were dissidents. Undermining unity They were sellouts...'

'No. They were just people. Ordinary people. Their crime was to come from the wrong tribe...'

'Exactly. They were scum. Always were. Still are. Cattle-stealing scum of the earth. People don't change.' He flicked his eyes from Daniel's face to his feet and back again. 'You know what your problem is? You can't see the big picture. You never could. You're highly educated. But you're pig-ignorant. All those years living in England. You've turned into one of them. You should be ashamed. You have no idea...'

Don't rise. Keep to the script.

'What I know is that my father went into Bhalagwe and never came out alive. What I know is that my sister went onto your sister's farm and came out dead, tossed over the fence like a piece of rubbish. Are you also denying you had anything to do with her murder?'

'Damned right I am. That wasn't me. Those morons who work for Nyarai - they don't know when to stop. If I'd had anything to do with it, she'd still be alive.'

'Somehow I doubt it. And while we're on the subject of your sister...why did she buy that farm? Does she feel a bit guilty about what went on there? Is she trying to stop the evidence from being dug up? And what is her name? Which one's correct? Hers? Yours? Neither?'

'Go fuck yourself.'

'Why have you kept her such a secret, Henry? You never told me you had a sister. Are you ashamed of her? Or what?'

Mliswa turned towards the doors again, and then turned back to face Daniel, as if something important had just occurred to him.

'You know something, Daniel? You don't realise just how lucky you are. If it'd been up to them you'd be dead as well. If I hadn't come looking for you, they'd still be scraping you off the bottom of that train. You should be thanking me, Daniel. Instead, you give me all this shit.' He waved the file in Daniel's face.

'Good story, Henry. If only it was true. You didn't save me from anything. Your tame gorilla, you see - the one who let me in. He was there, putting his boots into me when I was dragged out of the car, wasn't he? I recognised his voice. He also recognised me. He didn't even have to ask me my name at the gate.'

'You were also there. 'Take him halfway.' That was you. And then you just 'happened' to find me the next morning. Then, having 'saved' me, you encouraged me to go and find out what you wanted to know. You wanted to know why Patricia'd been on your sister's farm. And I was stupid enough to play ball.'

'Why didn't you ask your sister why Patricia was there? If, as you say, it was your sister's thugs who beat her, why didn't you ask her why Patricia went to her farm? I don't believe Patricia could have stood up to the treatment she got without telling them something. She must have...'

'She was dead before they got anything out of her.'

'Was she? Is that what your sister told you? If I was you I wouldn't believe a thing she says. After all, while you were being the big patriot, doing your duty stamping on all the cockroaches, she was telling the South Africans all about it. Sending them pictures of you and your friends. You didn't know that, did you?'

Mliswa said nothing.

'Patricia was looking for her – our - father's grave. But she'd read the file you've got in your hands.'

'So she knew. Patricia knew all about your sister, and

that's why she had to die. Your sister had Patricia killed. But you didn't know. You had no idea what your sister was up to. 'Till now. Now you know. How safe does that make you feel?'

Mliswa digested the idea for a second. 'Nyarai would never...'

Here goes. Get it right, Daniel. Give him the second helping of bait.

'Maybe. Maybe not. But it's not only her you have to worry about. What about her enemies. They take her down, you go with her. You're totally dependent on her. All this...,' He waved his arms at the surroundings. 'All this goes. You lose your business. No more shellfish, no more drugs, no more cash, no more house. You lose the lot.'

'No-one will believe you didn't know what she was doing. And even if they do believe you, it won't make an ounce of difference. They find out about any of it, you're finished. You can't afford for anyone else to find out what a traitor your sister is.'

A sneer spread over Mliswa's lips. 'Which is why you've had it, Daniel. Not me. You. Dead meat.'

Don't blink. Don't look away. Don't let your voice rise.

'Here's the deal,' Daniel continued. 'As you can see, that's a photocopy. That's your insurance, in case your sister does decide you're expendable. There's another copy lodged with my lawyer in England. It's insurance for me and the Sibandas. So long as none of us are harmed, that copy will stay where it is.'

'And where's the original?' Mliswa said, flatly.

Lie. Lie like you've never lied before. Convince him.

'That's the thing. It'll be at the Falls on Friday. I'd bet

anything on it. Your sister asked for a date with her old South African friend. I reckon top of the agenda will be how this whole thing has leaked out. I bet she has demanded that he bring the original. But you need that original as much as she does, if you want to truly safeguard your interests. The old hotel. On the terrace with a view of the bridge. Early Friday afternoon. You'll see her there, I promise you.'

Daniel looked intently at Mliswa.

Believe it, Henry. Go on. Make the decision.

Mliswa was silent for a few moments. He inspected his fingernails. Then: 'We'll discuss this further at the weekend.'

Daniel rejoiced. *You've swallowed it. Whole. You'll be there.*

'Meanwhile,' said Mliswa. 'You're going to remain as my guest.'

As I thought... Plan A.

Mliswa raised an arm and snapped his fingers. Butcher's-slab man opened the sliding door and walked through, followed by a taller skinnier accomplice that Daniel recognised from before. The man who had helped Mliswa carry him away from the railway tracks.

'Take him to the farm,' Mliswa said. 'Keep him there until you hear from me.'

He turned to Daniel contemptuously. 'See you Sunday. If you're lucky. If I'm feeling generous.'

Twenty Three

They travelled in convoy, Daniel's truck behind, driven by a third man who had joined the other two just before they left the house. Daniel sat in the back seat of the leading car next to the large man. The thinner man drove. There was no blindfold, no ties around his wrists. They didn't consider him a threat and they were correct. There was nothing he could do to change his predicament.

They drove fast and were through Gwanda in an hour. Not long after they drove past the crossroads and the police camp. Daniel saw the blue-painted rock as it flew by. A mile or two further on the convoy slowed and turned off the road, bumped over a cattle grid and through a bent metal gate which the driver of the first car opened and the driver of Daniel's truck closed behind him. And then a curving dirt track, grass on the *middelmannetjie* brushing against the underside of the car, which led eventually to the farmstead around which Daniel and Themba had crept only days before.

Days? Almost two weeks.

The cars circled the open area between the homestead and the line of sheds until they faced back down the track by which they had arrived. Daniel found himself being frog-marched to the brick-built storeroom. The padlock was opened, the chain loosened, and Daniel was shoved inside. The transition from bright sunlight to semi-darkness left him sightless, so he stood where he was, listening to the chain being pulled tight and the padlock being snapped shut.

His vision returned gradually and he looked around him.

Against the far wall, two human forms sat close together, motionless and dumb. Unresponsive.

He moved towards them. They sat, still not moving, scarcely breathing. It was Themba's sister and mother. He had never met them, but he knew it was them.

He tried to reassure them.

'It won't be long,' he said. 'We'll be out of here soon.'

But they didn't reply. Whether out of fear or contempt, Daniel wasn't sure.

Who can blame them. It was me who put them here.

* * *

He sat for some time against the wall opposite the two women, back against the bricks, knees drawn up to his chin, arms wrapped around his legs. What little light there was coming through the high windows was diminishing, so eventually he pulled himself to his feet and began to explore their commodious cell. There were various items of rusting agricultural equipment propped up against the walls. Towbars, chains, ploughshares. A rack of harrow tines sat vertically in one corner.

A single plate was on the floor near the door, small pieces of dried sadza encrusted on it. It must be the remains of something the women were given to eat, he supposed. But when, and had they had anything to drink? There was no evidence they had.

It was in another corner that Daniel found the untidy bundle of clothes. On impulse he picked it up. Below it were a pair of shoes. Trainers, slightly scuffed, a thin pink strip curving down each side from heel to toe. Women's trainers.

He unwrapped the bundle. A pair of jeans, a set of underwear. Nothing else. He gripped the clothing in his hands, stared at it, and found himself weeping.

* * *

Night fell.

The two figures opposite didn't appear to have moved a muscle since he arrived. He was sat once more against the wall and it was starting to get cold. He cursed himself for not looking round for a blanket, something to wrap around the women or himself. But the two women hadn't had any anything around them when he arrived, which probably meant there was nothing to be had.

He tried lying down at full stretch, but found he could keep warmer sitting up, so he dozed where he sat, waking periodically with a start every time his head slipped from his knees. He became aware of a noise outside, a little distant. There was laughing, the occasional shout and in the background the sound of party music. Their warders, he guessed. A crate of beer and a ghetto blaster were providing a distraction.

* * *

Daniel had no real idea of the time when he woke from his doze to hear the chain at the door moving. Ever so slightly. A dull click, metal upon metal.

His first thought was that it was their guards, having staggered across in a drunken haze to torment them. He could still hear the noise of laughter and music in the background, so they were still carousing. But it couldn't be them, he decided rapidly. There was no other nearby noise, no shouts, no stumbling around. Just that slight metallic click.

Silence descended once more, apart from the party in the background.

Wind, maybe, moving the door a fraction. Maybe that was it.

He closed his eyes again and tried to will himself to sleep. Then he heard it again. Definitely the chain, and he would have sworn it wasn't being moved by the wind. It was followed by another sound. A slight screech. A small sound, not far off silent, but extended.

Metal against metal, again.

And then a sudden clunk. A heavy sound. Industrial. Loud.

A moment or two's pause.

Another one, reverberating into the storeroom.

The chain was being pulled through its loops.

Stay? Go? Go.

Daniel braced himself, prepared to launch himself at the opening. The door opened.

And then through the gap emerged the familiar wiry frame of Themba Sibanda, a pair of long yellow-handled boltcutters dangling from one hand.

He was immediately over to his mother and sister, consoling them, helping them to their feet. Then he turned to Daniel.

'I'm so sorry,' Daniel whispered. 'I didn't know...'

'He's the manager. I saw him and just ran. The manager of this farm. He comes when the plane comes.'

'I know. I know that now. I'm sorry... but we must go.'

Themba fished in his breast pocket and withdrew two sets of keys. Daniel recognised one set as being for the truck he had rented. He assumed the other set must be for the second car in the convoy. He took them both.

'Where?'

'Kitchen table,' Themba replied. '*Bulalaed*... They're drunk.'

'Good.'

They left in single file, Themba leading his mother and sister, Daniel behind them all. They processed around the back of their erstwhile prison until they could see. The two vehicles were parked together where they had stopped, still facing towards the track.

The driver's door of Daniel's rented truck was locked. He crouched next to it so as not to present a silhouette against the window, and eased the key into the lock. It clicked, but no-one except Daniel was listening for it. He opened the door and crept onto the seat as low down as he could, reaching forward with his arms to find the handbrake. He released it slowly, compressing the ratchet button as fully as he could.

He withdrew a short distance, inserted the key into the ignition and freed the steering lock as gently and silently as possible. He reached forward again. Gearstick into neutral. Then he extracted himself fully, and keeping the door open, began to push the truck forward from his crouched position.

It took some considerable effort to overcome the inertia, but after straining to the limit from his awkward stance the truck was eventually persuaded to move. His efforts were immediately supplemented by those of the three Sibandas, who had moved to the back and begun pushing low down behind the tailgate.

The truck began to gain momentum. Daniel had to rise to his full height to see where it was going. He jerked slightly on the wheel to adjust the truck's direction, currently aimed towards a tree. He hoisted himself into the driver's seat at a run. Reaching for the key, he turned it and the engine burst into life. They were off, down the track, leaving the homestead behind.

There was now bedlam behind them. Daniel could hear the rising clamour as their guards fell out of the house and bundled themselves into the other vehicle, only to find that no-one had keys to start it. The noise intensified as the men started to shout at each other. Except for one.

Daniel could see him in the wing mirror, galloping up beside the truck, gaining on it with huge strides. He drew level, grabbed the roof rails and hoisted his feet onto the running board. His face was pressed grotesquely against the window, shouting. Daniel couldn't precisely decipher his threats, but he didn't need to. They were murderous in intent.

The man freed one hand and began to punch the glass next to Daniel's face. The window flexed with each impact of the man's fist. It wouldn't stand up to this kind of treatment much longer.

Daniel looked over his shoulder. He could see the two women lying flat in the back of truck behind him. The man, deciding on a different approach, began to try and swing himself over from the running board onto the open back of the truck where they lay.

Themba? Where's Themba?

The face at the window contorted even further. But this

time it wasn't in anger. It was a screaming mask of pain.

Daniel glanced behind him again. Themba was standing upright in the back, one hand gripping onto the truck, the other wielding the bolt-cutters. Daniel watched in the rear view mirror as he brought them down again on the thug's other hand, on his knuckles where he gripped the roof rails. He glanced sideways and saw the face recede from the window and the body fall away after it.

There was a deafening explosion as the back window of the cab shattered. The passenger window disintegrated at the same moment. Daniel heard another shot hit somewhere on the bodywork, a third just a loud noise with no impact felt. He looked quickly over his shoulder again. The women were still lying flat. They didn't appear to have been hit.

Alarmed. he saw another figure appear on his left.

But this time it was Themba, who had swung himself over on to the passenger-side running board. He opened the door and threw himself inside.

Daniel pushed his foot further down on the accelerator. He shouted to Themba, unnecessarily loudly in the confined space of the cab. 'How do we get out of here without going back on the main road?'

Themba yelled, equally loudly, and pointed ahead. Daniel wrenched the wheel and narrowly missed hitting a large rock on the side of the track.

They were bouncing along now, at a speed that would have been too fast had it been daylight. Daniel shouted again. He pointed over his shoulder with his thumb.

'No transport, but they have phones. They'll get Mpofu to block the main road. How do we get out of here without going that way?'

Themba nodded. 'There's another way. Further...' He peered intently through the windscreen. 'There. That side.'

Daniel couldn't see a thing.

Themba yelled. 'Now! Turn.'

Daniel swung the wheel blindly. The truck turned. Daniel could just make out the indistinct path of their new route.

'We can go fast,' Themba urged. 'It's straight, straight. Go straight.'

* * *

Straight it might have been, but less well used, the track was very difficult to follow. They appeared to be hurtling along, but when Daniel made an estimate from the wildly swinging speedometer they were not moving anywhere near as fast as it seemed. Even though there weren't any bends, driving took considerable concentration. The unevenness of the ground constantly bounced the wheels off course and Daniel was fully taken up with pulling them back again.

Themba pointed across Daniel's chest. Following his finger, Daniel saw the bush open up to his right. It took him a moment to recognise where they were. They were passing the one end of the airstrip. The end furthest away from where Daniel had lain up to watch the aircraft arrive and leave.

They kept going past the strip, bouncing their way forward, half-expecting that at any moment the night would erupt with gunfire and shouting once more.

Suddenly Themba hissed, whispering hoarsely for Daniel to stop and cut the engine. Daniel stood on the brake pedal. The truck lurched to a halt. They sat motionless on the track.

Themba pointed again. A dim glow was moving on their right through the vegetation some distance ahead of them.

'Where did that come from,' Daniel muttered angrily. 'Behind the house,' Themba replied. 'The one they use for the plane.'

The light stopped moving.

'There,' Themba whispered, pointing to a stand of bushes off to one side of the track. 'Behind there.'

Daniel drove slowly off the side of the track and nosed his way towards the cover. He drove behind it and turned off the engine again.

Ahead, they could still see the stationary headlights, and hear the low rhythm of the idling engine. Then the noise rose and the lights began to move. This time swinging towards them.

Daniel and Themba stopped breathing, eyes fixed on the headlights as they came nearer. There were two men standing in the back of the truck, silhouetted against the sky, scanning the bush on either side.

Slowly the lights came closer. Daniel found it impossible to believe that they could remain hidden from view.

But the truck drove straight past them and kept going until the lights were no longer visible and they could hardly hear its engine.

They watched it go. Daniel moved to turn the key in the ignition. Themba swung his hand across to stop him. He shook his head, saying nothing. They sat motionless and silent again.

Daniel could neither see no hear anything. But Themba already had. An agonisingly slow minute later Daniel heard the truck returning, and soon after that he saw the first glimmer of headlights re-appear through the bush behind them.

Again they sat, willing themselves to become invisible. Again, the truck drove past and the men in the back of it didn't see them.

The lights swung past them and were replaced by the twin red bars of the back lights. Daniel and Themba watched in disbelief as they shrank, until they finally disappeared.

Daniel heard Themba breath out slowly and deeply He looked across at him. There was a satisfied set to his lips. 'They can go. We will follow just now.'

* * *

Themba was guiding them now. They had crossed from the farm onto the neighbouring communal lands through a gate in the fence which their pursuers must have passed through only minutes before.

The countryside was much more open, the foliage grazed to ground level. The road was in more frequent use and consequently better worn. Daniel constantly fought the urge to go faster. But, as Themba kept reminding him, the last thing they needed was to catch up with the vehicle in front. So they pushed forward, past dark collections of huts and ghostly kopjes which seemed enormous in the dark, hoping against hope that they didn't turn a corner and find a car full of thugs in ambush.

The communal lands gave way to smallholdings, neatly fenced off from the road. The road had been graded and was much easier to drive along. Daniel switched the lights on – they would be far more conspicuous with them off – and they travelled towards the city through the outer suburbs.

Daniel looked across at his companion. Something had changed since he had last seen him. Mature enough before, he now had little of the adolescent about him. The boyish grin was gone. No more mischief in his eyes.

Head of the family now.

'My mother,' Daniel asked quietly. 'She found you with Father Barnabas?'

Themba nodded silently.

'I thought you'd be there. Tell me what happened.'

'We were staying by your mother. But her house is too small for us together. She said you told her of someone who could help us. We were ready to go. Full of thanks for the help.'

'But it was him. The manager. I ran away. I didn't want to leave my family but if I stayed we would all be in big trouble. I must run so I could go for them later.'

'I'm very sorry,' said Daniel. 'I thought he was a good man. I didn't know what he was like until a few days ago. And your father... I'm so sorry...'

Themba looked across at him and then stared straight ahead. Daniel saw tears welling up in his eyes.

'Where do you want to go?' Daniel asked.

'I will show you.'

'And now? What will you do?'

'We cannot go back. Not if he and that police is there.' He turned, almost pleadingly, to Daniel. 'What they did to my father... Can you fix them? Will you get them away from there?'

'I don't know. I just don't know.'

Twenty Four

I t was daylight and Daniel was very conscious that he was driving a truck with foreign number plates, no back window and a passenger side window reduced to a low jagged edge of diced glass, and was therefore an object of more than passing interest. He also couldn't forget the parcel tightly wrapped and secreted against the bulkhead of the engine compartment.

But there was no alternative. He had to press on.

He reached the road block way out of the city limits. From some distance up the road, Daniel could see two pairs of dented fuel drums standing in the middle of the road. They were crudely painted, white at top and bottom, black around the middle. A sagging grey military tent was pitched under the meagre shade of a roadside thorn tree. Daniel could see the cable of an aerial emerging from underneath the canvas, rising to where it was secured to a branch above.

Outside the tent a uniformed policeman rode on a wooden-backed tubular steel chair, pushed back until it was balanced precariously on its rear legs. His colleague stood by the barrels, dayglo vest visible from afar, cap firmly set, clipboard in hand.

There was nothing to indicate why the roadblock had been set up where it was. There was no local store nearby, no well-attended bus stop, no crossroads. But it did look like a semi-permanent outpost, which made Daniel feel slightly better. It didn't appear to be something thrown up in haste specifically for him. They wouldn't have bothered with a tent for that. There was no police vehicle parked nearby, not one that he could see.

And in any case, he doubted whether Mpofu's writ extended to this area. He wouldn't have wanted to alert the police in any other district. The risk of Daniel talking before he could be rendered into Mpofu's or Henry's gentle grasp were too great. Daniel spun all the logic through his head.

But until I'm through it...

The officer at the drums put up his hand, indicating that Daniel should halt. He bent to the window.

'Licence,' he said curtly.

Daniel fumbled around, found it, and offered it through the window. The officer inspected it, made a note on his clipboard, and handed it back.

'Papers'.

Daniel handed them over.

The policeman leafed through them, made more notes, and returned them. He pointed to the missing back window.

Daniel smiled weakly. 'Pothole,' he said. 'I hit a pothole. The glass shattered. I'll get it fixed.' He pointed up the road.

Please God let him not notice what's left of the passenger window. Or that bullet hole I felt hit the bodywork, wherever it is...

The officer strolled to the front of the truck.

'Lights,' he said.

Daniel turned them on.

'Full beam.'

Daniel complied.

The policeman started opening and closing his fingers. Daniel started at him blankly.

Oh. Indicators.

He obeyed.

The policeman changed hands and repeated the

command. Daniel followed suit.

How long is this going to go on? Is he soliciting a 'contribution'? A supplement to his salary?

The policeman bent down, disappearing from view.

What's he bloody doing now? Has something happened to that parcel? Is something showing?

But the policeman had only stooped to pick up the end of the strip of steel tyre-shredders which blocked the route through the drums. They clanked as they were pulled to one side.

Daniel was waved through. The policeman stared coldly at him as he turned right and left through the chicane.

Daniel accelerated onto the open road. He felt his pulse racing and had to tell himself to calm down, out loud. He changed up a gear, fixed his eyes on the road, and settled his hands on the wheel

Behind him, the police officer strode over to the tent and bent over the radio sitting on a trestle table inside.

* * *

Press on. Press on. Press on. You've got to make that appointment.

A sign on the roadside flashed past, giving the distance remaining to the Falls. Daniel glanced at the clock on the dashboard and the pointer on the speedometer. He did his sums. It was going to be tight. He pushed further down on the accelerator to see whether he could coax any extra speed from the engine. He couldn't.

The countryside should have provided a distraction. The scenery – mile after mile of teak forest – should have stilled his imagination, or diverted it elsewhere. But it had no effect. He found he was gripping the steering wheel as if it was about to fly out of his hands. The tension was playing havoc across his shoulders and up his neck.

He relaxed himself, rolling his shoulders and stretching his neck from side to side, flexing his arms and hands. But he could do little about his mind, which was examining all the possibilities of what could happen that day.

He tried a different tactic. He worked out how long it should take in minutes to cover various short distances. He began to count under his breath, and then checked his answers and the accuracy of his counting against the small white distance markers on the side of the road. The first time he tried it he reacted with alarm when the numbers appeared to be wildly out. But he patiently redid his calculation and was surprised at how reliably the subsequent markers appeared up ahead and then flicked past.

But there is only so long that even the most obsessive of brains can be diverted by such a ploy, and it wasn't long before he returned to his speculation.

* * *

Eventually, and not before time, a sign showed the turnoff to the airport.

Not long now.

Then the outskirts of the town, and the main road through it. Shops and kerb-side curio sellers. All things he recognised, although his last visit here had been years before.

Parking, parking, parking... where can I dump this truck?

That wasn't something he could retrieve from his memory.

He chose the car park at a mid-town supermarket. Mid-village, really. The border settlement was tiny, composed almost entirely of hotels. And what wasn't a hotel was a casino.

He parked in an unoccupied corner, and hoped he wasn't being watched as he raised the bonnet and fished around with one hand deep in the interior, in the space between the engine and the bulkhead of the cab.

It was still there. A weighty parcel, wrapped in a pair of his own trousers. He transferred it to his back-pack using the bonnet as cover. He locked the doors and, after a quick survey to make doubly sure he wasn't observed, shoved the keys up the exhaust pipe.

He started walking up the road. Across from him a pair of scruffily dressed men stood near a street light, one leaning against it. He glanced at them, then looked away, keeping his gaze fixed ahead of himself, trying to watch them from the corner of his eye. They stared brazenly at him as he walked past.

Muggers? Police? Neither? Both? He couldn't decide.

It was really hot now. Not more than a hundred yards further on and the sweat was flowing.

He turned towards a cluster of shops, intending to buy himself something to drink. He made his way between vehicles parked like a litter of pigs against the pavement. One of them, like the truck he had just abandoned, had an open back. Daniel looked into it as he edged sideways past it.

There was a bundle of clothing, obviously damp, and a scuffed fibre-glass helmet, swimming-pool blue, with a set of black webbing straps dangling from each side. Abandoning his shopping plans, he grabbed the bundle and the helmet and retreated the way he'd come.

Don't panic. Don't run.

He walked as nonchalantly as he could further down the street until he found a tree under which he could take refuge. There he examined his booty. There was a t-shirt advertising white-water rafting. A pair of shorts, industrial strength and Bermuda length, severely worn on the double-thickness quilted seat. A helmet that must belong to a white-water guide.

Bonanza.

A lone man walked purposefully nearer on the other side of the street. It looked for a split second as if he might be about to cross. Daniel felt his muscles tense. But the man continued on his way. Daniel wasn't even sure whether the man had seen him.

He changed into the shorts, kept his own shirt, and buried the rest in the back-pack. He resumed his journey. Within minutes the pilfered Bermudas were flapping dry around his thighs.

The road crossed a railway line, the steel buried in the tar, which looked gelatinous, almost liquid, in the heat. A hotel sat on the side of the road.

Daniel reached the turnoff to the old hotel on the opposite side. He stopped briefly to reconsider his plans.

Should I watch from this side? No. You've thought this through already. Don't change plans. Keep going.

Another casino, then the buildings petered out on both

sides of the road. He passed the last stand of municipal trees. The road curved away and then back on itself, re-crossing the railway line, with open scrubland on both sides. Only a few hundred yards from the one of the biggest waterfalls in the world, the cloud of spray now clearly visible, and it looked as if this particular stretch of countryside had never experienced rain. But there was an ominous discolouring to the sky behind the spray which amplified his already sensitised disquiet.

Another pair of loiterers watched him walk past. A man and a woman. Daniel wasn't precisely sure what gave them away. Their stares, perhaps. Alert. Definitely not vacant. Or maybe the man's strapping build which the rags he was wearing did little to disguise. But if he was unsure why he thought so, he was certain they weren't innocent bystanders.

Then the realisation struck him, as if a light had just been turned on.

Bloody hell. They're counting me through. Waving me through the checkpoints. Making sure they know where I am. Making sure I know they're watching. Making sure I keep clear. The bastards.

He kept walking. He passed the tourist entrance to the rainforest, then a short distance further on saw the low buildings of the border post.

He stood in a short queue to obtain a day pass over the border. This late in the morning, with the heat bearing down, there weren't many people ready to take a day-tripper's stroll to the other side.

Then the last stretch around another bend.

A sagging tent, this one dusty brown and fronted by a parapet of sandbags, guarded the approach to the bridge. There was a machinegun mounted on a tripod pointing over

323

the bags, a line of brass cartridges glistening on a belt. Behind it sat a soldier in camouflage, a beret sitting awkwardly on the top of his head, his cheekbones gleaming almost as brightly as the ammunition. The first line of defence against an assault from...? Daniel couldn't figure out who.

The bridge was now in front of him, some quirk of perspective foreshortening it. The two lanes of the road crossing were on the left, neatly tarred, with kerbstones blocked out alternately in black and white sloping gently towards the tar.

The railway line ran to the right of centre, protected on either side by waist-high steel barriers painted blue. And to the right of the railway, on the edge of the bridge, a pedestrian walkway.

Daniel began to walk along it.

Strong mesh in a bright warning yellow screened pedestrians from the drop on the right hand side. Except in the middle, where Daniel stopped. Here, a gate in the barrier led on to a bungee-jumping platform suspended out over the chasm. He peered over the edge. Below - a very long way below - dark water churned violently.

* * *

It's come to this. This is where it works. Or it doesn't...
The line of thunder clouds were now swollen on the northern horizon. As he had walked they had darkened, and they now looked like a vast angry bruise across the sky. This pregnant backdrop, deep amethyst in colour, made everything else seem more intensely bright. It was as if all he

could see had suddenly been flooded with colour.

It was a much better vantage point than he'd thought possible, but it wasn't built for comfort. The rock behind him was sharp and uneven. The earth beneath him was deeply corrugated by gargantuan serpentine roots which anchored the trees to the basalt bedrock. A paperbark tree reached over him like an oversized parasol. But while it shaded him it also trapped the heat. He was sweating as if he had just reached his perch by climbing up the cliff face in front of him.

The pilfered t-shirt was in a damp bundle next to him, abandoned in a vain attempt to cool himself down. Beads of sweat were now running freely down his back, sinking into the waistband of his shorts. The hair on his arms glistened. His legs shone with moisture. Again he shifted himself against the rock, knees drawn up to his chest, searching for the least painful position.

He fancied he could smell the sweetness of the spray behind him. But the scent was elusive, and there wasn't a breath of air to relieve his discomfort.

Drawing his hand slowly across his scalp and face, he wiped away the perspiration through three days' worth of stubble. He traced the scar on his head softly with his fingertips. It finally appeared to be healing. But the weals on his shins were still livid. They throbbed incessantly and he couldn't fully flex his legs to ease the discomfort.

Glancing to one side, he checked for the fourth or fifth time that the chalky swimming-pool-blue helmet was still buried under a pile of dead leaves in a crevice between two tuberous roots. It had been a silent colourful alibi as he walked onto the peninsula, but the pretext was no longer needed.

Or even valid. It was one thing to be seen with it on the path down from the main road. Here, off the path and with his presence no longer explicable, the incongruous colour was best hidden.

He knew that only someone actively searching for him would be able to pick him out amongst the rocks and vegetation. Even that would be a difficult task. All the same, he felt helplessly on show on the towering spines of rock rising like some overblown gothic cathedral from the black water boiling on three sides below him.

He looked over his right shoulder up the gorge. There, settled between the opposing cliffs like a jeweller's confection in filigree silver, the girders of the bridge reflected the filtered sunlight against the smoky spray rising in vast delicate clouds, like steam from a subterranean cauldron. It looked beautiful – nothing like its workaday appearance when he had walked across it.

He picked up the binoculars, shifted round, and, bracing his elbows against his knees, searched through the lenses until he found the span.

He adjusted the focus and then followed a lone figure pushing a low flat barrow, heaped with groceries, slung between a pair of bicycle wheels. He watched until the barrow and then the figure disappeared from view.

A hazy torpor descended over the empty crossing. No trains, no cars, no pedestrians, no cross-border traders.

Bored, he turned back in the opposite direction. Pressing his eyes hard against the rubber, he inspected the opposite side of the gorge. Though less sheer than the buttress on which he was perched, the facing bank still rose sharply from the dark waters below.

He could make out here and there amongst the patches of dun vegetation a path switching back and forth. He followed the traverses from side to side as they climbed the slope until he found the flagpole centred in the lenses, standing brilliant white through the haze. A flag dangled bleached and limp from its tip.

Around the pole on a stone-built viewing terrace sat a circle of fat red Alibaba pots. Dull green vegetation, unidentifiable over the distance, sprouted from the top of each.

Behind the flagpole and the pots he could see a substantial lawn. It was brown in patches and in need of watering. It ran up to the warm white walls and red tiled roof of the hotel, which sat like a *grande dame* casting a proprietorial eye over a late-imperial garden party. More imposing than the bridge, and just as incongruous in the surrounding primeval countryside.

Waiters clad in brilliant white, vividly coloured sashes brightening their uniforms, floated serenely up and down the steps of the veranda ferrying trays of drinks to guests, most of whom appeared to be seated unseen in the shade of the vast ancient trees which hid the most part of the central block of the hotel from his view.

A faint shimmer of smoke rose vertically from behind those trees as the lunchtime *braai* drums were stoked up. To the right he could see part of the car park to the side of the main building. Multi-coloured, highly-polished steel was just discernible through the shrubbery.

He remembered as a boy setting traps to catch birds on the fringes of the mission compound, where the trampled dirt ended and the bush began. What seemed then to be endless watching, hidden and still - although probably a fraction of the time he now imagined - until a sparrow, finally succumbing to temptation, hopped up to the pellets of mealie meal. Then pulling the string to dislodge the twig propping up the fruit box, catching the bird before it fled.

He focussed on the two short steel supports bracing either side of the foot of the flagpole.

Come on, bastards. You've all been invited and the party's about to begin. Where are you..?

He let the binoculars swing back on their strap, and fought the urge to sleep.

* * *

The lunchtime bustle on the lawns and the veranda had subsided, although there were still some customers sitting around a large table who were visible from across the river. An under-strength platoon of waiters ambled here and there, re-arranging the furniture, or just stood quietly with folded arms, alone or in pairs in the shade, waiting to be summoned. Tranquility had descended.

On the other side of the gorge, Daniel kept his binoculars trained on the gravel promenade which ran from the hotel down to the flagpole.

At the precise turn of the hour a woman appeared on the veranda.

After pausing to survey her surroundings, she descended the stairs to the lawn.

Daniel stared at her through the lenses. He could see her as clearly as if she were standing next to him.

328

She was draped from shoulder to toe in west-African style, the generous folds of cloth displaying a bright intertwining of deep purple vine branches on a loud yellow background. Her head was surmounted by a turban-like construction of the same material. It would have graced the most plutocratic of maharajas.

She looked little different from the multi-coloured promenade of other matrons that Daniel had seen during his vigil, some of whom were still decorating the terrace and the lawn.

But her bearing was different.

A waiter approached her obsequiously, offering to escort her to a table under the trees, but she waved him away with a peremptory twitch of her hand. He backed off - literally - stepping away while still facing her as if he was a palace flunkey in the presence.

That's it. She behaves as if she's royalty.

Her progress was stately and direct. Half way across the lawn she raised her left hand to her brow, as if shielding her eyes from the sun; an unnecessary gesture since she wore a pair of diamante-encrusted sunglasses that were more than adequate for the task. She carried on walking until she reached the stone observation deck around the flagpole.

She walked slowly past the mast to the low wall which marked the deck's outer limit and stood looking up the gorge towards the bridge.

So that's you. Nyarai Simango, or Nyarai Mliswa, or Mary, or whoever or whatever. More portly than in the photograph in Diedrick's file. But then who wouldn't be, more than a dozen years after the fact.

As from the photograph, Daniel could decipher no more

329

than that. The turban and sunglasses effectively masked any expression she might have worn. He watched, fascinated, as she stood rock still, gazing past him upstream.

She turned and walked back to the flagpole, where she turned again, as if to take one last look at the spectacular view. Her body was now shielding the lowest part of the flagpole from anyone looking at her from the direction of the hotel.

You've done this before...

Once more she raised her left hand. As she did, her right arm emerged from the folds of her sleeve and darted straight to the top of one of the tubes of steel either side of the flagpole.

Her hand hovered for a fraction of a second and then returned to her sleeve. All the time her neck was held firmly erect, her head pointing imperiously into the distance. Not once did her eyes or head follow what her right hand was doing. From behind it would probably have appeared as if she hadn't moved at all.

You could be a stage magician, with misdirection like that.

She swung round and began to walk back the way she had come.

Daniel watched her go.

As she moved, a dramatic choreography began to play out on the lawn. On that side of the river there must have been a soundtrack, but to Daniel it was like a silent movie without a theatre organ.

Three suited men advanced upon her. One directly in her path, the other two wide of him, securing his flanks. The centre man held up his palm towards her.

Halt. Like the policeman at the road block.

Except that this one's command was even more unconditional and menacing.

The turban switched rapidly to left and right. The woman turned sharply towards the border of the car park, quickening her gait.

The men adjusted their trajectories as she moved. They closed on her.

She tried to keep wide of them, but failed. She had no possibility of escape, even had she not been constricted by the swathes of her clothing.

The men were soon on to her. They stood in a semi-circle around her.

Close in. Crowding her.

Daniel could see the centre man demanding something of her. His mouth opened and closed rapidly, wildly. He was clearly very angry.

The turban swivelled and bobbed. She was equally agitated. She began to wave her arms, stabbing her fingers viciously towards the men in protest.

The standoff continued.

Until the man in the centre of the line slapped her hard - very hard - across the side of her face.

Daniel winced.

The group he was watching froze.

The two flanks stared at their comrade, then stared back at the woman. She had raised a hand to her face and was slowly massaging her jaw with her palm.

She retaliated. She swung round, putting her entire weight and effort behind her arm, and slapped him back.

Daniel flinched again, turning his head away in empathy. He could hear nothing, but his imagination filled in the sound for him. They must have heard that slap on the other side of town.

This time there was no stunned amazement. No pause.

Before Daniel could follow what happened, the woman had been bent into a headlock by one of her assailants, while the other two fixed handcuffs to her wrists, which were bent, extremely painfully it looked to Daniel, behind her back. Then they began to frog-march her between them towards the steps up to the hotel. Her turban lay discarded behind them on the lawn.

Daniel watched as the centre man, now behind the other two with their captive, suddenly raised his hand to his head.

She really did hurt you. You're feeling it now.

But it wasn't pain. The man stopped moving. He was concentrating, still holding his hand to his ear.

You're miked up. You're wearing an earpiece...

Abruptly, the two men in front also stopped. They wheeled round as one, turning their prisoner with them as they did. The centre man began to run, gesticulating to them as he moved. One of the others joined him, leaving his partner to take care of the prisoner on his own. He jerked her around. She resisted, and then rapidly complied.

Not sure what you twisted, my friend, but it worked a treat.

The other two men were now running towards the car park. Huge strides, flying leaps through the border shrubbery, and they were gone. The lawn was now deserted. The scene was suddenly empty. Any guests previously visible to Daniel had melted away.

Daniel saw a waiter poke his head enquiringly from the hotel interior, but he withdrew it again almost immediately. Another emerged from stage left, bent to pick up the turban, and retreated swiftly out of sight.

People know when it's healthier to make themselves scarce.

Daniel sat staring into space.

Who did you run off to chase? Antjie? Henry? Both of them? They were also invited to the party. Where are they?

* * *

Daniel began gathering up his small pile of gear. He pulled the t-shirt back over his head, and closed the fastenings on the top of the blue back-pack. He replaced his glasses on his nose. He dug the helmet out from under the pile of leaves and shook it to empty it of debris.

Carrying it one hand, with the back-pack in the other, the binoculars swinging across his chest, he started to climb back onto the spine of the peninsular and make his way back to the road.

After only a few steps, he saw a strong flash of sunlight out of the corner of his eye.

He turned.

There was a repeat flash.

Daniel dropped what he was carrying and raised the binoculars to his eyes. Frantically, he searched for the bridge, and when he found it, hastily adjusted the focus. But the image wouldn't sharpen. He remembered. Swearing, he removed his glasses and tried again. This time he could see.

The bridge was empty, but not for long. A car appeared from the left hand side, travelling at speed, closely followed by another, which tried to overtake it.

For a second - no longer - the two cars sped, wheel to wheel, towards the middle of the bridge. Then the overtaking car gained on its quarry and swerved in front of it.

The two cars collided, and then both hit the barrier separating the road from the railway.

Figures spilled from both cars and scattered, pursuers and pursued dispersing to all points of the compass.

Daniel looked on hypnotised as he saw a figure he recognised being attacked by two others. He was being punched and kicked, grappled with, as his two assailants tried to pin him down.

It was Boet, Antjie's chief thug, who he had last seen at the house on the beach. The beater-in-chief of Sollie Diedricks.

He wasn't having it all his own way now. But he still kept moving, dragging his attackers with him.

The trio tumbled over the blue barrier onto the railway corridor, flailing and kicking as they struggled. They were soon fighting up against the second barrier, using it for purchase as they wrestled until they fell over that barrier too onto the pedestrian walkway.

Now they were up against the yellow mesh fence.

Daniel looked on in horror.

He knew what was about to happen. He was willing them to stop with every fibre of his body, his muscles tensing and his body twisting involuntarily as he watched. He might as well have been trying to influence the trajectories of the planets.

On they struggled until the thug's attackers finally gained the upper hand. They lifted their flailing victim and rolled him over the fence.

He dropped, head over heels over head, rolling again and

again until his dive eventually flattened out just before he hit the water.

Daniel followed his tumbling body all the way down. The wild torrent into which he fell swallowed him whole without even a visible splash to mark his passing.

* * *

Daniel returned his gaze to the bridge, sick to his stomach.

Antjie, gazing downwards through the fence, her face stricken with horror, was being pinioned by two men, one or both of whom were probably redundant. She didn't look capable of further flight or resistance.

So. Two down. Nyarai and Antjie taken care of. But what about the third? Where is he? Where's Henry?

Daniel scanned left and right with the binoculars. Another figure was also being restrained, but only with token force. He also had no wish to join his colleague at the bottom of the gorge. And it wasn't Henry.

And between these two groups stood a solitary man.

Daniel recognised him immediately. The round earnest face, the bright, interested, even kindly eyes, the triangular smudge of a moustache on his upper lip. Mutambiro. Secret policeman. Factional fixer. Addressee of Daniel's parcel.

Daniel watched through his binoculars as Mutambiro raised his own. They stood motionless, looking at each other, promontory to bridge, bridge to promontory, collaborators in an awful theatre.

The message was as clear to Daniel as if they had been standing a yard apart. They might even have shaken hands, like a pair of lawyers. Acknowledging that a deal still stood, and was almost complete - the final clause about to be delivered upon.

Mutambiro lowered his binoculars, spoke a few words to those either side of him, and led them as they all walked back towards the left hand edge of the gorge.

Daniel let his binoculars fall back on their strap.

The air was suddenly cooler. Daniel felt a faint zephyr touch the sweat and hair on his arms. He turned his face to it, and this time smelt the moisture.

He opened the back-pack.

He took out the box of cartridges and hurled it over the cliff, the bullets spilling out and tumbling in the sunlight. The perlemoen shell followed, spinning horizontally out into the air like a stone in a game of ducks and drakes. And then the pistol. Butt over barrel, Daniel hurled it as hard as he could and watched it falling until it disappeared from sight.

Finished. Almost. No longer required.

He swung the back-pack over his shoulder, picked up the helmet and resumed his climb.

As he went, and without warning, the sound of thunder rolled towards him. Then the air filled with large fat raindrops, splashing loudly on the rocks around him, falling heavily on his head and shoulders as he climbed.

Twenty Five

T he weather was as bad as it had been before he left. If anything, the sleet was a little colder, the wind cutting that much more sharply into any flesh injudiciously left exposed.

Daniel Hove - Mr Daniel Hove in his reincarnation at St Botolphs - walked down Shoalview Terrace, hands buried in his pockets, head bowed, glasses and face spattered with driven rain. He refused point blank, on grounds of acute public embarrassment, to wear headgear of any kind, let alone the woollen beanie that some recommended. His shaven scalp was freezing as a result.

He continued down the pavement which was slippery under a thin delta of water flowing down to the sea front. He delayed, until the very last moment possible, removing a hand and a bunch of keys from his pocket to open the front door. The key missed first time, and his fingers got even colder, but the second time it slotted in and the door opened. He entered, removed his coat, slung it from the peg on the wall, and stooped to pick up his post scattered on the floor.

He walked along the hall and down the steps to the kitchen at the back of the house. The heating was on a timer and the rooms were already comfortably warm. He opened a drawer, grabbed a cloth from inside it, and wiped his face and head.

He loosened his tie, worn in direct challenge to a clinical health and safety ruling he considered absurd, set the kettle hissing, and sat down at the kitchen table.

Whatever the weather outside, his return to the hospital a

month before had brought with it a distinct change in the climate. However they might have considered him before, they - his management-level irritants - now viewed him in a different light entirely. His colleagues noticed it first; Daniel only once it was pointed out to him. It was quite simple. They were now scared of him.

He had described nothing. He had explained nothing. As far as the hospital was concerned he had taken several weeks off to mourn the death of his sister and to recuperate from his broken leg. For all they knew, or cared, he might have spent those weeks contemplating the universe from the isolation of a Hebridean island.

But his demeanour had spoken eloquently, if mutely, for him. Perhaps it was the almost imperceptible flare in his eyes when something they said annoyed him. Or his newly found willingness to challenge their ridiculous edicts.

Whatever it was, they now appeared to expect him to erupt at any moment, spreading carnage through the hospital corridors.

Ainslie, of course, had secured his own promotion in Daniel's absence.

But no-one, Ainslie included, had dared cross him since he had walked back into the department.

No doubt that would eventually change. But in the mean time he allowed himself to scoff privately.

Cowards.

Not in the sense that they would have behaved any differently from him, given the same set of circumstances. More that they had backed off in the face of a threat that didn't exist, that they had manufactured in their own imaginations. At least, that was how he saw it. Others, including the some of the more level-headed of his colleagues, were not so sure that the threat was imaginary.

Daniel neatened up the pile of envelopes. Two bills, which he opened, skim-read, and put to one side. A bank statement which joined the bills. At the bottom of the pile, a pastel-coloured envelope, brightly coloured stamps in the corner, his mother's handwriting across the middle.

As usual, she had precision-folded the contents to the exact dimensions of the envelope. More than once he had opened a letter from her to find that the paper inside had been shredded in the process. He rose and selected a slim filleting knife from the wooden block on the countertop opposite.

It won't do the edge any good at all, and six months ago I would have been risking a marital confrontation to use it... but stuff it.

He slid the blade into the top of the envelope, paring carefully to make sure he wasn't slicing the contents. The envelope open, he had to pull quite hard with his fingertips to ease them out.

Goodness knows how she got that in there in the first place.

It was a sheet of notepaper, the same colour as the envelope, folded in two. He opened it up. There was a newspaper cutting fixed to it with a paper clip. He flipped it up with his thumb. Beneath it on the notepaper she had scribbled a few words:

'I thought you might find this interesting.'

What could be so interesting that she didn't mention it when I phoned her yesterday?

He let the cutting fall back onto her note so he could read it.

339

It was from the Bulawayo daily newspaper, dated less than a week earlier.

'Double Tragedy in Gwanda', said the headline.

The newsprint was of an inferior quality and the print was indistinct in places, but he read on.

'Two prominent members of the Gwanda community were tragically killed yesterday, in what some in the town have called a freak accident which should never have been allowed to happen.

Dr Henry Mliswa, a well-known local businessman and doctor, and Inspector Deliverance Mpofu of the Zimbabwe Republic Police, died instantly when the vehicle in which they were both travelling collided with a moving train.'

Afterword

There was no Inspector Deliverance Mpofu. Nor was there a camp for any police officer to command at Jahunda. There was no Father Barnabas and no St Cuthberts mission.

But there was - still is – a place called Bhalagwe. What happened there is an open secret, and the legacy of the Fifth Brigade is still an open sore in Matabeleland thirty years on.

Saltwater shellfish – abalone – recorded as *Origin: Zimbabwe* still arrives in regular shipments in Hong Kong.

And the old hotel is still the doyenne of the riverside establishments at the Falls. Who knows who meets who on its lawns?

Printed in Great Britain
by Amazon.co.uk, Ltd.,
Marston Gate.